Rosie staggered back in fright. It was as though a void were closing around her—a presence so dark and ancient that her fear was matched by awe for whoever, or whatever, this man was. The obsidian pools that were his eyes loomed at her from the shadows, reflecting the hideous remnants of the ruined boy behind her. The twin images and the threat that they were telegraphing her fate turned Rosie's blood to ice.

The ground beneath her gave way and she was shocked to find her feet sinking into wet mud like quicksand. She gasped, in pain and frustration, as both her feet were sucked deeper into a hideous quagmire of blood and stench. Rosie clutched at thin air and screamed, thrashing in desperation. But all her movement achieved was to drive her deeper into the quicksand and a new panic took hold of her as she found herself up to her neck in the dark, stinking mud.

The huge man towered over her and she craned her neck back to look up at his face. His expression betrayed no emotion and she realized in that moment his eyes were covered with crude discs of obsidian glass. Perhaps designed to keep the light out—or to keep the darkness within. Rosie shuddered, wondering if his baser impulses might give him cause to extricate her from his oubliette. But he just stood there, immovable as a monolith and watched her sink into the ground. Rosie's screams became dirt in her mouth as she went under.

And fell.

THE SKINTAKER

FRAZER LEE

DEDICATION

For Laura, who has perfect skin.

PROLOGUE

Ohio. 1919

Rosie Shields turned eleven on November 11th, 1918—the day the Great War ended. The following summer she was blossoming into quite the pretty thing and was turning the heads of most of the young, would-be suitors at Sunday school. Her complexion was fair, her hair even fairer, and she possessed what one might call a "natural beauty." She was the pride and joy of Donna, her mother, and Herman, her father. They doted on her daily and often told her that she made their oil lamps last longer because of the way she lit up a room.

The Shields' family farm was vast, one of the largest in the region, boasting a large herd of cattle and more chickens and pigs than you could throw a recipe book at. To Rosie, it was her playground and she loved helping out with the animals. Her father had avoided the international call to arms, in support of the Allies, due to an accident with a temperamental bull when she was five. Rosie could still recall seeing her father's leg all hoisted up when she went in to give him his Saturday morning coffee. Her mother liked to take a drink come sundown on Fridays, and also liked to sleep in on a Saturday, but she was never mean with it.

The leg still troubled Herman now, but more so in the winter months when the chill got under his kneecap. Whatever the weather, he dutifully escorted Rosie to Sunday school, though she felt sure his motivation was partly to see if he could rile her Uncle Gregory with a bit of banter. Her father was an atheist, her uncle a pastor, and the two rarely saw eye to eye. Rosie had been born out of wedlock and her parents had still not married, both of which were situations that would be scandalous in less rural locales. To some locals they were scandalous enough, not to mention Donna's weekend libations. To any gossips at the gate, Rosie's parents said they were "saving up" to get wed, that they'd fix a date once the bank account had fixed itself. But Rosie knew they were spinning them a line—both her mother and father believed they did not have to get married to show their love for one another. House, hearth, and family were their commitments, and they took those commitments seriously.

Uncle Gregory frowned upon all of this, of course. After a brief stint as a missionary during the war, he'd followed his wife Francesca to her birthplace in Ohio. Gregory had met Francesca in France, where she worked in telephony for the Allies. Now a pastor's wife, Francesca still waxed lyrical about Paris and the "high life" as she called it. Gregory always fell quiet when his wife did this, something that her dad could not help but have a little fun with. Rosie liked having her father around.

That particular Sunday school on a scorching morning in July 1919 was a somber affair, but Rosie enjoyed the company. It was a summer's day like any other. She had something of a best friend thing going on with Esme Lanchester from the town, and together they delighted in running rings around the local boys. Her Uncle Gregory and Aunt Francesca led the service, which was administered in the Anglican tradition. Rosie listened dutifully to her uncle's sermon—

On the third day he rose again.

The resurrection of the body.

And life everlasting.

—delivered in his lilting Scottish brogue. Francesca sat poised at the edge of the congregation, ready to strike if one of the boys got too close to one or more of the girls. She looked like a raven, perched there in her black and gray frock, bonnet tied firmly to her head. Francesca looked like her sister, Rosie's mother, minus all the good humor. Rosie could not fathom why Francesca looked so cross all the time. Gregory was a good man, and a popular pastor, and together they shared the little house behind the chapel where Rosie took iced tea sometimes, on especially hot days like this. Rosie told her aunt that she liked to visit with them because their house was small, like a doll's house. Her aunt had packed away the tea things soon after and told Rosie it was probably time to go home.

That night had turned out to be one of the hottest on record, and it had taken Rosie several attempts to get to sleep in the cloying humidity. Her father had propped the window of her ground floor bedroom open, but there was just no breeze to make a difference. Eventually, Rosie had succumbed to the rhythmic song of the crickets in the grasslands outside her window. It was a summer's night like any other.

And then her world had exploded.

The choking smoke woke her, and it felt like someone had ripped out her throat while she slept. Blinking in the half-light she thought it strange that the light was flickering so. Hadn't her parents put out the light when they'd come in to say goodnight? Coughing, and struggling from her tangled sheets, Rosie walked over to her door and opened it. The wall of flame beyond was so intense that it knocked her from her feet. Fire tumbled into her room now, fed by the slight draft of oxygen from her bedroom window. She felt her eyebrows sizzle above her eyes, the stench of them burning making her gag. Rosie scrambled from the flames, hitting the back of her head against the little dresser where she kept her trinkets. Ted, her faithful bear for as long as she could remember, regarded the flames with indifference as they flickered, reflected in his black button eyes. Rosie struggled to her feet, knocking Ted to the floor. He went up in flames seconds later, and Rosie screamed as her bed sheets caught too, erupting into a dancing crackle of heat.

Instinct drove her to the open window. Perhaps she could clamber out. But even as the idea occurred to her, there came the sound of thunder from above and the ceiling rained down into her room. The upper floor had burned through and the floorboards had given way. A large wooden beam toppled right in front of Rosie and she shrieked. It landed where her pillows lay, setting fire to them and then the curtain at her side. She was stuck, pinioned between the beam and the window frame. She struggled, but it was no good, she could not twist her body around to tip herself out the window.

Rosie heard her mother scream, heard the desperate cries of her father somewhere deep within the tumult of flame. She screamed back at them, frantic. Then followed a terrifying sound, like a hot wave passing through the building as the breeze changed direction. A ball of flame shot past Rosie's field of vision, beyond her bedroom door and into the core of the house. She heard glass exploding, the cracking of timbers and the gust of yet more flames as they devoured her home.

The heat was unbearable, and Rosie felt the tears evaporate from her cheeks no sooner had they fallen from her eyes. She closed her eyes and tried to remember that morning's sermon. Something about resurrection. In the heat, the pain and the agony, Rosie prepared to die.

Then she felt hands on her shoulders. Strong hands, pulling her from the flames and out of the window. The breath was knocked out of her as she fell backward and hit the ground. She looked up at her Uncle Gregory's face, his expression one of agony. He held up his hands and Rosie saw he had burned them, badly, while extricating her from the fire. But all she could think of was her mother and father. They were still inside and she knew it. Rosie knew it still when the roof caved in and lay waste to all she had held dear. Her uncle sobbed in pain, and Rosie wished she could, too, but the shock and anguish had robbed her of any such demonstration.

"You're safe now," he said through his tears. But here, on the outskirts of the fire she felt as cold as ice.

Rosie Shields had turned eleven by the end of the Great War. But hers was now just beginning.

CHAPTER ONE

Amazon Rainforest. 1926

Nimbo gazed up at the tualang tree and wiped away the sweat that had gathered on his brow like dewdrops. He heard Pacon huffing and puffing behind him, playing catch up as usual. His little brother was the runt of the litter, all legs and no stomach to fuel them. Nimbo had begged his father, the chief, to allow him to hunt alone but his plea had fallen on deaf ears. Pacon was to be trained in the fine art of hunter-gathering and Nimbo was to be his tutor.

Teach him how to hunt, his father had instructed, *everyone must contribute to the greater good by placing food in the pot.*

He would never dare publicly dispute his father's wishes, but privately Nimbo questioned the wisdom of taking Pacon out into the rainforest again. Their last expedition together was meant to be a simple fishing trip but had ended in disaster. Pacon had somehow managed to tangle himself up in the reed bed and his subsequent splashes and frantic cries for help had scared away every fish within a mile's radius. Nimbo had returned to the village empty-handed that day, with both him and Pacon looking like drowned rats. Nimbo's name meant *rain cloud* in his mother tongue, gifted to him because of his ability to climb so high that he could poke the sky and bring forth the rain. But his name quickly became a cruel in-joke when the elders saw him soaking wet and dragging poor, pathetic, half-drowned Pacon back into the fold. They were the laughing-stock of his community, and all because Pacon couldn't keep his footing in the river they had bathed in since they were born. His little brother was a liability. Even now, Nimbo could feel Pacon's hot, panting breath on his neck. He was making enough noise to warn every possible source of nutrition of their presence.

Teach him how to hunt, thought Nimbo, *what a joke.*

Still, if that's what the elders wanted, then at least he could have some fun with his assignment. Nimbo turned to face his brother and frowned at the sight of him—his dark skin slicked with sweat and his eyes bloodshot and bulging from exertion. Nimbo disliked Pacon intensely. *Hate* was too strong a word for something as useless as his little brother. One did not hate a lame animal, instead one pitied and tolerated it until such a time that it was ready to lie down and die. Right now, Nimbo wished his brother would lie down for a bit and let him get on with the hunt. They were already a quarter-day behind schedule. Fighting the urge to hunt for the both of them, as he had done so many times before, Nimbo reminded himself of his promise to his father to teach Pacon, and of his promise to himself to have some fun with the scrawny brat.

"See this?" Nimbo pointed at a long, dark shadow on the forest clearing floor.

Pacon wiped salt sweat from his eyes and blinked. In their mother tongue, his name meant *idiot.*

"That's where you're headed," Nimbo finished, tracing the line of the shadow through the humid air with his fingertip until he was pointing at its farthest point.

Pacon shrugged and started—actually started—walking along the shadow as though it were a tightrope and he its walker.

Nimbo snorted and fell about laughing at the sight of his young brother. In all his twelve years he had never seen his brother act so dumb, and that was saying something.

Stopping in his tracks, Pacon turned and mouthed a single petulant word.

"What?"

Tears welled up in Nimbo's eyes and he fought valiantly to stifle his laughter.

"Wrong way, fool," he said, chuckling. "You have to go that way."

Nimbo pointed aloft at the treetop. The tualang was a younger specimen—lucky for Pacon as the adults could reach dizzying heights of two hundred, two hundred and fifty feet or more.

"I can't climb up there!"

Pacon's jaw almost hit the floor, making Nimbo laugh even harder. As his chuckles subsided, Nimbo put a brotherly arm around Pacon's shoulders and led him to the base of the tree trunk.

"If you want to eat tonight, you'd better get climbing. Don't worry, little brother, I'll help you reach the first branch."

He cupped his hands and gave Pacon a leg up into the tree. His sibling was so clumsy he lost his grip on the first branch and fell back, almost knocking Nimbo over.

"Fool," Nimbo groaned, pushing against Pacon's backside to get him back up into the tree. "Grab a tight hold of the branch, then pull yourself up and find the next one."

"I don't think I can—" Pacon started.

"Don't look down, only up," Nimbo snapped, reciting the advice like a mantra. He had, after all, told Pacon the same thing many times over the years—but always with the same resulting clumsiness from his younger sibling.

"Don't know why I bother," he hissed under his breath.

"How far do I have to go?" Pacon's voice was muffled by the tree's foliage. At least he had ascended more than a few feet this time.

"Just follow the hum."

"I can't hear anyth—"

"Well, if you stop chattering for a minute you might hear," Nimbo growled. "Now climb, and try to find the hive before it gets dark, will you?"

Pacon went quiet, save for the grunting that came of his exertion and the gentle rustle of the falling leaves as his body displaced them from the tree's gnarled branches. They rained down on Nimbo like confetti, displacing the cataract light of the sun through the trees.

"Found it!" Pacon hissed through clenched teeth.

"Great, now reach in and extract the goods, just like I showed you."

That last part was the hardest, and Nimbo knew it. He had used a hollowed-out melon skin to show Pacon how to extract the honey. But this time, his brother would have to deal with real-life swarming bees while extracting his golden prize.

"You have the cloth ready?"

"Mmmm." Pacon's reply was muffled and dreamlike.

Nimbo craned his neck to try and see what his brother was

doing. He could just about see him loosen the cloth wrapping from the drawstring of his loincloth. Good. He must get the honeycomb inside quickly, along with any bees that wanted to come along for the ride. Nimbo bit his lip as he watched Pacon reach into the hive gingerly.

"Come on, come on," he muttered under his breath. If only Pacon could do this one good thing, maybe their father would sing them a song, rather than the usual litany, that night.

"Owowowow!" Pacon's voice pierced the cloying, wet heat of the forest like a gunshot. He recoiled from the hive and the tree trunk, losing his grip on the upmost branch above him followed by the cloth containing what little honeycomb he had extracted.

The cloth tumbled and bounced through the branches until it hit the forest floor, spilling its precious golden cargo.

"Damn it!" Nimbo cursed. He started for the spilled honey, then stopped in his tracks as a louder sound erupted in the branches above him. Looking up, he saw the sky go as dark as an inkblot. The sound rose in volume and intensity, a heaving swell of thousands of tiny—and angry—little wings.

Pacon cried out, an awful exclamation of fear and pain. Nimbo saw the boy fall back from the tree as thousands of black bodies swarmed from the hive. They swirled around him like an ethereal cloak as he tumbled after the cloth, winding himself on branches as he fell. His heavy, uncontrolled descent led him to the thickest of the branches. He let out a piercing cry of agony as his back snapped against a low branch. Then he fell limp to the ground.

For a second, all was quiet, like that moment before a storm cloud breaks. Nimbo looked at his brother, saw the welts forming on the skin of his face, his chest and his arms. Their eyes met, his younger brother's glassy with tears and incredulity.

Then the droning of the bees returned with renewed vigor. Nimbo could feel the rush of them in the air, diving for him and Pacon, ready to wound their tender flesh.

"Run!" he said, reaching for Pacon through the swarm, intent on dragging him to safety. He did not hate his brother. He loved him. Even though he had brought the entire damned hive raining down on them like yellow death, he loved him. Pacon howled as Nimbo pulled him to his feet. The kid had fallen badly, maybe even displaced a few vertebrae in his back. He would have to pay a visit to the village healer—they both would if they got out of this alive.

Nimbo felt the skin at the back of neck burn white hot at the sting of the first of the bees. Others found the moist, tender spots beneath his arms where soft downy hairs had already begun to grow. Yet more stung his feet and calves as he ran. He did not look back for fear that they might somehow find entry to his eyes.

Careering through the tree cover, supporting Pacon as best he could, Nimbo crashed into a ditch. More like a crater, the dip in the land was devoid of life. Only dry grasses clung on there, such was the poor condition of the soil. This was one of the areas burned out by the fearsome, nomadic blaze farmers. They had cleared acres in and around the forest surrounding Nimbo's heartland. Nothing grew there now, and as a result he and Pacon were out in the open—sitting ducks for the bees and their harsh stingers. Nimbo glanced back and saw the looming cloud of bees gaining on them. They had no time to lose, and only one direction in which to go.

"Come on!"

Nimbo hoisted his brother's arm tighter around his neck and, driven by the violent buzzing at their backs, they pushed on across the arid ditch and into the thick tree cover beyond. The damp coolness of the trees soothed Nimbo's burning skin no sooner had they entered the forest. With that tiny glimmer of hope in his heart, he half-dragged, half-lifted his brother onward—toward the caves.

The caves were forbidden, he knew that, and from the moan of protest from his brother, Pacon remembered it, too. But there was no other choice; if they wanted to shrug off the bees, they needed to be somewhere dark, and somewhere wet. The caves fit the bill perfectly, and as Nimbo's toes dug into the moist red clay leading to the cave mouths, he dared to think they might even survive. Every village had at least one fatality from bee stings—enough of them could send the victim into shock and induce a fever from which they might never awake. If it was that or the caves, he'd risk the caves any day. The clay was like a mudslide at the entrance and it took two frantic attempts for Nimbo to drag himself, and his brother, high enough to get a handhold on the *curare* vines covering the rocks.

"No, no, smells bad in here," Pacon protested. He was shivering, already going into shock from the sheer number of stings that had penetrated his skin.

"Good," Nimbo replied. "Let's hope the bees hate the smell as much as you do."

With a single, lithe movement, Nimbo dropped to his haunches and kicked out his legs beneath him. With one hand clutching his little brother's shirt tight, Nimbo slid from the light of the forest and into the gloom of the cave with Pacon trailing after him. They slid down the wet clay chute for what felt like an age. Nimbo felt tangled roots brush against his arms and legs, the veins and ventricles of the forest high above. Nimbo's breath cooled in the back of his throat as the humid air of the rainforest turned to the damp murk of below ground. The muddy slope beneath him began to level out and he and Pacon slowed in their undignified descent, coming to rest in the pitch darkness of the cave.

"Pacon? You all right?"

His brother whimpered, a singularly pained and fearful sound. Nimbo listened hard for that dreaded droning of the bees and found only silence. Relieved, he felt around in the dark to get a sense of where they had landed. His fingertips and knuckles brushed against smooth rocks and stones. There seemed to be dozens of them littering the cave floor. His eyes were still adjusting to the darkness. Looking back to the cave opening through which they had tumbled, he could see a faint halo of light thirty, maybe forty, feet above.

His instinct was to climb back up there, to be back in the light air of the forest. The stench invading his nostrils was an unsavory blend of sweet and sour. It reminded him of the pungent algae that gathered around the makeshift jetty near to his village. In high summer the jetty was the smelliest place in the rainforest, a haven for mosquitoes. No such creatures buzzed in the cave. Despite the smell of rot and decay it was as quiet as winter. A chill permeated the sweat slicing the back of Nimbo's neck. There was no breeze penetrating the cave; the source of the chill must have been a feeling, instinct. And right now, that instinct was telling Nimbo to climb the hell out of there. Every fiber of his being was screaming at him to drag Pacon up and out into the azure sky to breathe fresher air—even if that air was swarming with fat, angry bees out for revenge. Nimbo squeezed Pacon's hand and began to pull him back toward the slope and its distant beacon of light. As he did so, he felt his younger brother's hand squeeze tighter, then let go. Nimbo turned his attention from the little emergency exit halo of light and saw another light source, deeper in the cave. A disembodied, flickering flame was dancing toward them, its light painting the cave walls orange. And what a cave it was, massive in scale and lined with paintings that had been fashioned in ochre, white—and blood red. The flame flickered closer, just two-score feet away now, and Nimbo glanced at the scenes depicted in the cave paintings. On either side of the cave they were surrounded by depictions of death, torture, and brutality. Human figures were pinioned, laid out, impaled on stakes for as far as the eye could see. Nimbo blinked their terrifying afterimages away and pulled again at his brother. There were worse things than bees in this cave, and he wanted out. At Nimbo's urgent touch, Pacon snapped out of his shocked state and together they turned and fled for the cave entrance. They slipped, tripped, and clambered their way over the detritus lining the cave floor. As the torch flame danced closer behind them, Nimbo took in the ruin at his feet in all its horrific majesty. He and Pacon were navigating a charnel carpet of bones—a femur here, a shattered ribcage there, and worst of all, hundreds upon hundreds of skulls. Human skulls. A gasp died in Nimbo's throat as he realized many of the skulls were smaller than the others; they had belonged to children.

"Climb, Pacon, climb!"

Nimbo's heart beat a frantic tattoo in his chest, half from terror, half from pure exertion as he pushed and pulled his little brother up the slope. The clay that had helped their descent was now hindering their crazed climb. Then Nimbo felt the heat of the flame at his heels, followed by the wrench-like grip of a massive hand. He lashed out with his foot, felt his heel connect with something hard and stubbly. A man's chin. So, their assailant was human after all, not some demon of the caves. This gave Nimbo hope—if it was human, it could be reasoned with, outsmarted. He swiveled his hips and turned over so he could rest on his elbows. Kicking out again, he saw the face of his attacker. It was a noble face, angular, as though hewn from shadows. Where its eyes should have been, Nimbo could only see the reflections of the flaming torch it still carried in its left hand. The flames danced in those strange black orbs, burning pure fury and intent. Nimbo wanted to kick the man back into the cave from which he had emerged, but that iron grip was still clamped around his other ankle.

"Leave him alone!"

It was Pacon. In his fear, Nimbo had almost forgotten his little brother was still at his side. He wanted to warn his sibling to just climb, that he should clamber over him if he needed to. To just escape. Because in the second that it took to kick the hulking man in the chin again, Nimbo knew this was a human being who couldn't be reasoned with, or outsmarted. The only thing that would save them now was pure luck or the favor of the Gods of Rock and Earth.

The gods were listening.

Before Nimbo could say a word, he saw Pacon bite down into the man's wrist with such fury that he would put a rabid dog to shame. The man cried out, a deep, strangled and inhuman howl unlike anything Nimbo had ever heard before. Pacon's bite did the trick. The man let go, instantly freeing Nimbo from his grasp. Grabbing a hold of his brother, Nimbo dug his heels into the clay and pushed himself and Pacon backward up the slope.

Twenty feet.

On and on he climbed, risking a glance over his shoulder to see the halo of light taking shape as they got closer to it.

Fifteen feet.

Ten.

Almost there. Nimbo sucked wet, humid air into his lungs. He felt light, giddy, the effort of the climb inebriating his senses. Nimbo roared as he dragged his brother the remaining few feet to the tunnel opening, then out into the blistering heat and blazing sunshine. Pacon landed on his back between Nimbo's legs. They had made it. Driven to maniacal laughter by his ordeal Nimbo looked down at his brother's face, ready to kiss him on the forehead with joy. They had survived the hunt; they could afford to go back to the village empty-handed because they had something more permanent than food to offer. They had a survival story, a tale that would be told to their children and grandchildren after them. But the kiss died on Nimbo's lips as he saw what had happened to his brother's face. Pacon's eyes had been gouged from their sockets. Looking up at Nimbo were two bloody pools. Pacon's mouth was locked in a silent scream, his cheeks and mouth livid with his own spillings.

Tears filled Nimbo's eyes. He clutched at his brother. Then, Pacon was dragged away from him, back down into the maw of the cave with such force that it toppled Nimbo. By the time he got back to his feet, Pacon's agonized screams had subsided and Nimbo was left alone in the forest.

He fled.

CHAPTER TWO

Buenaventura, gateway to the Amazon. 1926

Rosie Shields turned nineteen aboard an ocean liner bound for South America. Her aunt and uncle treated her to afternoon tea on deck, but they had been forced to withdraw when the weather had taken a turn for the worst. Rosie wouldn't have minded—they had traveled so much since she lost her parents that she had long since grown her sea legs.

Francesca had inherited her sister's farm, which she promptly sold to Mr. Lanchester who had kept his beady eye on the land for years. He was a local banker and Rosie's best friend Esme's father. Friendship could rarely endure such matters—the best friends drifted apart before the ink had dried on the deeds.

The money was put to, as Gregory had it, "higher purpose in the service of the Lord." That meant traveling from place to place while Rosie's uncle preached his heart out to anyone who would listen. Aunt Francesca had higher purposes of her own in mind, often taking in the stores while Gregory attended to his ministry. Following a brief stint north of the border in Canada, Rosie had spent her early teens in Cambridge, England when Uncle Gregory declared that they would be making a pilgrimage to the seat of Anglicanism. It was there he had answered his calling to a new post as missionary to the indigenous, and patently Godless, peoples of the Amazon rainforest. Rosie, too, was baptized into the Anglican faith, and took the sacrament—

Do you renounce the evil powers of this world which corrupt and destroy the creatures of God?

—her aunt and uncle's way of vanquishing the last remnants of atheist from her being.

Francesca had suggested they establish Rosie at a boarding

school in Cambridge, but it was decided that she could take lessons while she traveled with them. Their trip had no end date as such, and she was their charge ever since the moment that Gregory had bravely rescued her from the fire. And so, her aunt became her unofficial tutor, though the only lessons she seemed to wish to convey were those of etiquette, obsessed as she was by the notion of creating a well-mannered lady from the raw materials of a farm girl born out of wedlock. Perhaps in part because of this approach to schooling, Rosie had grown into a quiet, self-conscious young woman.

Rosie was an observer and when she looked at the outside world she saw, predominantly, faces. Her eyes accentuated the positives in each passing visage. The bridge of a nose smaller, cuter and more button-like than hers. The mysterious alcoves of high cheekbones that she would never possess. To add insult to injury, each facial landscape was clad in that precious commodity she coveted above all other things—perfect skin.

When the outside world peered back at Rosie, she knew it saw only the imperfections; the blemishes on her cheeks, nose, and forehead that testified so angrily to her skin condition. On her worst days, ugly pustules formed like a dermal minefield at the epicenter of a particularly bad flare-up. Today was, regrettably, one of those days.

The outside world saw that she was clad in a tainted canvas of altogether imperfect skin. She could see it—disgust, loathing—written on every bright and beautiful face that passed her by. It was for this reason that Rosie rarely went out. And when she did, when she *had* to—especially those situations that put her beneath the unwelcome, harsh glare of sunlight—she closed her eyes to keep the outside world at bay.

She was under the scrutiny of that dreaded sunlight now as she trudged after her aunt and uncle toward the mass of people gathered at the quayside. The area was a suntrap, offering no shade from the glare. A huge paddle steamer was docked at the railings, its massive wheel reminding Rosie of the Ferris rides at the fairgrounds back home. Ohio was a world away now. The first leg of their journey, from England to the mouth of the Amazon, had taken an age. Yet here they were, about to set sail or rather, paddle, once again. The prow of the vessel was decorated with peeling paint that bore the name *Amazonian Princess*. Rosie rather liked the fact that this princess was a little rough around the edges—she could identify with that.

She wished her clothing could hide her from the world a little better. Her aunt had insisted she wear the prettier of her bonnets, despite Rosie's protestations that the garment afforded little protection from the sun's rays. Fighting the urge to scratch and claw at her burning skin, Rosie glared after her aunt as she struggled to keep up. At least the rest of her body was protected from the glare, clad as she was head to foot in a dress too thick for the weather.

Catching up to her puritanical guardians, Rosie paused for breath and dabbed at her forehead with a handkerchief. She could already feel more pustules erupting there—little volcanoes that embodied her anger at being dragged out in the sun on what felt like the hottest day of the year. Rosie stood and glowered at her Uncle Gregory. He was in his fifties now, and gruffer than ever. He carried himself with the air of a man who believed he was always right, and was at that moment dispensing his wisdom upon a harried dock official. Waving his ticket like a duelist's glove in the man's crimson face, he proclaimed their right to board before, as he put it, "the passengers from the lower slopes." Her uncle's hands were clad, as ever, in the sable gloves he always wore in public to keep his scars hidden. Seeing the gloves never failed to remind Rosie of the night he had saved her life from the farmhouse blaze. A heroic act she would never be allowed to forget, well, not if her Aunt Francesca had anything to do with it. It was not that she was anything less than grateful, of course. Rosie adored her uncle even on his "difficult" days—it was simply that she did not feel, at the age of nineteen, that she needed daily reminders from her aunt about how lucky she was to be alive. And how she owed that life to them.

The memory of childhood flames ratcheted up Rosie's current temperature by a few degrees. She hissed through her teeth as she dabbed again with her handkerchief. The perspiration on her brow was worsening the rash that even now she could feel spreading across her forehead and up into her hairline. Uncle Gregory caught her glowering at him. He towered over her from his vantage point on the steps to the boarding gates.

"Whatever is the matter, child?"

The shrill voice was her aunt's, loaded with impatience and the strain that her corset was putting on her lower back.

"My skin, of course," Rosie hissed. "You both know how the sun provokes it."

Rosie watched as Gregory slipped a gloved finger inside his dog collar, wiping away the sweat that had pooled there, no doubt. Even God's ministers were not immune from the effects of the sun.

"Sunlight is God's gift to all creatures great and small," Gregory espoused. "It allows crops to thrive, and the Lord's servants to thrive with them. Without His blessing of sunlight mankind would still be trapped in the primordial dark."

"Like those poor fellows in Cattle Class, eh?"

Rosie grimaced at her aunt's quip. Despite her position as a missionary's wife, Francesca could be snooty at the best of times. Rosie knew that her uncle found Francesca's demonstrative attitude toward their position in society vulgar to the extreme, yet lacked the courage—or patience—to pick her up on it.

"Women and children first," Gregory said as he pushed past the sweating dock official.

"Quite," Francesca said. Then, taking Rosie by the wrist, began climbing the steps to the boarding gates.

As Rosie was dragged into the crowd, her eyes met the dock official's. He had kind eyes that, rare beyond measure, seemed to see past her blotchy skin and instead gazed at her with what looked like sincere pity. Rosie basked in his benevolent look for a moment, taking solace from it like the shade from a cloud. Then she was dragged ever on toward the boarding gate and the paddle steamer beyond that would deliver her to her destiny.

The air cooled the deeper they walked into the ship and, mercifully, so did Rosie's skin. The steamer was vast, a seemingly endless warren of creaking corridors, each one smartly clad in uniform cream walls and burgundy carpeting. Brass-rimmed portholes were set into the walls of the outer corridors at intervals, giving sporadic views of the dock and the teeming crowds boarding the vessel. Deeper in, these portholes became merely decorative, some framing tranquil little nautical scenes painted in oils beneath renderings of azure skies. Rosie liked these best of all, appreciative of their fake sunlight. Other portholes had been used to house menus and notices of entertainments in the ship's ballroom. Rosie's jaw dropped at the thought of an actual ballroom aboard a ship. But when she hesitated to take a closer look at the playbill, her aunt seized her by the sleeve of her pinafore dress and hurried her on. Uncle Gregory came to an abrupt halt around the next corner and dismissed the deckhand who had led them to their cabins no sooner than the doors were open.

Rosie's cabin was tiny, about five by eight feet at a guess, with the bulk of the room taken up by a cot bed set into the wall opposite another brass-framed porthole. This one looked out over the dock, and Rosie could just spy the outlet leading from the docks and onto the vast river beyond. The cabin smelled of polish and starch, and a full-length mirror gleamed in the corner. Rosie glanced at the crisp white sheets and royal blue blankets atop her bed. The pillowcases were sure to bring her skin out in a rash.

She was just about to ask her aunt if she could unpack her spares when Francesca turned to her with an overdone smile and said, "What a charming little boudoir. Quite sufficient for a young lady at sea, don't you agree, Gregory?"

"Certainly," he answered, his approving gaze settling on a modest wooden crucifix hanging from the cabin wall above Rosie's bed.

"I suggest we unpack our things, then find a vantage point above decks to observe our departure," Aunt Francesca said. At Gregory's nod of agreement, she continued, "Rosie, I shall knock for you in ten minutes."

"I'd rather watch from here," Rosie said.

"From here, child? Whatever do you mean? Through the porthole?" Francesca mouthed the word like it was a foreign expletive.

"Through the porthole," Rosie replied.

Francesca looked to Gregory for advice. He shrugged and made his way to their adjoining cabin.

"Suit yourself, child," Rosie's aunt said, before hurrying after Gregory.

Rosie shut the cabin door after them and bolted it. She turned and was faced by her mirror image in the looking glass. For a moment, she glimpsed herself as being beautiful, her fair complexion framed by tumbling pre-Raphaelite curls. Her shoulders were slender and her figure curved, but slim. The confines of her clothing accentuated the emergence of her breasts and hips. From a distance, Rosie thought she might look like quite a catch. Crossing to the mirror though, her heart sank seeing the work the sun had done on her tortured skin. Her forehead, cheeks, and the bridge of her nose looked as red as ripe tomatoes. If it wasn't for her skin condition, perhaps she would be perceived as beautiful. But what was it that people said?

Beauty is only skin deep. Easy for those with flawless skin to say.

Rosie took her shawl and draped it over the looking glass. Sighing, she kicked off her shoes, flopped onto the bed then stretched out on her front. Propping her chin up in her hands she gazed out across the bay. Alone in the cabin, enveloped in the cave-like retreat of her own making, Rosie waited for the steamer to move off. As the vessel's engines began to chug and hum, she felt her eyelids growing heavy.

When Rosie awoke, she felt as though someone were crushing the breath from her chest. As she came to, she realized the pressure was beneath her. She was still lying face down on the bed. When she opened her mouth to breathe, she gagged on a mouthful of thick, acrid smoke. Opening her eyes, she pushed her body up from the bed. Glancing around the room burned her eyes, as every inch was filled with billowing black smoke. She stumbled to the floor, feet searching out her shoes on instinct. She tripped over their familiar shape, and staggered headlong into the door. It buckled beneath her weight with the heat of a thousand fires but did not give. Remembering she had locked it, she reached for the little brass catch. Her fingers were seared by the heat; the metal was molten hot. The whole ship must have been ablaze. Crying out, she tucked her wounded fingers under her arm and retreated from the heat. Over her shoulder a vague glow permeated the fog of deadly smoke filling the room.

The porthole.

Her burned fingers made clumsy work of the little wingnut catches either side of the porthole. Rosie's efforts were made all the more difficult by the choking smoke that billowed around her. Feeling she might pass out at any moment, Rosie focused her resolve on the window catches, driven on by the heat of the blaze that was causing her cabin door to crack and splinter. Even if she could get the porthole open, she would still be trapped by the blaze, but the instinct to breathe clean air sent her body into autopilot.

One catch opened, then the other, and Rosie thrust her head

out into space. Cool night air washed over her face, along with a soft dampness that could only be sea spray. She breathed deep and coughed up claggy black smoke residue from her lungs. A crash, and distant screams, rang out behind her and she felt a fury of flames enter the room, lapping at her back like hot waves. She laughed, actually laughed, at the thought that she would die like this—with her head stuck out of a porthole above an ocean of water as she was burned alive by the inferno that was shaking the ship to its core.

Closing her eyes, she felt a tear escape from the corner of her eye. The tear burned against her sore cheek as it trickled down her face. Then, impossibly, she felt frantic hands at her shoulders, pulling her through the porthole.

But I'm too big, she thought, *I won't fit.*

Even as her mind formed the words, she felt the porthole stretch somehow, felt its brass orifice pushing her out and through into the cooling night air. Strong arms gripped her tight, carrying her to safety. She opened her eyes and, instead of the deck of a ship, she saw the scorched plantation outside her mother and father's house. Craning her neck, she could see the house ablaze behind her and could hear her mother's tortured screams.

She fought those arms then. She kicked and railed and screamed, *let me go, let me go, I have to save her, she's burning, she's burning.* But her savior held her fast and carried her farther away until the burning house was but a candle flame in her field of vision. Rosie was set down on the cold earth. She looked up into the face of the man who had rescued her from the fire. Uncle Gregory, his skin a slick of black soot and salt sweat.

He panted as he looked down at her and said, "You're safe, child, safe now."

Rosie spoke the names of her mother and father. Uncle Gregory looked upon the flames with resignation. She knew then they were both dead, and she an orphan. And Rosie wished she were dead, too. Wished with all her heart that her uncle had left her in the house to burn with her parents because she did not know how to live without them. Not understanding this, Uncle Gregory had knelt down beside her and cradled her in his arms.

"You're safe," he repeated.

Rosie could smell the burned flesh of his hands, ruined in

the blaze. She tried to push him away, desperate to be free of the charnel stench of blistered flesh and singed hairs, but he held her fast. Rosie wept floods of tears, but they were not enough to put out the fire.

CHAPTER THREE

Urgent rapping at Rosie's door roused her from her nightmare. She wiped drying tears from her eyes, artifacts from her bad dream, and crawled across the cot bed to look out the porthole. The undulating surface of the sea stretched as far as her eyes could see, reflecting the blue-gray sky above. She'd missed the steamer's departure during her impromptu sleep and could hear the steady thrum and splash of its big wheels in the water. In the cold light of the cabin she was resolute—she had endured the nightmare countless times since the night her uncle had rescued her and, along with her aunt, taken her in as their own.

Crossing to the door she could hear Gregory's clipped tones, brandishing her name like a weapon as the rapping continued. Rosie heard her uncle instruct someone to put a shoulder to it and thought it best to unlock the door. As soon as she did, a red-faced trio almost tumbled through the door—the first she recognized as the same deckhand who had shown them to their cabins earlier, followed close behind by her uncle and aunt.

"There you are, miss," the deckhand said, straightening his uniform. He looked even more put-upon than when she had seen him before—another unwitting beneficiary of her aunt and uncle's particular brand of social interaction. "Your parents were worried about you. Best not to lock yourself in like—"

"We are *not* her parents. Rather we find ourselves in the unenviable position of being her guardians. And I will complete the young lady's schooling if it's all the same to you," Francesca sniped, fixing the poor young man with a look that would freeze hot coffee.

The deckhand tipped his hat, first to Rosie then to her guardians, and sloped away.

"We missed the departure, thanks to you," Francesca said,

rounding on Rosie. "And everything was so chaotic we couldn't find anyone to help. What were you playing at, locking your door?"

Rosie glared defiantly at her aunt. The truth was, she cared not about missing their departure, all those crowds, all that noise, and the unbearable heat of the sun on her tender skin. She was about to articulate as much when her uncle fixed her with a stern gaze. Rosie faltered under his intensity and looked at the floor, mumbling, "I was tired is all. My skin...you know it exhausts me when it's so sore..."

"God saved you from the inferno, child," Gregory intoned. "The skin you are in is His creation, and a reminder of how lucky you are to be alive at all."

"Unlike my parents," Rosie said, her voice trailing off to a whisper as she recalled her dream. Unpleasant memories returned to her—screams, the roar of flames, exploding glass, and splitting timbers. She shook her head, willing them away and straining to hear the lapping of waves against the ship's hull.

"Unlike your dear parents." Aunt Francesca reached out and lifted Rosie's chin with her gloved hand. Her brow was furrowed as she peered down at Rosie, as though she were a parlor medium trying to read her aura. "To whom we are of course grateful for bringing you into the world."

Doubting the sincerity of her aunt's comment, Rosie longed to be alone again, even if that meant one more nightmare.

Better than the waking one I live in, thought Rosie bitterly.

But she had learned her aunt and uncle's limits over the years she had lived with them, and knew the best course of action was to feign compliance.

"I'm sorry, I didn't mean to sound ungrateful," she said.

Her aunt's fingers slipped from beneath her chin.

"Very well. But you are not to lock your door again for the duration of the voyage," her aunt said. "Your uncle and I are situated in the very next room. And tidy yourself up, girl, we will dine shortly and can't possibly have you out and about looking like you've just woken up. Uncle Gregory has been invited to say grace at the captain's table this evening."

With that grandiose statement, her guardians left. Rosie closed the door after them and fished out a small vanity mirror from her luggage. She was dreading the prospect of a social engagement, not least with the captain of the ship. Aghast at her tear-stained, red-cheeked reflection, Rosie wondered if it was worth trying to escape through the porthole after all.

The ship's ballroom was a grand affair. White-clothed tables were arranged in a tiered hierarchy, with the best tables overlooking the dance floor and grand piano. Crisply dressed waiting staff processed like worker bees in and out of the ballroom doors, which were flanked by huge bouquets of fresh cut flowers. Rosie could not help but think that the flowers would be long dead by the time they reached their destination. She scratched at an itch forming beneath the lace of her evening dress, its dark, heavy fabric more suited to a wake than a meal. Gritting her teeth, she hoped the ordeal would be over within an hour, but in her heart, she knew that she had a long evening of discomfort ahead of her. At least the red patches on her cheeks and forehead were hidden beneath a thick layer of face powder she had purloined from her aunt's meager stock of cosmetics.

Their waiter led Rosie and her uncle and aunt to the topmost table. Heads turned their way as they wove through the lower ranks and up into the echelons of high society. All around them diners silently questioned who these top-table newcomers were—eager for a glimpse of someone worth gossiping about. Seeing Gregory's dog collar many of the diners looked away again in an instant, his attire giving them all the details they needed about why he had been welcomed to the captain's table. Others ogled openly, and one or two of the male diners cast lingering looks in Rosie's direction. For once, she didn't mind. In fact, Rosie basked in the attention their brief celebrity had afforded. It felt almost good to be turning a few heads for reasons other than her blotchy skin. Rosie sat and unfolded her napkin in her lap while her aunt studied her every move. She was smiling, an expression that elicited nothing short of rapturous wonder from her aunt.

"Look, Gregory, she's actually smiling."

Gregory made a harrumphing sound and focused on the menu at his place setting.

"We'll make a lady of you yet, Rosie," Francesca continued. "But be warned, if this is the standard you wish to attain on a regular basis there is much work to be done. Much work."

"I'll enjoy it while it lasts," Rosie said.

"You're wise to," her uncle said from behind his menu.

"There'll be no silver service where we're going."

Rosie caught a look of displeasure as it flashed across Francesca's eyes. Her aunt would clearly much rather remain in this world, aboard the fake, floating manor house of the steamer with its tightly maintained class system.

"You look nice, dear," Francesca said to Rosie, sidestepping her husband's comment. "A little too much powder though—allow me to supervise your next application."

"I'm nineteen."

Rosie stopped herself from saying anything further, feeling relief as some other guests approached the table.

"And what is such a young lady doing on a tub like this?"

The voice was dark and rough, and as Rosie looked up to meet its owner for the first time, she saw he more than matched it in those same aspects.

"Frank Richter, at your service," he said, taking Rosie's hand and stooping to kiss it, but never once breaking eye contact with her. Rosie withdrew her hand sheepishly. The man was imposing and a little scary, even. His Southern drawl of an accent enveloped a pinch of German. He was dressed in a striking ensemble comprising a striped linen suit and a Stetson. Rosie could not decide if he looked more like a Wild West lawman, or outlaw gunslinger. The more he towered over her, the more she suspected the latter. He reeked of tobacco.

"Mr. Richter," Aunt Francesca announced, "I am Francesca McAllister, this is my husband the Reverend Gregory McAllister, and our charge, Rosie Shields. Do take a seat."

Richter made a show of greeting each of them with how-do-you-dos aplenty. When he finally sat down, it became apparent he had two other fellows with him whom he introduced merely as his "associates." One had beady eyes and a sinewy frame wrapped tight in a dark velvet suit. The other had the physique and large, overhanging brow of a manual laborer. Rosie looked at the man's hands in awe—they were both as large as dinner plates. He looked like he broke rocks for a living. Becoming aware that Richter was quietly smiling at her awestruck look, Rosie averted her gaze and fiddled with her napkin.

"I say. Is this the captain's table I see before me?"

The voice was stiff and nasal, with a lightness that made Rosie want to giggle. She looked up and saw that the speaker's face was no less jovial. Red-cheeked, with daffodil yellow hair that sprouted from beneath his straw boater, he looked to be in his early fifties but with eyes that burned with the youthful vigor of a man half his age. His body twitched uncontrollably as his words tumbled out of him as if they had been stored up in his head for eons, waiting for this chance to escape.

"Not very often one receives an invitation to dine with the Great and the Good. I am Cecil, Jeremy Cecil—professor to be precise."

The professor paused for breath and bowed ceremoniously to Francesca and Rosie, before nodding in an approximation of masculinity to the men. Rosie's aunt made the introductions and Professor Cecil joined them at the table, looking somewhat nervous and excited to be among company.

Presently, the captain of the vessel arrived. He cut a dash in his white linen uniform, with sparkling gold-braided epaulettes atop each shoulder and crowned with his captain's hat, which he removed with some ceremony before sitting.

"Ladies, gentlemen, thank you for joining me this evening, and welcome aboard." Rosie beamed at him, entranced by his dark, olive skin and the rumbling timbre of his voice. He looked like he had been born at sea and had a lifetime of naval adventures to tell.

To Rosie's disappointment, there were no such tales told during dinner. Polite small talk was the order of the day. After Uncle Gregory said grace, the talk turned to the innermost workings of the paddle steamer. By the time her dining companions had moved on to the history of Brazilian trade routes, Rosie's attention drifted to the denizens of the other tables. One table in particular caught her eye, as it was populated by a raucous group of Italian travelers. She marveled at the fuss they made over the arrival of each dish as it arrived, and the careless way that they poured their wine, with something approaching abandon. In truth, she wondered what it would be like to be among them, living life like some noisy great adventure.

"Hem-hem."

Her Aunt's fake cough brought Rosie's attention back to her fellows. Francesca frowned her disapproval at the Italian throng, just as the captain was waxing formal about how relaxed immigration policy was bringing ever more entrepreneurs into the region with each sailing. Under her aunt's watchful eyes, Rosie feigned interest in the conversation. She prodded her food with her fork and moved some of it around her plate without actually eating anything.

"So, what are you a professor of, exactly?"

Francesca's bluntness made her sound so rude at times, so confrontational, that Rosie could not help but squirm a little in her seat.

"Oh, oh…" Cecil spluttered on a mouthful of fish. He chewed, and then swallowed it down with a great gulp of wine before dabbing at his ochre whiskers with his napkin. "I am an acolyte of the photographic and phonographic sciences." Looking at each of the blank faces before him, he continued, "That is to say, I make pictures and audio recordings, *simulacra* if you will of the world around us. It is my intent to create an audiovisual record of the Amazon basin, its flora and fauna, peoples and customs." He reached for his glass with a trembling hand then set it down again as though afraid it might spill. "It's terribly exciting."

"Clearly," Francesca deadpanned.

"That explains the vast amount of luggage we carry for you in the hold," the captain said. "My crew needed some hammock time after lugging that lot in here, poor wretches."

"I hope the additional currency was enough to alleviate their exertions," Cecil replied.

Rosie detected sharpness in his voice, a calculating part of him that was otherwise hidden beneath his bumbling demeanor.

"Additional currency, eh?" the captain mused. "I shall have to have words."

Polite laughter rippled around the table. Rosie smiled, glad that the captain's quip had lightened the formal stuffiness of the meal at least.

"And what brings you and your daughter to the Tropics?" Cecil asked, glancing at Uncle Gregory, then Aunt Francesca.

"Oh, she is not our daughter, merely our charge," Francesca replied—a little too quickly for Rosie's liking.

"We are here to spread the Word," Gregory said, gruff as ever.

"The Word." Cecil made a meal of the term, searching for meaning.

"Of God," Gregory said.

"Oh! You're missionaries?" Cecil replied.

"Aye. Faith has taken me from the shores of Loch Shiel in

bonnie Scotland, to the seat of our faith in Canterbury. Then on to Ohio and now to the Amazon, where..."

"Who could argue with a faith that has you so well-traveled," Cecil quipped.

Gregory chose to ignore him and continued, "...where we are to convert the natives to His teachings."

"Why? Convert them, I mean."

All eyes were on Richter now, especially Gregory's—which Rosie noticed had narrowed with something bordering on contempt for the man.

"Heathen paganism is a hangover from the last century, Mr. Richter. Those who walk with the Word walk a divine path. We wish only to share that blessing with others."

"Have you met any tribespeople before?" Richter asked.

"Not as such, no. Unless you count Scots—there's many a tribe over there."

Uncle Gregory's attempt at a joke fell flat. Rosie watched her aunt fidget uncomfortably in her seat.

"Well, you'll have your work cut out for you, that's for sure," Richter said. "The Amazonians are very set in their ways. They have divine paths of their own, sacred routes through the rainforest known only by them and their kin."

"And you have walked these paths I take it?"

"But a fraction of them. It is said that a man would have to live ten lifetimes to walk the entirety of the rainforest and even then..." Richter paused to wink at Rosie, "...he'd be lost most of the time."

Muted laughter rippled around the table. To Rosie, it was a discomfiting sound, and one that accentuated the fact that she and her guardians were strangers in a strange land. The rainforest sounded increasingly like some vast alien world, and one that she was not sure she wanted to become lost in.

A cool dessert of exotic fruits from a huge platter followed the lull in conversation, after which the captain proposed a toast "to health, wealth and happiness" for his passengers. Each of them responded with gusto before downing their drinks, with the exception of Rosie. She attempted to refuse a flute of champagne, but Richter took one from the waiter's silver tray and slid it across the table to her.

"You never know when you'll get the chance to enjoy such fine things, young ma'am," he said, "especially where you're headed."

Rosie looked to her aunt for guidance on drinks decorum. She had not been allowed to partake back home. A sharp nod from Francesca told her that, in company, she had no choice but to take the drink. She spluttered as the bubbles from the champagne surged up through her throat and into her nose. The others laughed as though she were a child spitting at her first taste of castor oil. In a way she was—the champagne marked only her second experience of drinking alcohol. She dabbed at her nose with her napkin, a little disconcerted by the knowing twinkle in Richter's eyes as he watched over her like a bird of prey.

"Are you an explorer, Mr. Richter?"

Her aunt's customary bluntness had something of a disquieting effect on the group.

"I don't know about that," he said, "what do you think?"

"I think you dress like one."

Rosie blushed, partly from the sudden flush of alcohol in her system, but mostly because of her aunt's brazenness.

"I'm more a hunter than an explorer, truth be told."

"And what is it that you hunt?"

"Whatever I am paid to by my employers."

He fixed Francesca with a mirthless grin.

"Oh, and in whose employ are you, if you don't mind my asking?" Francesca asked.

"I do not. I hunt on behalf of a consortium of the wealthy—an elite group interested in exclusives of all kinds, but especially of the big game variety. Rarer the better."

Professor Cecil's ears pricked up at this. "Fascinating. So, your presence in the Amazon is to hunt and kill rare specimens? And take them back to your masters? Is that so?"

Richter's eyes narrowed to slits and his grin widened, revealing two perfect rows of teeth. "That's how it is."

"I must confess I did wonder when I saw your munitions boxes being brought aboard." Cecil looked hot under the collar. He harrumphed and waved his glass in the air for a refill. "I say, Captain, what is the shipping company's policy on carrying firearms aboard your vessel?"

The captain glanced at Richter. Rosie discerned unspoken tension between them.

It was Richter who replied.

"The people I work for *own* the shipping line, Professor. They own the table at which you are seated, the napkin in your lap, and the bubbles in your glass," he said, before downing the remainder of his champagne. "Now if you'll excuse me, my boys and I better get some beauty sleep. Ladies…"

The hunter made a show of kissing Francesca and Rosie's hands once more, while his silent companions flanked him like bodyguards.

"So soft, like the petals of a freshly-opened flower," Richter murmured as he held Rosie's hand in his calloused fingers. "Fragile as a butterfly's wings."

Rosie did not like the way he was looking at her through those narrow eyes of his, nor did she find his touch agreeable. She slid her fingers from his grasp before he was quite done with her. He tipped his hat to Rosie and then he and his fellows were gone. Rosie shivered involuntarily, catching a draft of outside air from one of the dining room windows. Evening was drawing in, in hues of purple and gold, over the river.

In the stillness, she saw Uncle Gregory consider his glass.

"God made the air in these bubbles. *He* is the owner of all things," he said.

A band had gathered on a low stage nearest the status tables. They launched into a jaunty rag, which Aunt Francesca took as a cue.

"Hem-hem. Rosie, it is perhaps time you were to turn in," Aunt Francesca said. She waved her hand in front of her as if to dispel Richter's lingering presence from the close atmosphere cloaking the table.

Rosie bade goodnight to the remaining diners and followed her aunt back to their cabins, noting that even the raucous laughter from the Italian table had died with the sunset.

CHAPTER FOUR

Rosie was glad to cast off her formal dress and stifling underclothes, enjoying the slight breeze that undulated through the porthole of her cabin. It was still hot but bearably so, now that she was unburdened of her restrictive frock.

She sat propped up in her cabin bed, half-reading the book of Psalms her aunt had foisted upon her. What she wouldn't give for an adventure novel, or epic romance, to while away the hours but her aunt and uncle would never allow such an indulgence. Listening to the rhythmic *thrum* of the paddle steamer's engine, Rosie let her book fall closed and ran her fingers across the nape of her neck. The warm breeze tickled her there like a phantom hand and she smiled at the sensation. But then the pleasant moment was gone, replaced by the sensory memory of Richter's rough fingers enclosing her hand like a vise. She blinked away the memory of those narrow eyes, studying her like a predator might survey its prey before closing in for the kill. He was a hunter, he'd made that very clear at dinner, and Rosie wondered if his base pursuits had given him cause to forget how to behave in polite company, or if he saw every encounter as an opportunity to prove himself the strongest will present. Her Uncle Gregory had made his dislike of the man evident through his uncomfortable silence. Normally her uncle would at least try to exchange pleasantries, in his own gruff way of course, but his silence when faced with a dominating fellow such as Richter spoke volumes.

Men were nothing short of a mystery to Rosie—their attitude toward life, their changes in mood, their bluster and innate rivalry all completely alien to her. She had never experienced a courtship and, though there were stirrings within her to the contrary, she hoped she might never have to endure one. Deciding the draft from the window was now an annoyance rather than soothing, she got out of bed to close the porthole and quickly dashed back beneath the sheets. Clutching the lace neck of her nightdress in her hand to keep it away from her skin, she drifted off to sleep.

The breeze woke her from her slumber.

Strange, she thought—still half-asleep—*could've sworn I closed the porthole.*

Then she felt strong hands on her body, weighing her down, and she panicked fully awake. The scant light from the porthole revealed the young deckhand's face, poised above hers, his expression a mask of expectant lust. What she had mistaken for the breeze from the porthole was in fact his breath, which came in sharp, excited rasps. She could smell strong liquor on his breath, rum or the like, and its heat burned her eyes. Rosie tried to cry out, but the sound imploded inside her dry throat as he let go of one of her wrists to clutch her neck. She used her free hand to lash out at his face, trying with all her might to simultaneously kick at him. The assailant shifted his weight above her, trying to pinion her legs with his knees. All the while his grip on Rosie's throat threatened to strangle her last breath away. He thrust his lower body against hers, making clear his intentions. She felt his heat and his arousal and for a moment she thought she might pass out from lack of oxygen. Then, she had her nails inside the flesh of his cheek, drawing blood. He yelped like a startled puppy and let go of her throat just long enough for her to take a blessed breath. Humiliated, he resumed his attack with renewed ferocity. But his sexual anger had tilted him a fraction away from her lower body and Rosie felt her knee connect with his manhood. There was a strange snapping sensation against her knee and she saw his drunken eyes bulge from their sockets.

Rosie scrambled from her bed and raced to the cabin door. But the deckhand was not about to give up yet, especially after she had wounded him. He clawed at her hair like a rabid wolf, entwining it in his hand like a leash. He pulled, hard, and the force spun her around on her heels. She screamed as he dragged her across the floorboards before throwing her onto the bed. Rosie tried to get to her feet once more, but he backhanded her with a cruel force that belied his modest stature. He dabbed at the blood oozing from the scratches on his face and tasted it. Licking his lips, he laughed.

"Now I'll make *you* bleed," he said, bloody spittle bubbling on his wet lips.

He unclasped his belt, removing it from his trousers and stretching it between his hands like a weapon.

"I'm going to enjoy you, little firebrand that you are," he cackled as he approached her.

Rosie tried to retreat, feeling only the hard and unyielding cabin wall at her back. She screamed then, the force of it cracking her voice.

The cabin door burst open, taking Rosie and the deckhand by surprise. Before either of them knew what was happening, a tall, swift figure crashed into the room, felling Rosie's would-be rapist with a single blow to the back of the neck.

"Are you all right, ma'am?" the man said.

Rosie stared in disbelief at Richter, holding a revolver in his right hand. He had knocked the deckhand unconscious using the butt of the revolver. She managed, amid her dissipating panic, to nod at Richter. Then amidst a small chorus of agitated voices, her Aunt Francesca and Uncle Gregory entered via the main cabin door through which her rescuer had arrived. They both looked at Rosie, then at the fallen deckhand, and finally to Richter.

"Rosie?" Francesca said, incredulous. "The communicating door was locked. We heard your cries but could not enter."

Richter crossed to the communicating door and found it latched.

"This fellow must have locked it when he showed you to your room earlier," Richter said. "His foolishly misguided libido led him back here, several drinks later by the looks of things."

"The rascal must be thrown off the ship," Francesca said, crossing to Rosie and frowning at the girl's neck, where Rosie imagined angry bruises were already forming.

"I am fine, Aunt Francesca," Rosie said. "He frightened me is all. My honor is still intact, even if my nightdress is not."

Her aunt tutted at the ripped fabric of Rosie's nightdress. She reached for a crocheted shawl hanging from the end of the cabin bed and draped it around her niece as though it were armor.

"The beast," she said.

"I'm sure the captain will have plans for his rehabilitation that will make him wish he'd stayed in his hammock tonight," Richter muttered, grabbing the boy by the ankles and dragging him from the room. He paused at the doorway and fixed Rosie with a paternal look.

"Best keep that door of yours locked for the duration, miss. Heat, drink, and beauty can have an ill effect on the weak-willed."

Rosie nodded again in agreement.

"Aye. An ill effect indeed," Gregory echoed, "thank you, Mister Richter, for your timely intervention."

"You're sure you're all right, miss?" Richter asked.

"Yes, I am, quite all right thanks to you, sir. I doubt I shall sleep but I do feel exhausted."

"That's the adrenalin," Richter said. Then, to Rosie's guardians, "You should be proud of your little girl here, it looks like she put up quite a fight."

Rosie could feel herself blush. "Perhaps I'll lie down for a little while now."

"Then you'd better do as the gentleman suggests," Francesca said, "keep the door locked, dear Rosie, and we shall leave the communicating door ajar."

Rosie winced at Francesca's sage advice. It had been her aunt and uncle who insisted she leave her door unlocked after all. Rosie wondered how different things might be if her parents were still alive to look after her. She had wondered that all her life. But now she was passing into womanhood, the burden, it seemed, was ever increasingly hers to bear. She wondered how she could possibly feel so alone with her aunt and uncle so present in her life. But the truth was she felt more alone in the world than ever before.

Her aunt and uncle filed out of Rosie's cabin after Richter and the still unconscious deckhand, leaving her wrapped in her shawl atop the bed. As soon as they'd gone, Rosie crossed to the porthole and opened it. She loosened the shawl, allowing the slight breeze from the movement of the steamer to soothe the contusions on her neck. A great soughing sob welled up in her chest and soon her cheeks were drenched in tears. Rosie sighed, the breath rattling a little in her tightened chest as she did so, trying to calm herself. She knew she was in a state of shock after her ordeal because she had felt this way before, long ago when she was a little girl, plucked from a burning house and cast adrift in someone else's world.

Looking out across the ripples unfurling across the glassy surface of the water, Rosie waited for the coming dawn.

Rosie refused to take breakfast in her cabin, making a show of her resolve. Her aunt and uncle seemed to approve of her attitude toward what Francesca referred to as "last night's unfortunate commotion." She made it sound as if Rosie had been entertaining in her cabin rather than being attacked by a drunken sailor. Rosie was about to protest when she thought better of it. Any display of emotion, one way or the other, would undermine her mental state in the eyes of her guardians. The more willing she was to get on with things, the more they might be inclined to leave her alone to her devices. Or at least that was the way it worked for her in the past. Playing the compliant niece might even earn her a parasol for their trip through the scorching hot jungle. She could hope.

After breakfast, Rosie packed her small suitcase. She had only been allowed to bring clothes, and had no entertainment aside from Francesca's book of Psalms, but Rosie had managed to smuggle one tiny piece of contraband inside her luggage. Glancing at the communicating door in her cabin to make sure no one was watching, Rosie unclipped the cotton lining inside the lid of her case and retrieved her forbidden treasure. She unfolded the small sheet of paper, enjoying its softness on her fingertips from years of clandestine readings such as this one. There, as ever, was the stark headline—a little faded now with age:

LOCAL FARMERS DIE IN TRAGIC FIRE

Below the headline was the picture of her family home. She had the imprint of its shape on her mind's eye. It looked stately, standing proud against the rolling fields she used to frolic in as a child. Portrait shots of her mother and father had been laid out either side of the farmhouse photograph. And there above the brief account of her parents' demise in the inferno was a sub-heading:

"It was God's Will"—Child Saved by Brave Pastor.

Rosie had remembered seeing her aunt acting suspiciously with the newspaper soon after her parents' funeral. Seeing a section of the paper had been cut away from the front page, Rosie had put two and two together. Her aunt was trying to protect her. She searched out the newspaper clipping in the garbage—it still bore a few stains from the potato peelings that had been thrown in after it—and had treasured it ever since.

Rosie kissed the photographs and closed her eyes in prayer for the mother and father she had barely known. She clung to the paper so that it might somehow communicate all of her lost memories of them to her. But her mind was a blank; the paper was all that remained of them, of their memory. Their ashes were long since scattered, and here she was a million miles away. She was thankful to her uncle of course, thankful for his bravery and what he had done for her. But sometimes Rosie felt as though she had been rescued from the fire, only to burn outside of it anyway. Her fingers found the sore, raised lumps on her face. The marks and lesions on her skin were her stigmata, the price she must pay for having been saved.

Hearing her aunt's voice, Rosie folded the newspaper cutting and tucked it back into the lining of her case. Her little secret. Her totem. She packed the last of her clothes and shut the case tight.

CHAPTER FIVE

Above decks, the paddle steamer was a flurry of activity. Deckhands hauled luggage onto every available space adjacent to the platforms used to exit the vessel. Passengers crowded the prow of the ship, eager to catch a glimpse of the port as the steamer reached the end of its journey. They had gone far beyond the mouth of the Amazon now, and Rosie still marveled at the huge distance between the river's banks. Tall trees formed a wall of green either side of them, beneath a brilliant blue canopy of cloudless sky. The sun was on the up. By midday it would be high in the sky, blasting the rainforest with its rays. Through the heat shimmer, Rosie saw plumes of steam rising from the trees like mist. They were breathing. Rosie pulled her bonnet forward as far as it would go, in order to protect her face from the sunlight.

Many of the passengers seemed oblivious to the verdant display that Mother Nature had created for them. They were focused entirely on locating their luggage and jostling for pole position in order to exit the vessel first once it had docked. Such behavior made Rosie chuckle. They had, after all, been sailing for an age—what difference would a few minutes make now that they had almost reached their destination? As the steamer chugged on through the water, signs of life began to reveal themselves. Floating huts lined the riverbanks on either side of the steamer—villages on the water, connected by a maze of wooden ramps and narrow rope bridges. Native people made their way across them, to and fro, carrying huge baskets on their heads laden with fruit, fish, or pulses. Rosie had never seen their like, especially as they were half-naked, wearing only simple skirts or tabards. Modesty forced her to look away, but not for long. The lithe people fixated her, and she was astonished at the skill with which they carried each load. She could barely imagine how heavy the overladen baskets must be, and yet the people carrying them did so balletically—as though the contents were merely feathers.

The steamer slowed, with a great grinding roar of its engines, big wheels thundering and kicking up spray as the vessel changed course. The port revealed itself amidst the surrounding floating villages and was teeming with life. Children splashed and played in the water, darting about between ranks of narrow rowing boats like excited shoals of fish. A joyous cacophony of cries started up as the children greeted the paddle steamer. Many of them began waving, and Rosie waved back, finding their apparent fascination with the arrival of so many strangers infectious.

Her aunt called to her—they were docking now—and Rosie peeled herself away from her vantage point to catch up to her guardians. As she navigated the narrow, crowded walkway to the main deck, Rosie spied Professor Cecil. His face was red as beetroot as he huffed and puffed, dragging a large wooden trunk behind him, followed by two deckhands who were struggling along with his many remaining boxes of equipment. Cecil blinked the sweat from his eyes, muttering under his breath, and looked like he might expire at any moment. Rosie rushed to his side.

"Good morning, Professor. Can I help you?"

"Oh, my dear girl, I couldn't possibly...I mean to say, it would be quite ungallant..." He set the wooden chest down for a moment, retrieving a white handkerchief from his waistcoat pocket to mop up the sweat cascading down his face. "If you would be so kind, my dear."

Rosie was about to grab hold of one of the side handles on the chest, when her uncle waded in. He placed his gloved hands on her shoulders and gently, but firmly, moved her to one side. Without a word, he grabbed a handle and helped Cecil heave the chest all the way to the disembarkation ramp and down onto dry land.

Cecil clapped a pink, sweaty hand on Gregory's arm.

"My dear fellow, most kind, what could I have done without your help I do not know."

The professor cast a disapproving look at the deckhands as they deposited his boxes in disarray, and without ceremony, on the ground.

"These blaggards could do with taking a leaf out of your good book, that's for certain."

Cecil tutted, reluctantly tipping the deckhands with a few

coins. They both lingered for more, but he waved them away as though they were insects.

"It's nae bother," Gregory said, himself perspiring.

"Now, where is my welcoming party?" Cecil said, scanning the crowd gathered around the jetty.

Rosie listened intently as Cecil spoke to a group of native speakers in their own tongue. The words sounded exotic to her, and musical to such an extent that the stilted, formal conversations she had experienced thus far paled by comparison. After a few back-and-forth exchanges with the natives, Cecil threw his hands up in the air and guffawed. Wiping the mirthful tears from his eyes, he turned to Gregory.

"I say, old chap, these fellows are to transport my equipment as far as the next village. Your mission house is adjacent, so why don't we travel as a convoy? A few extra cases won't matter a jot, and you good people are traveling so very light."

Uncle Gregory, being a proud man, was not the type of person to accept a favor. He stiffened, and looked prepared to refuse when Francesca stepped in.

"Most kind of you, Professor, that would be marvelous, a great kindness, thank you." At her husband's stern look, she added, "We will recompense you for the bearers' fees, of course."

"Nonsense," Cecil said. "It is all paid for. Besides, the entire trip is costing me a fraction of the bally tip those seadogs embezzled from me." He winked at Rosie, apparently enjoying having the audience for his starring role as an Englishman abroad.

She smiled back, warming to the professor. Rosie found his exuberance amusing, especially as she was used to the prim and proper ways of her aunt.

"That's settled then," concluded Cecil, hearing no argument to the contrary from Rosie's guardians. "Let us see if we can tap those Italians for a cup of proper coffee before we make our way."

Rosie watched the luggage bearers lashing the boxes and cases together before heaving them away from the dockside. There was not an ounce of fat on each of the men, their bodies tight from years of labor such as this. Taut muscles rippled beneath skin so dark olive in color and so perfect that it looked like the offspring of an artist's oil brush. But despite their athleticism, most of the men looked too thin, their ribcages visible beneath their pectoral muscles. Remembering Cecil's comment about the bargain price he had procured them for, Rosie wondered if the men earned enough to eat properly. Her thoughts were beginning to take the shine from her admiration for the professor, if he was indeed taking advantage of these poor people. Not realizing she had been staring at the men for some time now, Rosie wondered why one of the men was staring back at her. He grinned at her from beneath a greasy mop of thick black hair. All but three of his teeth were missing. Rosie quickly averted her gaze. What must they think of her? Looking at them as if they were beasts in a zoo. The man said something to his fellows in that curious musical tongue of theirs. Rosie felt herself blush, turned and followed after her aunt and uncle. The men laughed, sharing a joke, and got back to their work.

She found Professor Cecil in his element, sipping strong, shallow coffee called *espresso* at a crowded bar. The ramshackle structure had been constructed entirely from timbers and grasses, and gave the impression it had taken root at the dockside and sprouted from the ground. The smell of the coffee was overpowering, awakening Rosie's senses. Even though it was only eleven o'clock in the morning, the sun's heat was already making her drowsy. How she longed to try a cup of whatever the professor was having, but her aunt would never allow it. She was fond of reminding Rosie that stimulants were too strong for the weaker sex. Rosie resented the fact that she and her aunt had to stand by while the men quaffed cup after cup of the stuff. They had all the fun. Francesca handed Rosie a small tin cup of water from her own canteen. It was tepid, but it was all they had. She sipped at it, wishing she could drink a cool, crisp soda pop like the ones they had back home.

Glancing around the morass of dockworkers and arrivals giving their patronage to the coffee concession, Rosie noticed a few young local women had joined the throng. They looked strikingly exotic to Rosie with their black hair tied in braids or swept up in bouquet-like arrangements atop their pretty heads. Each had applied bright red lipstick to their lips and rouge to their faces, along with heavy black mascara. They looked like painted birds as they flitted among the scores of men leaving the steamer. The effect was accentuated by the backdrop of lush rainforest vegetation that encroached upon the dirt path leading away from the dock. Laughter, shrill and melodious as birdsong, rang out as the women led the men a merry dance. They looked so comfortable in their own skins, so free with their bare arms and risqué displays of cleavage. Rosie could not imagine how that freedom might feel, unconsciously pulling her arms around her upper body. She flushed a little when she saw one of the women lift her skirts up, revealing her shapely legs beneath, before being carried off into the foliage by one of the deckhands to rowdy applause and wolf whistles from his fellows. Elsewhere, men from the ship, crew and passengers alike, cracked open bottles of liquor and began drinking as they waited their turn with the women.

"Locals putting on a parade I see," Professor Cecil said, with a twinkle in his eye.

Seeing what Rosie was looking at, Francesca yanked her around in the other direction, back to the coffee bar.

"A parade of base sin," Gregory said, every syllable loaded with his disapproval.

"Oh, quite. Quite," Cecil said.

"Shall we be on our way?" Francesca asked, though her tone made it less of a question and more an order.

"Capital idea. We shall follow in Darwin's footsteps," Cecil said, as he dislocated himself from the bar and broke into caffeine-fueled activity. He uttered short, sharp instructions to his luggage bearers in their tongue and, doffing his hat, led the way along the path into the rainforest.

As she followed, Rosie took a parting glance at the rush and swell of humanity lapping at the Amazon's shores. Among the crowds of people, she spied the familiar faces of Richter and his men. The deckhand who had attacked her in her cabin was with them, struggling under the weight of their supplies. He looked to be in a bad way, with a livid cut across his right eye and another making a rosy bloom of his lower lip. His sullen eyes met hers momentarily. Then he was gone—ushered off into the shadows of the tall trees by Richter's aides.

CHAPTER SIX

The walk through the rainforest became more arduous and, as the morning gave way to afternoon, Rosie and her companions had slowed their pace to a crawl. None of them were used to walking in such humidity and Rosie could see that even Uncle Gregory, a keen hiker, was struggling. Dark patches of sweat stained his clothing beneath his armpits and he had even unbuttoned his waistcoat—a rare release from his ingrained Victorian restraint. Aunt Francesca wafted a paper and lace fan in a vain attempt to cool herself, but the energy it took to repeat such an action appeared to be making her hotter, not cooler.

Professor Cecil looked to be suffering most of all, his stocky frame seemed to be dissolving in the wet heat, and he took ever more frequent stops at the side of the path to drink from his canteen and mop his face with an enormous white handkerchief. Their guides observed all of this with looks of quiet amusement and Rosie wondered how ridiculous she and her lobster-faced companions must look to them, struggling through the humidity that they had no doubt known all their lives. At least her aunt had allowed her to wear a lighter cotton dress today; she would have expired by now in the formal gown she'd been forced into for the boarding party.

Rosie caught a glimpse of red and a squawking cry through the trees—a parakeet on the wing, slicing its way through the foliage like a colored dart. The sound and movement alarmed her, and she had a sudden memory of the deckhand's vivid wound. It was accompanied by the unwelcome sensation of his weight upon her in her cabin the night he'd attacked her. She rubbed at her neck, a reflex action, and found perspiration there—slick and cold beneath her now trembling fingers. *A state of shock* the doctor had called it when she'd had the shakes as a child following her rescue from the fire. Rosie hadn't understood what it meant then, of course, but she had an insight now. And how she dearly wished that she could loosen it now from her being, just shrug it off like an unwanted garment.

The professor had stopped to rest once again and, taking advantage of the fact, Rosie removed her hat and used it to fan her face and the pockets of red fury that were no doubt erupting there. The deckhand had been beaten and wounded as a result of his cruelty upon her. He had cuts and bruises to show for his crimes, and perhaps they would become scars in time. But Rosie's wounds were more than skin deep. Her wounds went much deeper.

"Come along, young lady."

Rosie was so embroiled in her thoughts that she had not noticed her aunt and the others had already started off again through the trees.

"The professor promises us we have but a short way to go before we reach the mission house. Just beyond the next ravine, whatever that entails."

Replacing her hat, Rosie caught up to the others. As the group of travelers broke the tree line, they saw for themselves what Cecil's comment entailed. The trees tailed off giving way to a slope of earth and rocks, at the end of which an elderly rope bridge was strung across a deep ravine—a natural valley formed by the flow of a tributary of the main river. As they walked closer to the edge Rosie could hear the distant rush of water. The pit of her stomach churned at the sight of the river snaking through the valley floor, far below. They had to be two hundred feet or more above the water.

"We cross the bridge, walk a little further and we are there," Cecil said as he swabbed further torrents of sweat from his face and neck. "Not afraid of heights, I hope?" he said to Rosie, looking a little wary of them himself.

Rosie tried to take solace from the fact that a well-traveled man such as he should be afraid, too, but found that it did little to calm her nerves. Their guides were already busying themselves, organizing the passage of the luggage across the bridge.

Professor Cecil spoke up in that strange native dialect, then explained to Gregory, Francesca, and Rosie, "Women and children first."

"Oh, we're quite happy for them to go first, aren't we, dear?" Francesca said.

Rosie just nodded, feeling a little nauseous. Her aunt handed her the canteen of lukewarm water. She took a few sips, the water's warmth adding to the coil in her belly. The travelers watched on tenterhooks as the luggage bearers worked in unison to ferry the luggage across the bridge. The process took fifteen minutes or more, with much cajoling and physical effort from their guides. Then it was their turn. Uncle Gregory decided Professor Cecil should go first, followed by Francesca and Rosie. He would cross behind them in case they, in his words, "Took a turn."

His assumption that the fairer sex might find a rope bridge crossing too much to handle made Rosie more determined to complete the task without exhibiting any indication of fear. As the puffing professor creaked his way across the first few planks of the bridge, Rosie saw Francesca hesitate. Righteous indignation ignited in Rosie like a spark. Instead of waiting to be led, she forged ahead of her aunt, turning to offer her hand for support. Francesca's face betrayed her fear and she gladly took Rosie's hand. Over her aunt's shoulder, Rosie saw that Uncle Gregory looked impressed at his niece's bravado.

Good, let them all be impressed, Rosie thought as she steadied herself against the taut rope banister with one hand while supporting her aunt's outstretched hand with the other. She took step after shaky step across the planks, some of which were so green with moss and lichen that she almost lost her footing crossing them. Up ahead she could see the faces of their guides, watching from their improvised bleachers of luggage and equipment crates. At such a distance their features were indistinct, but their eyes blazed with the reflected light of the azure sky. They looked like a pack of hungry wolves sitting there, waiting.

A sudden cry from up ahead and the bridge rocked sideways with a violent motion. Something was wrong with Professor Cecil. Rosie looked ahead and glimpsed the rotund man as he dropped through the center of the bridge. Fragments of wood clattered down from the hole, where the bridge used to be, beneath him. Agonizing moments passed until she heard the broken planks splash into the fast-moving river far below. The professor flailed and spun as he grabbed the rope supports at the foot of the bridge. He was dangling above the void, crying out in shock and terror.

Rosie was at his side before she even acknowledged the urgent shouts from her aunt and uncle telling her not to move, to wait. She vaguely heard them hollering at her that she'd fall, too, and that the bridge wasn't safe, but she was already crouching next to the hole, reaching down for the professor's hand.

"Reach through, Rosie, and, when I grab your hand, pull." The professor struggled to speak. "You can do it."

"I don't know if I can..."

He looked up at her, his mouth agape, before glancing at the river hundreds of feet below as though to emphasize the dreadful alternative.

"You alone can save me, dear girl. Just reach through and pull!"

Rosie needed no further spur to action. She reached through and held out her hand. Cecil grunted with effort as he swung and reached upward with one free hand, the other still locked around the coarse rope of the bridge. Rosie's fingers brushed his, but the professor's pudgy digits were so slicked with the sweat of exertion and fear that they passed through hers like smoke.

"Try again," Rosie cried, "but you must reach higher!"

The professor narrowed his eyes in concentration. Rosie knew he must realize this was his last chance. A man of his dimensions simply couldn't hold on much longer. He made a strangled growling sound and swung again, beads of sweat mimicking the spray from the river below as they were cast from his fingertips.

This time, Rosie managed to grasp Cecil's hand. The sweat caused his fingers to slip again and Rosie cried out as she struggled to keep a hold of his hand. Cecil took his chance and pushed his other hand off from the rope to grab on to Rosie. He caught the sleeve of her cotton dress. Rosie felt it tear and tried to pull him up. The professor grunted like a pig and kicked his legs as Rosie wriggled backward. Her sleeve gave way, but his upper body was safely atop the planks now. He looked into Rosie's eyes with an intense look of gratitude and relief. But this turned to new terror as the plank beneath his chest splintered and cracked beneath him. Feeling the light cotton fabric of her cuff sliding from her skin, Rosie held on to Cecil's other hand for dear life. Then her aunt and uncle were with her, each grabbing hold of the professor's clothing and dragging him to safety farther from the broken section of bridge.

Breathless, they each looked at Rosie in a mixture of awe and admonishment. She smiled back at them, relieved that the professor had been saved. Their guides returned, checking each plank of the bridge before they trod on it. They helped Rosie and the others across the three-foot hole made by the professor's impromptu descent, then the rest of the way to safety on the other side of the ravine.

Cecil was profuse in thanking Rosie for her lifesaving intervention, his chest heaving through his tattered waistcoat that had been shredded by his fall. Apparently not knowing what else to do with it, he returned her errant sleeve to her. As Cecil's breathing slowed to his normal huffing and puffing, one of the guides spoke to him. The professor replied and the guide spoke again, his comment eliciting chuckles from his fellows.

"What did he say?" Rosie asked.

"Oh, he said the River God will be angry that I did not fall as fate decreed. And that I might pause and give thanks to the Forest Goddess for making trees and rope strong enough to keep me," Cecil replied, smiling. "I just reminded him that I do not worship any deity but prefer to put my faith in science."

Rosie nodded. Then one of their guides surprised them all by speaking English. His words were heavily accented, but their meaning was clear, as he fixed Rosie with those twinkling eyes of his before turning his attention back to Professor Cecil.

"She is your proof that God exists."

For once, Rosie did not feel herself blush. She felt emboldened, and icily calm. Folding her torn sleeve in her hands, she used it to mop the sweat from her brow. Her exposed arm felt cool above the moisture vapor from the river, each downy hair standing to attention atop her skin. She peered down and along the ravine and saw a rainbow had formed over the water, like a bridge of multicolored light. Smiling, she watched it shimmer in the heat haze. Perhaps this was what the freedom of the joyous, painted women back at the port felt like. Sensing her aunt and uncle's watchful eyes upon her, Rosie pointed out the rainbow. They looked mystified by her mirth. Feeling more prepared than ever for the final leg of their journey, she left them to marvel at the sight and strode onward.

CHAPTER SEVEN

"There! Through the trees!"

Rosie looked in the direction that Professor Cecil was pointing and glimpsed stone structures there. Cecil was positively exploding with delight, hopping from one foot to another and wringing his hands together like an excited schoolboy on Christmas morning. As they continued walking, the structures became clearer. They looked to be the ruins of an ancient temple, their man-made silhouettes rather incongruous against the rainforest's wild backdrop. It was a magical sight, to Rosie's eyes like something from a Romantic oil painting. As they drew nearer still, the crumbling edifices revealed their finer details—each was carved with depictions of tribal worship, hunting, and symbols that Rosie could not fathom.

"It's a temple," Cecil announced, giving answer to Rosie's thoughts. "One of the oldest in the region, ancient in fact, yes. It dates back thousands of years, the backbone of time if you will in this part of the forest. Local stone quarried from the surrounding valleys and dragged up here by tribespeople over decades."

Rosie looked to her aunt and uncle, who both looked as awestruck as she by the sight. Collectively, the oldest artifacts of human civilization they had seen thus far had been confined to museums. These buildings were real, and Rosie could not help but imagine the human toil it must have required to drag each huge stone up here into the forest.

"The carvings are exquisite," Francesca said, impressed.

"Aren't they just?" Cecil agreed. "They depict the life and times of the *Myahueneca.*"

"The who?" Rosie asked.

"The indigenous people in this region go by that name. Their numbers are many, living in pockets all across their lands. They are excellent hunter-gatherers, yes."

Cecil ran his fingers across the surface of a fresco depicting a hunting scene, the stone stained green with moss and lichen. "This pictograph represents their ancestors on a blowpipe hunting expedition—you will perhaps recognize their prey?"

"They ate monkeys?" Rosie said, incredulous.

The professor chuckled. "And still do. Especially howler monkeys, the major source of protein for the landlocked villagers in this region. I read that the Myahueneca can mimic the calls of every species of monkey in their territory. Something I would dearly love to put to the test while my recording equipment is up and running."

Rosie smiled at the unburdened glee in Cecil's voice. It was something of a tonic to offset the fact that the locals ate *monkeys*. She strolled around the base of the temple, losing herself in the manifold textures and hues of the structure and the thick tree roots that snaked their way all around it. Reaching an archway set into the building, she instinctively looked up and saw more carvings of tribespeople. Unlike the hunting scene, where the figures were lithe and active, this section showed them on their knees, subjugated beneath a towering figure. The looming figure was in turn surrounded by animal configurations. She could make out the shape of a parrot, a big cat of some kind, a spider, a snake, and a tortoise in the stone menagerie. It reminded Rosie of a replica totem pole she had witnessed at the museum with her aunt and uncle, back home.

Feeling a sudden presence over her shoulder, Rosie turned to see her uncle frowning at the carvings.

"Pagan idolatry," he said.

"Spot on, absolutely," Cecil chimed in. "This is one of their deities. He is Master of the Hunt and Watcher Over the Forest, the Lord of Shapes. In the Myahueneca tongue he is known as *Skintaker*."

The name gave Rosie unfathomable chills. She rubbed at the gooseflesh pricking her forearms and backed away from the archway, eager to be free from its long shadow.

"Heathen nonsense," Gregory grumbled.

"That's what the Romans said to Jesus Christ about His Father, I'm sure," Cecil said with a twinkle of his eyes.

Rosie watched as her uncle simply shook his head and turned his back on the temple.

"There is much work to do here. God's work," he said. "Perhaps that is why my predecessors chose to install a mission house here, so close to this…temple."

"Perhaps," Cecil said, though his tone hardly suggested agreement. "It often seems the case that the new religion springs up wherever there are old gods to conquer."

"New religion? I assure you that Christianity is hardly new."

"And I assure you that to these people, it most certainly is new. The worship of their deities stretches back behind the curtain of time, to an era pre-dating Christ. Their beliefs are as constant as the flow of the river that informs their livelihoods. They have ever been a vital part of their daily lives and rituals."

"They are simple effigies, nothing more."

"Like Christ upon the cross in churches the world over."

"We prefer a simple cross all on its own in the Anglican faith, Professor." Gregory glanced up at the carvings once more. "As I said, there is God's work to do here."

"You will have your work cut out for you, sir," Cecil said before quickly adding, "but if anyone can achieve it, it is most certainly a man of your conviction."

Though visibly rattled, Uncle Gregory seemed satisfied with the professor's well-timed flattery. After witnessing their indignant exchange, Rosie stifled giggles and felt gladder than ever she had seen fit to rescue Cecil from his fall at the rope bridge.

Dusk was falling over the forest by the time they reached the mission house. The building was stilted and formed the hub of a complex of vine-covered wooden walkways and rope bridges. A large, man-made clearing had been created to accommodate the structures, affording a view of the sky that would be impossible elsewhere in the dense rainforest. Yet every part of the complex was bordered by the distant tree line, a constant reminder of the permanence of nature at the mission's doorstep. The guides hoisted the travelers' luggage onto the steps leading up to the main house, and took their rest in the cool shade beneath the eaves once their labors were completed. Some smoked pungent hand-rolled cigarettes, or little pipes. To Rosie's eyes, they looked like a strange troupe of carny roughnecks. She decided to keep such thoughts to herself, blaming a day in the heat.

Professor Cecil was busy making noises about the lateness of the day—his final destination was a tribal village several miles further away from the mission. Rosie saw her uncle and aunt exchange silent glances, their subtext clearly one of resignation, and presently they invited Cecil to remain at the house for the night. His luggage bearers were to stay, too, before resuming their journey in the morning. With their arrangements made, the staff began meal preparations while Gregory led Rosie, Francesca, and Cecil on a visit to the chapel.

Rosie had never seen a church on stilts before, and she mused that the resulting structure looked as though it were levitating itself to reach higher to the heavens. A ramshackle wooden building with dozens of cracks and holes in its walls the chapel had some charm, especially the makeshift weather vane that topped its uneven steeple. The carved, wooden cockerel that perched there amidst the arrows pointing north, south, east, and west in the non-existent breeze was clearly a local craftsman's interpretation of a Westerner's ideal. The bird had taken on something of a tribal form through its interpretive carving and, similar to the animals carved in stone at the ancient temple, it looked like it had migrated from a totem pole.

Following her uncle inside, Rosie found the chapel to be a blessed haven of cool darkness. She remembered a trip to midnight mass one Christmas Eve, back in Ohio, on a night when the drifts were making ladders up the sides of all the buildings in town. The refreshing chill she had felt on that night had nothing on what she was feeling in this place. She looked up at the high, slatted windows and watched dust motes dancing in the orange light of sunset. The chapel was the only place that had given Rosie total reprieve from the sun since setting foot on dry land and she felt grateful for it. Her uncle looked down at her from the pulpit, which he was trying for size, and nodded to her serenely. He had mistaken her look of euphoric relief for one of holy worship. Rosie turned away, pretending to study one of the musty hymn books perched at the end of a pew.

Uncle Gregory led the way to the rear of the chapel, where the rainforest had been cut back in order to create a cemetery. The area was no more than twenty feet square, and much smaller than the cemeteries Rosie had seen back home. Wooden crosses, carved from local wood, poked out from the leaf-strewn ground at varying angles. Rosie noticed that each cross was entwined with roots from the encroaching forest, a reminder that the trees could be cut back but never tamed. They stood at a reverent distance while Gregory intoned the Lord's Prayer, his chin tucked into his chest in supplication. Prayers over, Rosie listened dutifully while her uncle spoke of the men and women buried beneath their feet. The dead were their predecessors and, according to her uncle, each had suffered great hardship in order to establish a church in such a remote site. Gregory seemed humbled to be following in their footsteps, and made vocal his intention to continue their great work by filling the chapel with songs of praise.

Of course, thought Rosie, *he'll need to assemble a congregation first.*

As the others left the cemetery and prepared to return to the mission house for supper, Rosie lingered by the graves, reading the names and dates inscribed there. A gentle breeze rustled the leaves like whispers from the dead. As a chill passed over her skin, it dawned on Rosie that she, her aunt, and her uncle might be buried there with them someday. Companions for the lonely dead—more names for crooked wooden crosses that lacked the permanence of the ancient stone temple looming in the distance. Until now, it had not occurred to her that theirs could be a one-way trip.

Rosie quickened her pace as she left the graveyard.

STRATUM CORNEUM

*H*is fingers worked the boy's still-warm flesh. His nerve endings felt alive as they traced the olive-colored landscape. He felt every pore, each follicle, as it passed beneath his fingertips. Life had once pulsed beneath this smooth, slick surface. The boy had played, fought, hunted—all in preparation for an adulthood that would, now, be denied him.

At this, he sighed.

His head pounded and his eyes ached. He extricated his fingers from the boy's corpse, reluctantly, and rubbed at his temples before removing his eyepieces. He flipped them over and regarded his distorted reflection in their black glass domes. His breath fogged the image and for a moment he saw himself as though he were gazing through a fog of time. He was indistinct, a memory, or a myth.

Perhaps he was all of those things. He rubbed at his eyes and felt how sore they were becoming. Reaching over to his table, filled with the bowls, jars and tools of his art, he picked up a rag of soft leather and used it to wipe his eyepieces clean. They sparkled blackly in the flickering torchlight of his cave. He wore them again, feeling his vision grow clearer—but he knew not for how long.

He reached down, his hand as steady as a tiller's, and prized open one of the boy's eyelids.

Beautiful.

The dilated orb reflected the fire of his alchemy. It would not go to waste.

He took his favorite blade and began to cut.

CHAPTER EIGHT

As night fell, the interior of the mission house grew as dour as the sky outside it. There was no electricity at the compound and the only light came from the fire in the hearth and the flickering flames of oil lamps and candles. A mirror hung above the mantel, reflecting and amplifying their combined glow.

Rosie watched shadow forms dance across the paneled walls of the dining room. She liked being in the shadows, she always had. Although it was still humid, the air was cooler in the dining room, ventilated via open shutters that gave access to balconies either end. She could see the light of the half-moon through one of them, making a halo around the dark shapes of the treetops beyond. Even at night, the view from their lofty, stilted viewpoint was breathtaking. Rosie began to feel part of the forest, sensing that this was how its true denizens—the monkeys, snakes, and spiders depicted in the temple's iconography—saw the world around them.

The staff brought supper in on carved wooden trays. It was simple fare of broth and unleavened bread, with flagons of cool spring water. Rosie took a sip of water to refresh her palette before eating. Her cup, like the trays their food had arrived upon, had also been carved from wood. The craftsmanship was exquisite and she could only wonder how much time such a feat of work had taken. She rolled the whittled curve of the cup between her hands, watching the reflection of the firelight on the surface of her drink. Aunt Francesca made the distinctive coughing noise that signaled her discontent. She made it clear she was quite unimpressed with the tableware, and instructed their servers to locate the glassware in their luggage before the next meal.

When the staff had scurried away Uncle Gregory folded his hands and said grace. Rosie smirked quietly when she saw

Professor Cecil had already bitten off a huge mouthful of bread, through which he struggled to utter his amen at the prayer's close. The meal passed quietly but conversation sparked with the arrival of the glassware—and wine to pour into it. Rosie refused a glass, preferring to keep a cool head in the humidity. Professor Cecil seemed to take her refusal as permission to refill his glass a second time, after which he proposed a toast.

"To young Rosie Shields," he blustered, "whose quick thinking saved me from becoming Amazonian alligator feed. And to you, her guardians, for sharing her, ahem, burden when gravity proved the, erm, better of us."

Rosie's aunt and uncle smiled politely and joined Cecil in his toast. After that, they made their polite excuses about having much unpacking to do and hastened to their rooms, but not before reminding Rosie to retire at a sensible hour. She murmured her compliance, though she had no intention of sleeping anytime soon. The professor's toast had reminded her of the rope bridge crossing adventure and, although she was physically tired from their journey, her mind raced. She saw the same adrenalin behind Cecil's eyes, which gleamed at her in the firelight.

"I find I must digest before I can retire," he said to Rosie in that peculiar English way that seemed to warrant a reasoned excuse for any behavior one might deem as being different to the norm. "Perhaps you'll help me unpack some of my recording equipment? It will pass the time and you may find it, ahem, enlightening. Unless modern technology bores you? Please tell me if it does, I shan't be offended."

"I'd love to," Rosie said, taking his arm.

They adjourned to the lobby where Cecil's cases and crates sat in towering disarray. He set about cataloguing the characters and numerals stenciled on the sides of the luggage until he found one box in particular. Rosie watched, expectant, as the professor prized the lid open using his pocketknife amidst a shower of wood shavings that had been deployed as packing material. Huffing and puffing as usual, Cecil extricated what looked like a large, tan suitcase from the crate.

"A box within a box," Rosie said, intrigued.

"And what a prize this box contains," Cecil replied, his breathing heavy. "It weighs quite a bit. Most ungallant of me again, but might I…"

"Oh, of course," Rosie said, grasping one of the case's side-mounted handles.

Whatever the professor had stashed in there was certainly not what someone might normally transport in the suitcase. Between them, they struggled over to one of the larger packing crates and carefully lifted the suitcase onto the lid. Rosie waited as the professor took out his handkerchief and mopped his brow. Then he released the clasps at the front of the case and lifted the lid to reveal its contents. A turntable was built into an enameled metal housing, slightly left of center and adjacent to that was a golden S-shaped arm.

"A phonograph?"

"Correct," Cecil enthused, "a Victor Orthophonic to be exact. Although we refer to them as gramophones in my country."

"It's very grand," Rosie said, stroking the tactile bronze letters spelling out "Victor" on the base plate.

"One of only two in existence," Cecil said. "I had them specially modified to record sounds as well as replicating them. Observe," he said and released the catch on a little brass cover, "this houses the recording cylinders. Quite efficient, and quite portable—with a little elbow grease so to speak, yes."

"You have some records inside the lid, could we play some of them?"

"Oh, I'm afraid they are not recordings in the musical sense, my dear. Not traditionally so, anyhow."

"Really? I'd love to hear them all the same."

"Well, so long as we don't disturb your uncle and aunt. Of course, that means carrying this beauty into the parlor."

"I'm game if you are, Professor," Rosie said.

He blushed a little at her enthusiasm before saying, "Right you are then. But if I slip a disc, on your head be it."

Laughing, they carried the machine into the parlor, lid still open. Their mirth attracted the attentions of members of the waiting staff, who looked perplexed by the technological marvel contained in Cecil's luggage. Rosie and Cecil's efforts became light work, having acquired two helpers, and the phonograph was soon in pride of place atop the dining table. The staff made to leave and Cecil intervened, instructing them to return with nightcaps. He then set about extending a fan-like contraption that was revealed to be a horn for amplifying the unit's sound.

Their drinks arrived, on a silver tray and in glasses this time. Rosie did her best to refuse, but the professor would have none of it.

"Gin and tonic, holy water for the Caucasian abroad," he said.

"Is it really? Don't let my uncle hear you say it."

Cecil chuckled. "Oh, even your gruff old uncle would approve of imbibing quinine in our current location. Especially useful at nightfall, when the mosquitoes are prone to make their descent. Us whiteys make for a delicious feast unless, of course, our bloodstream is filled with good old G and T. Cheers."

Rosie sipped her drink, finding it refreshing, and cast her eyes over the discs stored inside the lid. The records had no labels, blank save for a sequence of numbers on the paper sleeves. Rosie selected one at random and watched as Cecil placed it on the turntable before turning the phonograph's crank handle. The machine whirred into life and Rosie watched, transfixed, as the needle descended into the record's black groove. Crackles burst from the retractable horn and Rosie giggled, imagining the device was filled with popping corn. The crackling gave way to the unmistakable melody of birdsong.

"Beautiful, isn't she?" Cecil said, seeing the joy on Rosie's face.

She did not reply, unsure if he meant that the phonograph or the bird's song was beautiful.

"Nightjar," he said, "one of the first animals I recorded as a matter of fact. Ah, and this..." He paused a moment, until a chirruping, croaking sound erupted from the phonograph's horn. "Hazard a guess as to what is making this unique little call?"

"I really have no idea," Rosie said.

"Guess."

"A frog?"

"Oh bravo, Rosie! *Bravissimo!*" The professor clapped his hands and beamed at Rosie. "Specifically, it is the call of *hyla cinerea*. The green tree frog in everyday parlance, quite."

The recording continued, and Cecil described the characteristics of the animals making their calls along with minute details about where and when he had recorded them. Rosie heard him say something about howler monkeys, but then found her senses drifting away from the tinny sounds of the phonograph, her young ears picking up on more subtle sounds out the window. She crossed to the balcony and listened intently to a distant cacophony of shrill cries that ebbed and flowed with the passage of the night air. It was as though the creatures in the forest outside were answering the calls recorded on the professor's machine. Rosie felt stranded between two worlds. The fake world of recorded sound, dulled as it was by the wall panels around them, was a shadow of the carnal ferocity teeming beneath night's canopy outside. Her arms turned to gooseflesh as she realized just how much the rainforest terrified her, but also how much it exhilarated her. She stood there trembling, serenaded by a feral chorus of cries, for some time before she noticed that the professor's recording had finished. He stood a respectful distance away, clutching his liquor glass. When Rosie turned to face him, an unspoken understanding passed between them—that the alien world on their doorstep was frightening, humbling, and above all else, alive.

Her mission house quarters were befittingly Spartan, with a carved crucifix the only decoration on the log cabin walls. The windows were heavily shuttered and, having no glass in them, did little to muffle the sounds of the rainforest. The night air was too muggy for sleep, and so Rosie kept her oil lamp burning as she made vague attempts to read her aunt's book of Psalms. She wriggled in her bed again, uncomfortable on the lumpy straw-stuffed mattress. Once or twice, a large moth dive-bombed at her, casting phantasmagorical shadows on the wall as it did so. She swatted at the creature until it flew to the other end of the room, but when it came back—attracted no doubt by the flickering light of her lamp—she was forced to admit defeat. Extinguishing the lamp's flame plunged her into total darkness. No light crept in beneath the door, as it usually did back home, and night outside was black as a void. The total darkness accentuated the sounds outside, and Rosie felt rather pleased with herself to know the names of the creatures making several of the cries. The howler monkeys were the most prominent, their conversation rising to a frenzied pitch once or twice before dwindling. Perhaps whatever it was that was bothering them had moved on. Rosie drew her sheet around her, not wishing to imagine which kind of creature could rattle a group of howler monkeys so much. She lay still and waited for her eyes to close against the darkness.

CHAPTER NINE

Richter watched the young deckhand as he struggled to light their campfire.

The beating he'd endured at the hands of Richter's men had started with his face and spread out to his extremities. His fingers had not been exempt from Keyser's attentions. Those same hands with which the boy had tried to pin the redhead down in her cabin now trembled as though he had arthritis. Maybe now he'd learn to choose his conquests more carefully, or at least his timing. It amused Richter to see the young deckhand wincing with pain. He watched as the kid tried again to spark the kindling by striking two stones together. The blood slicking his hands caused him to lose purchase on the stones and he cursed as he dropped them into the still-unlit fire. Hearing Richter's laughter, the deckhand glowered at him.

"Something the matter, boy?" Richter asked.

The young upstart looked from Richter to Keyser and then the others. His defiant look drained from his face as Keyser balled his fist and smacked it into the palm of his other hand—a languid threat. The deckhand's petulance disintegrated with the hint at another beating, and he set about retrieving the stones from the stack of twigs and broken branches. Richter's men teased the boy as he began striking again, but their ridicule gave him new focus and a few moments later the boy's shaking hands gleaned a single spark. He crouched as low as his injuries would allow and blew into the dried grass at the fire's edge. The grass caught, cinders glowing orange, and the deckhand kept them alive by wafting his hands like a fan. He crouched again and blew and, pretty soon, the fire was ablaze.

"We can cook now," Richter said, giving his men the nod.

The natives among them brought the howler monkeys they had

hunted earlier and began skinning them. Richter's eyes narrowed at the sight of sinew separating from bone. It never ceased to impress him how similar all creatures were beneath their skins. Rabbits looked like pigs, and pigs looked like humans just as soon as their coats were off and the butcher had done his work. Their guides lashed the exposed carcasses to wooden poles, which they then balanced atop the stakes driven into the soil either side of the fire. The monkey flesh began to blister, little droplets of fat sizzling on the flames below. Richter gazed at the reflected fires in the dead creatures' eyes and allowed the smell of their immolation to wash over him. The monkeys' bodies were just protein now, fuel for a larger and more important hunt. He knew the native men believed that ingesting monkey flesh would give them the animal's power to navigate the rainforest, to climb its tallest trees and swing from its highest branches. He did not share their faith, but was party to such power. Even now, Richter fancied himself atop one of those high branches, at the summit of the food chain and looking down on all creatures great and small. He looked at his fellows, busying themselves around the fire, each one an integral part of his plans for the hunt to come. Everything had its place in this rainforest, even the young deckhand they had taken with them from the steamer. The kid would have his uses in the days and nights to come.

When Richter was done eating, he would sleep for as long as the humidity allowed. And in the morning, he would set about occupying his place in the vast territory that surrounded them. He listened idly to the calls of the howler monkeys beyond the clearing—warning calls, telling their fellows that hunters were abroad amidst the trees.

Let them howl, he thought. *Let them speak "killer."*

The hunt was always more compelling when his quarry knew that he had its scent. Richter inhaled the night air.

It smelled of meat, and murder.

CHAPTER TEN

Rosie felt rested after her night's sleep. The mattress on the bed in her room had proven surprisingly comfortable, shaping itself to her body as she'd settled in under the covers. She had awoken to an exotic chorus of birdsong and other animal cries, which provided a sweet tonic to the disquieting call-and-response of howler monkeys the previous night. The mission house staff brought a bowl of spring water to her room and Rosie set about washing and dressing for her first full day as a resident of the rainforest.

She found fruit and strong tea waiting for her in the dining room, and Rosie helped herself to energetic portions of mango and bananas. She helped her aunt unpack some of their things but got the impression she was rather getting in the way. Sloping off downstairs in search of some other distraction she found it in the form of Professor Cecil who was cataloging his vast array of recording equipment, attended all the while by a young houseboy who spoke little English. Cecil seemed glad of the help, dismissing the servant boy the instant that Rosie offered.

The next hour or so (marked by the chimes of the grandfather clock that ticked loudly beneath the curve of the staircase) was something of an induction for Rosie as she learned all about the twin disciplines of film and sound recording. Cylinders for recording the sounds of the jungle were labeled, ready for use, and stacked alongside virgin film stock that lay tightly wrapped like sardines in little cans. Rosie almost knocked over the little pile of film cans when she reached for Cecil's white china pencil, observing how his face reddened while he struggled not to berate her for her clumsiness. She apologized profusely and withdrew while he busied himself rearranging the equipment. The professor had an enthusiasm for his work that was infectious, but Rosie felt she must keep a respectful distance from him due to his tendency to fly off the handle if things were anything less than "just so" in their arrangement. He clearly felt bad about his impatience for, no sooner than had he repacked the itemized equipment, Cecil asked if Rosie might like to accompany him on a recording excursion. Rosie accepted his offer, excited at the prospect of seeing the magic of film and sound recording at work in the field. She rushed upstairs to tell her aunt, who promptly instructed her to go to her room to change into more "practical" clothing.

I'm nineteen, not nine, thought Rosie.

Biting her lip to stop the words from coming out, she ducked out of her aunt's room and went to her own.

By "practical" Aunt Francesca of course meant one of the modest, heavy frocks they had lugged along with them for their trip. Rosie cheated, opting for the only two-piece in her wardrobe. With her slip and blouse beneath, she could always remove the top layers should the heat and humidity get the better of her later on—which of course they would. Pausing to fasten her hair beneath her bonnet, Rosie studied her reflection in her hand mirror. It rather dismayed her to see the familiar redness making an irritable rainbow of her forehead and cheeks, especially as she was to spend much of the day out of doors. All she could hope for was that the trees would provide enough shade to keep her condition from getting any worse.

Professor Cecil awaited her at the foot of the stairs, dressed head to toe in safari khakis complete with pith helmet. He looked as if he were going to war, or would have done if he were carrying a rifle rather than a recording device. Cecil apologized as he gave Rosie the lightest of the bags to carry along with a spare canteen filled with water, which she slung over her shoulder via its long leather strap. Along for the expedition were Pedro, one of the staff and an excellent guide according to Cecil, and Jorge the young boy she had met earlier who did not speak much English. Pedro heaved a large box, which had been fitted with shoulder straps, onto his back and she recognized it as the modified Victor. Jorge had been entrusted with Cecil's movie camera and hefty tripod. Rosie felt sure the combined weight was too much for the youngster and tried to intervene, offering to help split the load. Cecil reassured her the boy was used to such work and, despite his diminutive stature was in fact as strong as an ox. She watched astonished as Jorge loaded himself up with equipment and trotted out of the mission house like a pack mule. With Pedro in the lead, they processed out of the clearing and onto a path that bore its way deep into the rainforest. They traveled quietly, their footfalls falling into a kind of rhythm as they each defined their pace. Cecil was slowest, mainly due to his propensity for rest breaks so he could mop his brow and take great gulps of water. Rosie recalled reading somewhere that in the heat, one was better off sipping rather than gulping down water. She did exactly that and found herself adjusting to the humidity rather than dissolving into a perspiring mess as she had done during the long walk to the mission house the previous day. Her thighs and calves still ached from that trek but, as she began the climb to higher ground, it felt good to be putting them through their paces once more. With each step, she felt like she was working off her sedentary days aboard both the ship and paddle steamer. Her skin was still sore, though, and she moistened a handkerchief with water, gently dabbing at her forehead and cheeks to cool them.

"That looks sore."

Cecil had caught up to her. Then, seeing her expression, began to retreat the way he had come. Rosie put away her handkerchief and tried to soften her expression.

"I'm sorry," Cecil said, "I didn't mean to pry."

"And I'm sorry. You startled me, that's all."

"How long have you suffered from *acne rosacea*?"

"Acne...what?"

"*Rosacea*. It is that which ails you, is it not?"

Rosie's heart began to thrum. The idea that there might be a name for her pain was something of a revelation to her.

"I'm not sure, Professor. My doctor back home said it was growing pains, something I might grow out of. He prescribed plenty of sunlight, but that seems to be the worst thing for it. If you know anything otherwise, I'd be very grateful..."

"Bloody provincial quacks, if you'll, ahem, pardon my French."

"Of course."

"Quite. Sunlight can be of benefit for some skin conditions of course, but for others, yours included I imagine, it can be something of a trigger."

"A trigger?"

"Yes, well, it's not an exact science you see, but you yourself said the rays of the sun can make it worse?"

"I did. It can."

"Well then, scientifically speaking, if you were to remain in shady conditions, low humidity—like perhaps a cave—mightn't your skin become much improved?"

"I have no idea. We're in the rainforest after all."

"That we are," he said, glancing around the lush green of their environment with evident pride. "Perhaps when the rains come, we can keep you indoors, monitor your condition."

Your condition. Rosie didn't know whether to laugh or cry. Ambiguous tears welled up in her eyes.

"Oh, my dear, I did not mean to upset you. Please…"

"You didn't, Professor. Upset me I mean. It's just…I never dared even think I had an actual, bona fide 'condition.' My aunt keeps telling me it's a phase, something connected with childhood trauma."

"She could be right," Cecil mused, "at least partly. Traumas of the skin can be manifestations of mental anguish." He fell silent then, apparently unsure of how to broach the difficult subject of patient history. Rosie decided to make it easier for him.

"You want to know if I suffered any such trauma?"

He nodded, blushing profusely in that archetypical British way of his.

"My parents died in a fire, when I was little," Rosie said, "that's why my aunt and uncle raised me. I was so red the next day that I thought my skin had been burned by the fire, but my uncle saved me before the flames could get to me, so…"

"So?"

"It has always been a bit of a mystery. And as it flares up from time to time, like today, I was always made to feel it wasn't anything serious." She paused for thought, then a terrible idea took hold. "It isn't anything serious, is it?"

"Not life threatening, if that is your meaning. But rather a burden on your self-esteem I should imagine?"

Rosie nodded.

"You are an incomparably beautiful girl, Miss Rosie, I want you to remember that."

Now it was she who blushed. She reached again for the cool, damp handkerchief.

"You're very kind, Professor."

"Not at all. I also want you to remember that you do not suffer alone."

"I don't?"

"Not at all. History has borne witness to a long and distinguished roster of *acne rosacea* patients throughout the ages."

"Such as?"

"Are you familiar with W. C. Fields?"

Rosie knew the entertainer's name instantly. "The Broadway star—from the *Follies*?"

"The very same. Quite."

"I thought his liking for alcoholic drinks gave him a red nose?"

"A common misconception. *Rosacea*, my dear. Just like you. His curse is that the more he appears, the more famous he gets. And the more famous he gets, the more visible his condition—but the general public is ignorant of his actual plight."

He offered Rosie a sip from his canteen, which she refused, eager as she was to hear him continue.

"The medical fraternity is not so ignorant, however. I recall attending a symposium on diseases of the skin in London, though I must admit it is memorable due to the delicious teacakes they served there.... But I digress. Messrs. Willan and Bateman, medical fellows and specialists, were among the first to study such dermal matters closely. They proposed that your condition was treatable via topical solutions of alcohol, although I'm sure you know these to be ineffective."

Rosie flinched, recalling the alcohol rubs she had endured at her aunt's hands. Francesca had finally admitted defeat when Rosie's entire face broke out in pustules.

She nodded in agreement.

"The latest research theorizes that emotional triggers are to blame, though others still are looking into the effects of mites that are said to live on the natural oils secreted by the skin."

"I would be sure to have an extreme emotional reaction if I were to learn that mites were living on my face, Professor."

"Brave girl, do not be alarmed. Our bodies are hosts to many a strange, microscopic creature."

Rosie felt a little queasy all of a sudden. She reached for her own water canteen and took a couple of sips to steady her stomach.

"Someday there will be a cure, do not doubt that. You can rely on scientific method to find an answer for what ails you."

"And in the meantime?"

"In the meantime, you must do what pleases you, Rosie my dear girl. For only in joy can you find respite from the emotional triggers that imbalance your fleshly vessel."

Professor Cecil gave their guides the nod that they were ready to continue.

"Now if you'll allow me, Rosie? To show you true joy."

CHAPTER ELEVEN

They broke the tree line after a little over an hour's walk, descending a gentle slope into a clearing that had formed around the fallen trunk of a massive tree. The tree was split at its base but still connected to its roots and appeared to still be growing, even though it was lying down. The gossamer strands of spiders' webs had caught dewdrops, which glistened in shafts of sunlight like tiny gemstones. Bright shapes circled overhead and Rosie used the flat of her hand to shield her eyes from the sun and get a better look at them. They were macaws, dozens of them, their rainbow wings making a dazzling show as they swooped and flapped from one tall tree to the next.

"Perfect," Cecil whispered, and set about instructing Jorge on where to set up the camera.

Rosie watched intently as the professor removed the lens cap and extended the concertina housing the lens. He pointed it at a group of the birds perched on a long branch.

"Would you like to try, Rosie?"

She did not need a second invitation. Crossing to the camera, she listened to Cecil's instructions and took a look through the viewfinder. The world had been plunged into stark contrast, her peripheral vision framed out by the matte box. It was a curious way of looking at the world, as if through a window. Just as Rosie withdrew, she saw a fleeting movement in the trees, a large, dark shape and the glint of an eye among the leaves. Returning her gaze to the viewfinder, she found the shape had disappeared. Whatever it was, it moved fast.

"See something interesting?" the professor asked.

"No, I...must have been mistaken."

The snap of a twig startled them, and the birds. Several of the macaws took to the wing, flapping and squawking to higher branches above the fallen tree. The professor widened the tripod legs and tilted the camera back, shooting a few seconds of footage of the flying birds before choosing another angle and repeating the process. While Cecil was preoccupied with the macaws, Rosie peered into the trees where she had seen, or thought she had seen, the large, dark shape. She saw no shape, only the pattern made by blotches of sunlight as they fell across the leaves.

Must have been a trick of the light, she thought.

Then, she noticed something extraordinary. A pair of smaller birds had landed atop the far end of the fallen tree trunk. One of them was the most beautiful creature she had ever seen. Its feathers fanned out in front of it like an umbrella and were of the most vivid, dazzling hue, like the azure of the sea she had sailed upon just days ago. The little bird hopped and spun on its delicate little claws, apparently performing a mating dance for its comparatively drab companion. Rosie watched open mouthed as the brilliant azure feathers gleamed like precious stones when the sunlight caught them through the tree canopy.

"Professor," she whispered, hoping he could hear her above the whir of his camera. He didn't, so she risked raising her voice, repeating his title, *"Professor."*

He popped up from behind the camera, blinking at her. She nodded in the direction of the beautiful azure-feathered bird and saw his jaw drop just as hers had moments before. Wordlessly, he gestured to Jorge to help him move the camera around and disappeared behind the viewfinder again while working the crank handle. Rosie watched the mating pair continue their dancing courtship, convinced that they would fly away just as soon as the camera's glare was upon them. But the dance went on and she observed with bated breath as the professor got his footage. A few moments later, the plainer of the two birds fluttered away, disinterested. *Must be the female,* thought Rosie, smiling. The prettier of the birds hopped away in pursuit of its would-be mate, and Rosie heard the whir of the camera slow to a stop before the professor let out a great *whoop* of triumph. Red-faced, he dashed out from behind his contraption and approached Rosie with open arms, embracing her with such force that he knocked the wind out of her lungs. After releasing his grip, he clapped his hands together and performed a little dance of his own.

"You, my dear, are an absolute treasure," he panted.

"What were those birds?" Rosie asked. "They were so beautiful, especially the one with the azure feathers."

"Birds of paradise," Cecil replied, "the little azure fellow being the male, of course."

"I thought as much," Rosie said, smiling again.

"In full plumage, and rather amorous, to boot. Quite the display he put on, what? Quite, quite, yes."

"I've never seen birds like that before, Professor."

"A rare sight, indeed. But now, thanks to you the world at large can enjoy them. Oh, but if only we had the capacity to make our films in the same colors which our eyes bear witness to. Would that not be something? Of course, we can artificially color them in, frame by frame. But such a process, however painstaking, can never truly replicate the splendor that we just saw with the naked eye."

"Still, you captured them on film?"

"That I did, my dear Rosie. And I didn't even require a cage to do so!"

The professor laughed at his own joke, the shrill sound echoing off the branches of the trees. He returned, still chuckling, to his equipment and began setting up the audio components.

"Now to add nature's soundtrack to our little magnum opus," he said, flipping open the lid of his customized Victor phonograph. "If you'd be a dear and fetch one of those recording cylinders."

Rosie retrieved one of the cylinders from the canvas bag and clambered over the fallen tree's branches to pass it to him. He loaded it into the phonograph, which gleamed like some fantastical alien device from a pulp science fiction magazine in the wilds of the forest. He unpacked a sectioned metal pole from one of the other cases and fastened it together, revealing it to be a microphone stand. Cecil then retrieved the device's microphone array from a smaller box and mounted it on the stand before connecting it to the recorder. Rosie had seen similar microphones at music halls, a central lozenge-shaped receiver suspended on springs from a metal outer frame.

"Why don't you record the sounds while you are filming?" Rosie asked.

"Because all we would hear on our recording would be the whir of the camera," Cecil replied, "and that would make for rather a wasted journey. Now, if you could all find somewhere comfortable to sit still for a few moments that would be capital. And if you have to cough, now would be a good time."

He repeated his instructions in dialect to Jorge and Pedro, who instinctively cleared their throats as they hunkered down where they had been standing. Rosie sat sidesaddle on the huge tree trunk and, when they were settled, the professor activated the recorder via the brass crank handle on its side. Sitting silent in the rainforest made Rosie more aware than ever that the landscape around them was teeming with life. She could hear the whisper of air through the leaves above and around them, and the soft plink of dewdrops falling from the leaves to the forest floor. Animals chattered in the distance—more monkeys, presumably—amidst the shrill calls of bright birds. Underpinning all the sounds was the constant bass drone of insects, some of which buzzed past her ears like tiny aircraft. Each nuance added to the whole, as though the rainforest were composing a living symphony that had no end, and no beginning. She lost herself in the sounds, feeling her heart rate slowing to a meditative pace, and almost jumped out of her skin when the professor stopped the recording with a loud click.

"Thank you for your silence," he said to Rosie before extending his hands in appreciation of the forest. "And thank you for your beautiful performance, bravo! Now let's journey back to see, and hear, what we got, yes?"

Rosie reluctantly climbed down from her peaceful spot on the tree trunk and helped pack away the equipment. She moved one of the boxes from the base of the fallen tree and spied something brilliant out the corner of her eye—an iridescent turquoise feather, fallen from the paradise bird's plumage. She picked it up and gasped at its beautiful pearlescence. Hearing her, the professor strode over to see what she was looking at.

"A rare totem," Cecil said, "you must keep it, my dear, as a souvenir of our expedition."

He fished a clean white handkerchief from his breast pocket and held it out so that Rosie could place the feather inside. It gleamed with all the color of a thousand butterfly wings. Cecil folded the handkerchief around the feather with great care and handed it to Rosie, who tucked it away in the pocket of her shoulder bag. She looked a *thank you* in the direction that the courting, quarreling birds had flown. Glad that she had come along for the experience she set off after the professor and their guides, feeling as light as the feather that she now carried with her.

She felt joy.

CHAPTER TWELVE

The journey back to the mission house had seemed a lot shorter. By the time of their return, Rosie had badgered Cecil into staying for dinner. Her aunt and uncle had, at her behest, extended their invitation for him to stay. And so, they sat together at the dining table while their guest, the professor, recounted their adventures in the rainforest that day. After they had dined, the conversation moved to the subject of the paradise bird feather, which Rosie produced from the protection of Cecil's handkerchief. The colors glimmered in the light from the fire and lanterns, and even Uncle Gregory looked mesmerized. He quoted from the Bible, something portentous about God having dominion over all creatures, before passing the feather to Francesca, who cradled it as if it was about to snap in her hands. Her aunt baulked at Rosie's suggestion that she could ask one of the staff to help her weave it into a pendant or else affix it to her bonnet. Rosie noticed how much the suggestion, that she wear the feather as an adornment, made her uncle scowl, too. She loved him, but could not help taking delight in shaking his Victorian values whenever the opportunity arose. Rosie supposed the idea of wearing plumage was to Gregory akin to making herself into a painted bird, like those sultry women from the port. She blushed a little, remembering the sinful scene upon their arrival. The room felt humid and airless and she had a sudden desire to take some air on the balcony. She was relieved beyond measure when the professor suggested, rather showily, that they accompany him to the drawing room in order to examine his day's work.

They arrived to find a projector and screen were already set up in the drawing room, evidently with some help from Jorge, who stood dutifully next to a tray of drinks. They each took their seats as the professor fussed and fidgeted with the equipment. He chattered all the while, describing how he had established his "darkroom," as he called it, in the house stores to the rear of the kitchens. Tonight's presentation would comprise of the footage from their expedition into the rainforest, after which they would be treated to a couple of reels from Cecil's prior travels. To Rosie's delight, the Victor phonograph had been set up on a trestle table next to the film projector.

Cecil instructed Jorge to start the audio cylinder playing; then the projector flickered into life and the show was underway. Shadow shapes danced across the walls of the room as the film started, accompanied by the noise of the phonograph. Rosie guessed what the soundtrack might be before it started, and smiled at the sounds she had heard just hours ago while sitting on the fallen tree trunk in the forest. The sound was scratchy and tinny through the amplification horn, reminding Rosie of all the times she had listened to the ocean in seashells as a child. The whir of the projector behind its flickering beam was mesmerizing and, as the first few frames of the jungle footage were revealed, Rosie felt herself utterly transported. The combined effect of sound and vision was alchemical, taking her back to the calm and quiet of those moments in the rainforest. There were the macaws, arcing across the sky as the camera followed them. Then the footage jumped abruptly to another angle, and another. All the while the sounds of the forest chirruped and droned from the phonograph, just as they did in life. But then something changed on the soundtrack, like each and every sound had become muffled somehow, dropping several octaves. All eyes were on Jorge, silently accusing him of committing some kind of sabotage upon the phonograph. He looked back blankly, clearly turning the crank handle at the correct speed just as the professor had instructed him. The deep drone turned to a crackle, then became a howl of white noise that set Rosie's teeth on edge. Aunt Francesca shrieked at something on the screen and Rosie narrowed her eyes to see a dark shape flicker in the shadows of the trees beyond the foreground image of frolicking birds.

"What was that?" Francesca said, afraid.

Rosie shook her head dumbly.

"The noise, man! Put an end to this infernal noise!" Uncle Gregory implored, his hands covering his ears. He appeared not to have seen the shape on the film, as his attention was instead on the phonograph.

The professor crossed to Jorge and pushed him away from the

phonograph. The soundtrack came to an abrupt stop and Rosie heard a fearful whimper escape from her aunt's throat. Rosie looked back to the screen and caught a final glimpse of the dark figure in the trees. It looked like a tall man, utterly dark save for the glint from the impenetrable black of his eyes, or the places his eyes should have been. Every hair on Rosie's body stood on end at the sight of him. An icy chill passed right through her. Then, the shape moved and was swallowed by the trees. The film was caught up and mangled in the projector, spooling around the mechanism like spaghetti.

"Hellfire and botheration," the professor exclaimed, rushing to the projector in order to try and salvage his precious film. He muttered further expletives when the film snapped apart in his hand as he tried to free it from the metal jaws of the projector.

"Language, please, Professor Cecil, there are ladies present," Uncle Gregory boomed.

"Quite. Of course, please forgive me," Cecil said, flustered. "Jorge, pour some stiff drinks, my boy, I think we're all in grave need."

Upon Jorge's blank look, he repeated himself in dialect.

At that, Rosie burst into hysterical laughter, partly as a result of nerves. She felt as though those hideous eyes were still peering out at her from the projector screen, even though it was now blank. She saw the same fear and uncertainty in her aunt when their eyes met, an unspoken acknowledgement that they had both witnessed something that the men in the room had missed. Professor Cecil was busy trying to remove the rest of the film from the projector in order to project another reel, when Gregory helped his wife to her feet.

"I think that concludes our cinematographic, erm, event for this evening," he said to the professor.

"Are you sure? I have some wonders of the Adriatic to show you."

"I'm not sure we are quite equipped to take any more excitement this evening, Professor," Gregory replied in a tone that offered no quarter. "Rosie, I suggest you retire also."

For once, she was in agreement with her uncle and so they left the professor to his chaos of spooling film.

Once she was alone in her room, Rosie tried to blink away the memory of the film and those eyes that, even now, seemed to be penetrating her.

She checked, and rechecked, that the shutters were closed tight.

CHAPTER THIRTEEN

Morning broke over the rainforest, bright orange and yellow. A pale moon was still visible in the sky, looking out of place against the color spectrum of morning. Richter remained on his bedroll, enjoying the sight from beneath his mosquito net. He watched as a large spider crawled across the moon on the surface of his net. The sight of the silent predator reminded him he was hungry. He shook off the net, stretched and yawned, ready for the hunt.

Keyser was already preparing the weapons, and Richter greeted him with a nod. The hulking man was not big on conversation, preferring to take orders rather than ask questions—one of the reasons Richter had deemed him perfect for his current expedition. Errol was still sleeping, the weasel, and Richter kicked him where he lay as he passed by. The sleeping man grunted, groaned, then opened his eyes.

"Wake the deckhand. Time for his initiation."

Errol nodded, rubbing the sleep from his eyes, and got up to rouse their young guest. The bruising around the kid's face was settling in. Richter admired Keyser's handiwork in the way an art connoisseur might look upon a painting. The deckhand's lips were dry as a bone, the cut on the lower lip still angry as a rose bloom. Richter handed the kid his water canteen and watched as the boy slaked his thirst greedily. It was already almost ninety degrees Fahrenheit and morning had only just broken.

"Sip, don't gulp," Richter instructed. "Going to be a hellish hot one today, especially when we put you through your paces."

"Paces?" the deckhand asked.

Richter and the other men laughed.

"Today we are going to see how well you hunt, boy," Richter said.

"Hunt what?"

"Whatever the rainforest throws at us. Hopefully something we can all eat, eh? Our group is like any other tribe. We march on our stomachs, so we must keep them filled. Each man has the responsibility to bring food to the fire, and today is your turn."

"But I've never hunted before."

"That's not altogether true though, is it?"

The deckhand shifted uncomfortably on his feet, glancing at the faces of the men around him. Richter could smell the fear emanating from the boy's pores. His sharp eyes picked out the momentary lick of the boy's tongue against his damaged lip. The kid's mouth must be drying up from fear, and memories of his first, and second beatings.

"That's what you were up to aboard the steamer, isn't it?" Richter asked. "Hunting. For pretty redhead pussy, I'd say. Blood rushed to your head, did it?" Richter turned to his men. "We all know which head that was, don't we boys?"

He laughed at his own joke, and they did, too, enjoying the act of victimizing the weakest member of their group.

"What's your name, kid?" Amidst the violence, Richter had neglected to ask.

"Seamus."

"Ah, that explains why you like redheads so much. Irish on your mother's side, is it?"

The kid nodded.

"Listen, Seamus, your task today is simple. Hunt and kill food for our camp or we'll all go hungry. If we go hungry, we might just have to eat you. Understood?"

Seamus nodded, his eyes betraying fear that Richter's threat might be real.

Let him believe it, thought Richter. *I've done far worse.*

He collared the petrified deckhand and marched him over to Keyser, who was handing out spears. The weapons had been cut from nearby bamboo and sharpened using a machete.

"Take one," Richter said.

Seamus took a spear, looking up at its sharpened tip as he held the shaft in his fist.

"Lift it like you're going to throw it," Richter said.

Laughter echoed off the trees as the deckhand lifted, and then almost dropped the spear.

"Again," Richter said, "and find the balance this time."

Seamus struggled to keep the weapon steady. He pivoted it in his hand and nearly dropped it again. Richter wondered if his suspicion that the boy didn't know his ass from his elbow was to be proven accurate after all.

"You'll get the hang of it," Richter said as they set off into the forest. "Or else."

Fatigue was setting in by the time the sun reached its maximum altitude. Even Richter, who prided himself on his patience during all things hunting, was beginning to think their efforts might be fruitless. Seamus was a first-degree klutz, treading wherever a noisy twig lay in wait to be snapped and clutching his spear like an oar in a storm. Richter suspected his bargain with the steamer captain—to take the boy on as sentence for his crime—was turning out to be more of a sentence for himself. It felt like hours since they had broken camp. Checking his pocket watch, he learned that it had been longer than he'd imagined. He was just about to take Keyser aside for conference when the big man hissed in alarm.

The tall, thin trees parted as a dark creature burst out from between them and galloped across the forest floor.

"*Wangana!*" Richter cried.

He saw Seamus's eyes fill with yet more confusion.

"Wild boar," he clarified. "Spears at the ready, boys."

The brown-black boar slammed through them, knocking Errol from his feet. Keyser hurled his spear at the animal, going wide. Richter gestured at Seamus to follow him and they took off together through the undergrowth, chasing after the boar. The forest was a labyrinthine whirl of green and wet, and Richter ducked and weaved through the trees in a desperate attempt to catch up to the boar. The tubby creature was much faster than appearances might suggest, the little hooves on its four legs digging into the forest floor like running shoes on a racetrack. After propelling itself at an awesome pace through the stick-thin trunks of saplings, the boar descended a steep incline into an area clear of trees and some thirty feet in diameter. As Richter gave chase, he saw the lie of the land was like a crater, likely to have been caused by weather erosion. It was the perfect place to trap a wild boar, if they could only keep up. He yelled at Seamus to circle, praying the half-witted boy would understand his intention to ensnare the boar in a pincer movement.

Richter pushed himself into a leap, collapsing his body into a roll as he hit the dirt. He used the spear as a prop with which to push himself at the boar, without losing much momentum. He felt his hat fly from his head as he speared the animal with his weapon. But the brute was intent on outrunning them and, as Richter skidded chin-first into a pile of dead leaves, he saw its hind legs pushing the animal on up the other side of the incline. Remarkably, the creature was dragging the entire length of the bamboo spear behind it. The weight must be slowing it down, but Richter did not know if that would be enough for them to catch it. He'd lost boar in deep woods before, and they had been wounded with buckshot.

Pushing his body up from the forest floor, Richter retrieved his hat and got to his feet, ready to sprint. Then he heard a feral screech from the beast and saw Seamus drive his spear down into the meat of its neck, right between the shoulders. The weapon was embedded with such force that it burst through the boar's throat and pinned it to the ground. Its little legs were still pumping like pistons as Richter approached, then it breathed its last and fell still on the ground where it had met its maker. Richter stooped and cupped the animal's neck, which gushed blood over his hands like a broken barrel might leak wine.

He stood and faced Seamus, who looked to be in a state of some shock.

"Your first boar," Richter said, "well done."

He slapped the boy's face. First one cheek, then the other, painting each bright red with blood.

Keyser and Errol caught up, both sweating and out of breath. They looked in surprise at the dead boar at Seamus's feet.

Richter turned and looked at them.

"He'll do," he said.

CHAPTER FOURTEEN

Rosie was met with her uncle and aunt's typical stoicism when it came to discussion of the events during the professor's cataclysmic film show. Twice, over breakfast, she tried to raise the subject of the dark shape she and her aunt had seen projected large as life on the screen, and twice the subject was summarily changed. They had made it clear to her that they desired no further discussion of the matter, and their meal continued in an uncomfortable silence. The professor scurried in, pink-faced and so late that his morning coffee was already cooling. Rosie made efforts to ask after the condition of his apparatus, but he, too, remained curt on the subject. She caught him glancing at Francesca, his brow wracked with guilt, and she wondered if he hadn't already been briefed that the subject was now out-of-bounds.

Rosie felt sure that her guardians meant to protect her from any further distress, but the stalemate around the dining table gave her cause to believe that she had seen something odd on the film after all. If she hadn't, wouldn't they be gaily laughing its presence away and making light of the tangle of film and the awful cacophonous soundtrack? Finishing her boiled eggs and juice, Rosie excused her presence from the table and retired to her room where she intended to read.

Her aunt had other plans for her, however, and Rosie soon found herself perspiring beneath the brim of her bonnet as they tackled the huge weeds that had taken hold around the threshold to the chapel. Inside the building, Uncle Gregory was supervising the house staff who had been instructed to clean the interior to make it fit for purpose. Rosie had kept the feather in her bonnet, enjoying the way it glimmered in the daylight. Her aunt had already made her disapproval of such adornment abundantly, yet silently, clear. Rosie was thankful for the latter. She gardened in silence, until her aunt surprised her with a question.

"Are you happy, Rosie? With your uncle and I?"

Rosie balked at giving an answer. That her aunt even cared for her opinion was strange enough, but the suddenness of the query had rather pinned her to the spot. She opted to sidestep the question by giving her aunt cause to ask another.

"In general, you mean? Or here, specifically?"

"Oh, both I think," Francesca replied. "You must think it odd, for instance, to establish a mission all the way out here?"

"I think it odd to have a chapel with no congregation," Rosie said, still on guard, "but Uncle Gregory would fill it with pigeons if he had to."

Francesca laughed, a sound like a snapping twig. Rosie had never noticed how deep the worry lines around her aunt's eyes were, giving the impression that crows' claws were gouging there.

"True," Francesca replied, before sighing. "I wonder if we might be happier at home. It's awfully humid here, and it'll only get worse when the rains come. Bound to wreak havoc with your poor skin…"

This struck Rosie as most irregular. Her aunt had never exhibited the slightest interest in her dermal welfare—the "phase" that she was to grow out of. What was the old dear playing at?

"You mustn't feel that you can't approach your uncle with any concerns you might have. About your wellbeing, I mean. He won't deem them unreasonable, I'm sure, especially matters of personal health."

So *that* was it, then. Her aunt already hated life in the rainforest, after just a couple of days, and wished for Rosie to be the conduit for her disapproval. Rosie dug her knees into the dirt and tugged at a thick root stem that seemed to go deeper than the chapel's stilts.

"I quite like it here, actually," Rosie said through gritted teeth. "Yesterday with the professor was the most fun I've had in ages. And I learned more in one day than I did in several at school."

"Brave girl," Francesca said. "You do your uncle proud with your dedication to his cause. But if things here get too much for you, please remember he is your pastor as well as…"

Rosie felt sure the silence was her aunt tripping over the word "father." She felt a longing to be back amongst the trees, making films and recordings, and learning about wildlife. Anything but this.

You hate it here so much, thought Rosie, *then tell him yourself.*

She had to admit she was rather enjoying her aunt's futile game play.

"...as well as your guardian," Francesca finished, to Rosie's relief.

"I will do my best to remember that," Rosie said, getting back to work on the weed stem, without much luck.

"I'd better check on how our lunch is doing. Your uncle will turn his nose up at anything too exotic."

Francesca rose, dusted down her skirts and walked away, leaving Rosie to the remaining tangle of weeds.

A few moments later, the chapel door creaked open. Rosie peered up from beneath her bonnet to see Uncle Gregory towering over her. He bade her good morning, descended the steps and headed for the mission house in Francesca's wake. Rosie wondered how long he had been standing on the other side of the door, and just how much of their conversation he had heard.

At lunch, Gregory said grace then invited Rosie, Francesca, and Professor Cecil to join him for a sermon in the chapel. Rosie suspected this unscheduled worship had been concocted to show off the newly-cleaned building. She and her companions murmured their compliance through mouthfuls of lunch, and Uncle Gregory seemed happy.

Accompanied by the staff, they processed across the clearing and up the wooden steps where Gregory stood, statuesque for a moment, before flinging open the doors with a flourish. From Rosie's vantage point on the lower steps, he looked like a vaudeville magician performing some grand illusion. She followed the others inside and looked around to see every surface had been scrubbed, or polished, to a dust-free shine. The altar cross glimmered in the light from the high windows as she took her place in the pews with her aunt and the professor.

From the lectern, her uncle delivered a speech in his mightiest baritone, the content of which was concerned mostly with the subjugation of all heathen religions under the Word of the one true God. Gregory leaned forward as he described the desire to smash all false idols in the name of the Lord, taking great relish in his vengeance-laden verse. Rosie thought it might be a shame to ransack the temple ruins they had seen on the outskirts of their mission camp. They had, after all, stood there for centuries before Christians such as they had arrived in the region. She wondered if such thoughts were un-Christian of her. If she'd possessed the bravery to voice them, there and then in the chapel, she wondered if her uncle would brand her a blasphemer and lock her up in her room until she repented. She was tempted, almost, to test her theory out, if only to combat the extreme boredom that was setting in as she listened to the droning voice of her guardian-cum-pastor. He was now extolling the virtues of the family unit and railing against the heathen proclivities of tribal peoples who were known to take more than one wife.

"We are all equal beneath the eyes of the Lord," he said, emphasizing the word "beneath."

Rosie stifled a yawn as he arrived at the finish, saying, "Let us pray."

She lowered her eyes and clasped her hands together. Hearing the distant voices of howler monkeys outside, her thoughts wandered to their agile forms in high treetops. She imagined lithe hunters stalking them from the forest floor below, brandishing blowpipes Professor Cecil had described to her on their field trip.

Let us prey, thought Rosie, an anarchic smile curling her lips.

The prayer ended and she said "Amen" with the rest of her uncle's intimate congregation. She lifted her gaze to find him smiling, open armed, at them.

"Tomorrow, we will take His Word unto the heathens," Gregory enthused. "The good professor has agreed to guide us to the nearest village of sinners awaiting absolution. Come, take your rest, for the journey is arduous and our holy work will take time and great effort."

As the others walked back to the mission house in post-ceremonial silence, Rosie stopped to try and pull up the weed root that had outwitted her earlier. She wrestled it with both hands but it snapped clean off. Its roots were too stubborn and went too deep.

CHAPTER FIFTEEN

They rose with the dawn, and Rosie washed and dressed before venturing out of her room to find the mission house buzzing with industry. The staff had loaded packs with the essentials for their journey, and each one looked fit to burst at its seams. Aside from the obligatory food and drink, which vied for space amongst the professor's audiovisual gadgetry, Rosie was curious to see khaki tents, rolled up around their broken-down frames.

"Are we camping?" she asked Cecil, who was trying to shoehorn a wooden map tube into a reluctant backpack.

"Only if the rains come," he replied. "The tribal village is a half day's journey from here. A lot can happen in the skies above the rainforest in that time. Did your uncle not mention it, my dear?"

"Oh, no one tells me anything," Rosie said in a hushed voice. "Little girls should be seen and not heard, my uncle always says." She leaned in closer to Cecil, like a conspirator. "Can I tell you a secret?"

"Of course."

"I stopped being a little girl a long time ago."

The professor blushed a little, and barely stifled his great guffaw of a laugh.

"You promise not to tell anyone? My aunt and uncle don't know," she said.

"Oh, mum's the word, my dear, mum's the word."

Rosie winked at him then helped him to force the map tube into his bag. She rather relished the idea of camping out in the rainforest, away from the rather stuffy, creaky wooden cocoon of the mission house. When the staff had loaded themselves up like pack mules and flung open the main doors, Rosie licked her lips, straightened her bonnet and marched outside feeling like an intrepid explorer of old.

This is how Sir Ernest Shackleton must have felt when he strode out into the great white unknown, thought Rosie, *ready for anything that nature could throw at him.*

As she settled into the pace set by their guides, she tried not to think about how Shackleton had died—from the ravages of alcohol and heart failure—just a few years ago in '22. And, try as she might, Rosie struggled not to think of the names on the grave markers behind the chapel back at the mission compound. All around her the trees were closing in as the forest became thicker. Each tree trunk looked like a grave marker in waiting, ready to be felled, cut, and engraved with another name, then another. A macaw let out a cry across the treetops and it sounded like a warning. Rosie quickened her pace to keep up with the others.

The journey was taxing in the heat and they stopped early for luncheon in a shady glade of trees. True to form, Professor Cecil located a picnic blanket in one of his many pieces of luggage and laid it out on the forest floor for the ladies. He and Uncle Gregory retired to the makeshift comfort of a couple of tree stumps, each overgrown with a cushion of vivid green moss. Rosie was uncomfortable on the blanket, feeling the twist of roots beneath it, and expressed her wish to sit on a tree stump like the men. Her aunt, still as frosty as ever after their exchange outside the chapel, forbade such an act, deeming it too unladylike. Rosie marveled that someone could maintain such a frosty disposition in the heat of the rainforest. Disinterested in her lunch of potted meat and the dry flatbread that was a specialty of the staff, she watched her aunt swatting at the flies that buzzed beneath her bonnet, tutting loudly at the creatures as though they were errant schoolchildren. Any private pleasure Rosie gleaned from the sight was at an end when the swarm of flies fanned out and began bothering her. She felt a sharp sting on her neck, just above her high collar, and realized one of the insects had bitten her.

"Sand flies," Cecil said rising, as he, too, was under attack.

"All creatures great and small," Gregory said before one of the creatures stung him on the arm. "Bastard!" he yelled before he could stop himself, his curse echoing around the trees.

"Hell's teeth," Cecil said, "I'm being eaten alive. I am quite aware that there is ample portion of me to go around but still..." He yelped at another sharp sting.

Amidst the hubbub, Rosie fancied she heard the sound of

a twig breaking. Her eyes searched the forest and she felt her heartbeat quicken when she saw a shape moving through the trees. She was about to vocalize her concern when she realized the shadowy form was just a monkey, swinging from branch to branch before climbing higher and out of sight. Their picnic at an end, Rosie helped as they hurriedly packed up their belongings and prepared to evacuate from the sand fly nest they had inadvertently opted to take lunch upon.

The rest of the walk was fraught, thanks to the sand flies that followed them for much of the journey. After an hour of frenzied swatting and intermittent cursing, Rosie and Francesca took to wearing napkins around their faces as makeshift scarves. Rosie's skin burned beneath the fabric and she felt the dismay of another rash making a cratered landscape of her face. Hot pain swelled beneath her shoulder blades where the flies had feasted on her fair flesh. She could only imagine that her blood, and that of her companions, tasted exotic to the creatures, and Rosie found herself wishing for one of the professor's gin and tonics. He looked to be suffering as much as she, swinging his map holder as if it were a surrogate machete as they pushed on through the forest. Rosie wondered how on earth her guides knew where they were going. She glanced over her shoulder, taking care to hold her napkin-scarf in place, and was baffled as to how anyone could discern landmarks in such a landscape as this. The way back looked exactly the same as the way ahead, a crush of tall trees and smaller saplings, each competing for the high sun's nourishment. She did her best not to entertain morbid thoughts of being lost in the forest, but fatigue, and the almost desperate pace at which they traveled, caused them to creep into her consciousness regardless. Droplets of perspiration began to seep through her improvised facemask, and she was about to beg for a rest stop when one of their guides shouted, "Myahueneca!" His voice was filled with joy, and the unmistakable sound of relief.

Then, through the regiments of tree trunks, she saw it.

The village was ten times the size she had imagined, even glimpsed from its outskirts. As they rounded the natural curve of the pathway through the trees, Rosie could see the encampment had been constructed around a long hut with a sloping roof of branches and interwoven reeds that gave it the aspect of a huge thatched cottage. The walls were formed of mud, dried over timber frames, like those of the smaller, satellite huts surrounding the long building. The small huts were roughly circular, with the same roofing, and—unlike the long house, which hugged the ground beneath it—had been built on stilts. Sloping ramps and low ladders, like the ones back at the mission house, gave entry to the dark doorways of the stilted dwellings outside, upon which hung animal skins, fruit, and plants that were drying in the sunshine. The village occupied dusty flatland that had been cleared of trees to such an extent that the ground shimmered with the heat. As she stepped out of the shade of the forest and onto the baking earth, Rosie could feel its heat penetrating the soles of her shoes. The sun was at its zenith, and she felt gladder than ever for the veil that still clung to her sensitive cheeks.

Their guides gestured to them that Rosie and the others should remain at the outskirts of the settlement while they made the approach. She listened to her breathing as she watched them walk into the clearing, toward the long house at its center. They carried themselves like cats might approach their prey, taking short, stealthy steps and apparently prepared to flee at any given moment. They had almost reached the shadow of the long dwelling when they stopped still in their tracks.

One by one, tribespeople emerged from the long house, forming a human wall—in welcome or warning Rosie could not decipher. She had never seen their like before. The men wore jewelry of wood and bone in their ears, which stretched the lobes into new configurations. Some even had nose piercings and all of them had brown ink designs on their half-naked bodies. Their athleticism was pronounced, with not an ounce of fat between them, and Rosie felt relief to see that they at least wore loincloths to protect their modesty. The women among the gathering group were less covered, with breasts of every shape and size on display for all to see. Rosie felt a prickle of shame burn beneath her veil. She felt embarrassed for them somehow, though she could scarcely understand why. Compared with the painted women back at the port, the females before her possessed a natural power and defiant beauty. They looked proud in their nakedness, their costume augmented by large earrings and neck jewelry, which appeared to have been fashioned from bone, wood, and woven reeds decorated with bright feathers. Rosie glanced at her uncle and saw him avert his eyes from the display of flesh before him. Aunt Francesca regarded the scene with cool indifference, wafting her face with a fan from her handbag as if she were enjoying a day at the races. Their guides spoke in dialect to the villagers and waited while a spokesperson disappeared inside the long house. He emerged a few moments later and conversed with the guides who, in turn, gestured to Rosie's party that they could enter the village.

Aunt Francesca folded her fan away and linked arms with Rosie, who could feel the gaze of the villagers penetrating the fabric of her veil. She must look as alien to them as they did to her, perhaps even more so. All round her, hushed voices spoke in the language she felt she could never hope to understand. She looked to Professor Cecil for clues and found him smiling.

"They are bestowing upon you a name already," he said, beaming. "White Angel."

CHAPTER SIXTEEN

"Hem-hem."

Aunt Francesca's hiccoughing sound conveyed her utter disapproval at such a moniker as "White Angel" being given to her charge.

Rosie thought it best to remain quiet and continued hiding behind her veil. They came to a halt a few feet away from the long house and stood patiently while the village spokesperson made several pronouncements. Though she could not understand the content of his monologue, she felt sure of the general meaning. Each sentence ended louder than the last, until the spokesperson had whipped his fellows into a frenzy of whoops and cheers. Then, from the shadows of the long house a man appeared, in full tribal dress adorned with the exquisite paradise bird feathers Rosie had seen in the forest. He moved strangely, dancing his way across the short distance from the shade to his visitors. Rosie's stomach turned to see that the cartilage of his nose had been pierced with what looked like a bird's beak. It wobbled and shook above his top lip as he sang some words at the top of his voice, which was higher and more feminine than Rosie had expected. He finished his weird performance by shaking out his limbs and folding his body almost in two, before fixing each of them with wild, staring eyes.

"This is their shaman," Cecil said.

"Shaman?" Uncle Gregory interrupted.

"Their equivalent for you," Cecil replied, "but he is both their pastor *and* their doctor."

"Ah, a *medicine man*?"

"Quite. And he bids us warm welcome in the domain of the tribe."

Rosie detected a hint of animosity in her uncle's exchange

with the professor resulting, she suspected, from Gregory's fierce dislike of anything he might deem un-Christian. He would have ample scope for dislike in this village by the looks of things. She glanced at her aunt, who looked so much like a fish out of water Rosie wondered if she might expire on the spot. Not one of them, Rosie included, knew quite what to do or to say. The shaman then broke the disquieting silence with some loud clucking and whooping sounds, rather like those of the roosters she used to hear on her parents' farm, and gestured for them to follow him inside the long house.

"He wishes for us to have an audience with their chieftain," the professor said.

Rosie could still feel the gaze of the entire village on her back as she passed over the threshold. The air inside the long house was cool and inviting, cut through with heady scents of herbs and boiled meat from the ashes of a large fire pit at its center. The internal structure of the building was formed of a backbone of tree trunks, lashed together with vines. Sturdy beams that jutted out at angles from the column-like trunks supported a thatched roof. A round hole in the middle of the roof provided a chimney for the fire pit below, and Rosie looked aloft to glimpse a perfect circle of brilliant blue sky as she passed beneath it. Each column and beam formed a natural seating area, made comfortable with dried grasses and animal skins. Three men were sitting cross-legged and straight-backed, awaiting them, in the farthermost of these areas.

The shaman stooped as he approached the three men and glanced over his shoulder. The meaning of his gesture could not be clearer; he wished for Rosie and the others to follow suit. Professor Cecil went first, being more accustomed to such rites of passage than his fellows, followed by Rosie's aunt and uncle. Rosie laughed inwardly at their pride, which apparently allowed only the merest slope of their shoulders rather than a full stoop. She herself adopted the stance demonstrated by the professor. Although she found it difficult to walk in a strange half-curtsying gait it seemed the thing to do in the presence of the imposing trio at the end of the long house. They had an innate reverence to them, their dark eyes gleaming from the shadows of the alcove like owls' eyes on a full moon night.

The shaman spoke in rhythmic whispers to his masters, who regarded their visitors with looks of slight amusement. Presently,

Rosie and her fellows were invited to sit, forming a semicircle before the village elders. The men were perhaps in their early sixties, though it was hard to tell. Rosie had never seen elderly people in such a state of vitality before. Though the skin of their arms was sagging a little, their bodies looked tight as drums beneath—presumably the result of their lifetimes of hunting and gathering. They were adorned with similar carved jewelry and feathers to the people outside, but theirs were fancier and far more intricate in accordance with their status in the community. The man at the center of the group must be the chieftain, as his body jewelry and head dress were complimented by bright body paint the color of turmeric. His cheeks and forehead were slicked with the stuff, the effect of which was to make him look like a wise old bird of prey. Though his expression was stern, Rosie could sense a softness in his dark eyes that went some way toward explaining why he had been elected leader of the community. He looked like a benevolent leader, authoritative yet kind.

Rosie listened, bemused, at the foreign exchange that ensued between the professor and the elders, with the shaman as its conduit. Finally, Cecil turned to Gregory and advised him.

"The chief welcomes us to his village and invites us to take sustenance here."

"All those words to say so little?"

"The dialect here is complex. Luckily their medicine man has traveled and his conversational skills with him."

Uncle Gregory grunted. "And our mission here in the jungle? You told them about that, I trust? Told them the doors to our chapel are open, as are the doors to His kingdom?"

"It is perhaps prudent to learn a little of their ways before imposing yours," Cecil replied, as democratically as he could.

The fact that he had said "your ways" rather than "ours" was not lost on Rosie. Here, perhaps, the definition of the two men could be made. The professor was a man of science and his presence among the people of another culture represented great opportunity for study. Her uncle was a man of the cloth and his purpose here, indeed the purpose of their entire trip, was one of conversion. Rosie was reminded of the night when she had felt stranded between two vastly different worlds, the civility of the mission house and the feral nature of the rainforest. Her feelings were not dissimilar now—caught, as she was, between the secular and the divine worlds of the two men, the two father figures either side of her. She had always been raised a Christian and had a quiet respect for her uncle's faith, even though it was somewhat tempered by her interests in science and technology, which the professor was helping to draw out of her. The tribal environment into which she had been thrust was providing her with a third wheel of belief to consider. Their customs must date back before the beginnings of Christianity if the temple ruins were anything to go by. Perhaps they would remain long after missionaries and scientists had departed from their shores. Either that or Christianity, science, and the savage could find a way to coexist. Rosie supposed each culture had reverence for the land and nature, in its own way.

Lost in her thoughts, Rosie felt a tingling in her legs and realized they had gone to sleep. She rocked on her knees, which prickled with pins and needles. Rosie felt terribly urbane all of a sudden, a city girl kneeling in a mud hut and not used to sitting without a chair. Rosie saw the same discomfort in her aunt's eyes as she frowned at her over the brim of her face scarf. Recalling their conversation at the chapel, Rosie felt a little sorry for her aunt. She was sure that the act of kneeling on the dirty floor of a mud hut must have been stretching Francesca's devotion to the limit. Rosie watched the poor woman clinging to the last shreds of her dignity while the menfolk talked via their interpreter.

"The chieftain has but one more request of his honored guests," Cecil was saying to Gregory. He paused, listening to the birdlike ramblings of the medicine man, before translating once again. "The women do not cover themselves, and he wishes very much that ours do not veil their faces."

At this, Gregory stifled and glanced at Francesca, his look a mixture of apology and the seeking of approval. The shaman continued speaking and Cecil filled them in.

"The act of masking is one that is reserved for ritual and rite, if you will. We are to be the recipients of such a tradition, a welcome ritual in our honor. The chieftain asks if we accept?"

Francesca nodded silently to Gregory, who grunted in his customary way.

The professor smiled, looking like he was enjoying the exchange, and spoke a few words in dialect directly to the chieftain, who clapped his hands and looked at Francesca, then Rosie.

Reaching to the nape of her neck, Rosie found the knot holding her scarf to her face and began working at it with her fingertips. Her Aunt Francesca did the same, removing her veil first. Rosie untangled the last of the knot and, trying not to wrinkle her nose at the amplified smells in the long house, pulled the scarf away from her face.

Seeing her, the chieftain gasped and turned to his fellows, chattering excitedly. They each pointed at her in an overt manner that might be deemed rude in polite company but seemed to be the accepted way of things in the wild. The chieftain gestured at her face, then at the markings made upon his own in that vivid turmeric make-up. Rosie did not require Cecil's translation to tell her that the chieftain thought the marks caused by her skin condition reminded him of his own. She longed to veil her face again, feeling all eyes upon her, but dared not in case it was the wrong thing to do.

Presently, Cecil spoke. "The chieftain welcomes you, Rosie, to the tribe and asks how long you have walked with the spirits."

Rosie could feel her aunt and uncle's gaze upon her. She did not look, fearful she would feel like a little girl again if their eyes met. She kept her eyes forward and dared making eye contact with the chieftain, who was beaming at her.

"What does he mean by that?" she asked.

Cecil conversed with the men, none of whom could take their eyes off her.

"Your tribal markings, as he calls them, make you a spirit walker in their eyes. Your skin has been kissed by the sun and bathed in the rainbow…"

Cecil paused as the shaman spoke again. When the man was done, the professor translated, as if for Rosie alone.

"Such markings are made by nature, and nature is to be praised for them. The chieftain says that Great Spirit who dwells in all things within the rainforest brought you here across the rainbow bridge, to us…I mean to *them*. Yes, quite."

Rosie tried to take in the meaning of the words as Cecil's eyes gleamed at her.

"You are to be initiated into the tribe, Rosie."

CHAPTER SEVENTEEN

Uncle Gregory demonstrated admirable restraint, waiting until they were outside the long house before making his feelings known on the subject of Rosie's surprise initiation. As she'd expected, her uncle forbade any such thing, and instructed Professor Cecil to issue a polite refusal to the tribal elders. Rosie felt a surge of relief—the idea of initiation was quite frightening to her and conjured the images of tribal scarification and witchery she had glimpsed within the pages of *The Geographical Digest* before her aunt had confiscated the magazines and consigned them to the kitchen to be used as kindling. Rosie felt a part of those forbidden pages somehow—it was as though their half-glimpsed pagan world had pulled her inside and made her part of their secrets.

Following her uncle and aunt outside, she had been greeted as though she were a deity, with the women in the tribe actually kneeling before her and singing sweet songs upon seeing her reddened face. The condition that had brought her daily shame back home was providing an embarrassment of adulation here on the other side of the planet. For Rosie, one form of unwanted attention had merely been supplanted by the other. She felt doomed to be under scrutiny wherever and however far away she traveled.

To her surprise, Cecil stood up to Uncle Gregory by informing him that he need not worry about the initiation. Rosie listened intently as he described the rite after the village shaman, underlining that it was a metaphorical rite of passage involving only song, feasting, and tribal dance.

"Pagan nonsense," Gregory spat. "My niece will have no part of such animalistic pursuits."

"Then I suggest we leave," Cecil sighed.

"You suggest what?" Gregory looked as shocked as Rosie felt hearing Cecil's drastic words. She certainly admired his bravery in speaking so frankly with her uncle. Few men would even dare. But what she had seen of the professor so far placed him firmly in the "not regular men" category.

"If the pursuits and practices of these noble people—people who have embraced us into their village and offered to bestow upon us the very great and rare honor of a tribal welcome—if their pursuits are distasteful to you then I suggest we leave now before we can offend them, and your predecessors, any further."

"Make sense, man," Gregory said. "Offend my predecessors? How?"

How like him to focus on his predecessors rather than the tribal people around him, thought Rosie, biting her lip so that little girls might be better off seen and not heard.

"The early settlers here took the time to get to know these people. Weeks were spent mastering the rudiments of language and custom until a dialog could be entered. Sadly, during that time the bacteria your European friends brought with them had been introduced into the delicate ecology of the village. In short, dozens died, of influenza and other ailments brought here by those very missionaries seeking to 'save' them."

Cecil's words hung heavy in the humid air, adding to its heat. He glanced at Rosie, looking remorseful for blowing his top, and then moved closer to Gregory in order to speak more quietly.

"In spite of this dubious history with outsiders, the Myahueneca have accepted us with open arms, into the very bosom of their culture. I put it to you that the least we can do is to pay them the respect of attending their welcoming ritual. What they wish to do is no different from your saying grace before supper, or taking the sacrament in church…"

"I am not a Catholic, Professor," Gregory said.

"Neither am I," Cecil replied, "but I respect the beliefs and practices of those who are Catholic. Or Anglican—or Myahueneca."

Gregory turned to Rosie, his brow heavy as a storm front.

"Do you have issue with any of…this? Speak, child. It is not our intent, your aunt and I, to subject to anything that gives you recourse to fear or anxiety."

Rosie wished he had said those words before they had boarded the ship, before making the decision for her to leave her home. But he had not demonstrated this concern for her well-being then. Partly in dismay at that fact, and partly for solidarity with the professor, she replied to her uncle with a shake of her head.

"Francesca?"

Rosie's aunt stiffened and her eyes narrowed, sharpening her nose to a point. After a protracted and uncomfortable silence, she let out a thin sigh and said, "If you must see fit to bring us to this Godforsaken place, then let us do whatever is required to improve our lot within it."

"Thank you, my dear," Gregory replied. "It seems you have your wish, Professor."

"Quite," Cecil said, before talking in tongues with the medicine man once more, who smiled at each of them in turn then led the way into the communal arena just beyond the long house. The professor offered Rosie his arm, which she gladly took. She was feeling unsteady on her feet beneath the twin glare of both the sun, and the tribal community.

CHAPTER EIGHTEEN

Rosie's walk to the dusty communal arena, where the welcoming ritual was to take place, was mercifully short and she was glad to be seated. This time Rosie was invited to take her rest on a three-legged seat that looked like a milking stool but felt like a throne compared to kneeling on the ground. Her aunt and uncle beside her, Rosie thanked the professor for his arm and watched the preparations of the people who dashed to and fro around them.

The pre-ritual atmosphere was one of nervous excitement with much laughter and chatter from the women and children. The majority of the men stood in the shade of the long house, an area that appeared to have become an unofficial dressing room. Rosie watched the men as they applied handfuls of tribal make-up to their fellows' skin. The paint, which looked more like a paste, had been mixed in deep red hues. Rosie wondered if they always wore it this way, or if the desired effect was to better match her own ruddy complexion. Shadows danced before her eyes and she looked up to see that a gaggle of infants had gathered around her, singing in shrill voices as fragile as eggshells. She smiled at them and they giggled at her acknowledgment, before draping garlands of long green stems topped with fiery orange flowers around her neck. Rosie thanked them for their unexpected gifts with handshakes and listened as they continued their song.

"*Heliconia*," Cecil said, pointing at the garlands around Rosie's neck, "beautiful, are they not?"

"Very," Rosie said, "and their song is beautiful, too. What are they singing about? Do you know?"

The professor listened intently for a few moments, lifting his index finger and letting it rise and fall with the tempo of the children's song. Rosie chuckled at him, amused to see him conducting his juvenile choir in such a fashion. He closed his eyes and the words of their song began to form on his lips.

He nodded and said, "They are chanting your name, I believe."

"White Angel?"

"Oh, you remember. Very good, Rosie, but then you are a quick learner, yes quite. But no, they have already seen fit to rename you now that you have removed your veil and revealed yourself to them. They are very excited, you understand, so it is hard to translate into a single word..."

"Feel free to use as many as you need," Rosie said, intrigued. She would be lying to herself if she didn't admit that she was enjoying the attention a little now. It felt like a great honor to be the subject of such a beautiful song. Rosie hoped she could remember its melody and store it away for future memory.

"Roughly translated—very roughly you understand—they sing of a white angel who has swum the river's mysterious depths, and risen on rainbows."

Rosie's jaw dropped.

"A very pleasant song indeed, yes!" Cecil said, laughing and clapping at the children.

Rosie smiled to herself behind her garlands, enjoying the delicious floral scent at her throat. The song was indeed beautiful, and its meaning filled her heart with glee.

The children had a further gift for Rosie. Two cherubic infants knelt before her with a wooden bowl filled with a white paste. They dipped their fingers in the paste and held them up so Rosie could see.

"Make-up? They want to paint my face?" she asked Cecil.

"They do indeed," he said.

"But what about my skin?"

The professor conversed for a while with the children in their strange dialect, then turned to Rosie.

"They say the paste contains the calendula, a precious medicinal flower. When the girls of the village show their coming of age signs, they apply the paste."

Rosie shot the professor a puzzled look.

"*Acne*, my dear. They say the make-up helps. Who is to say it won't help your skin, too?"

Rosie considered Cecil's words, then smiled her permission at the children, who whooped with delight and set about dabbing at

Rosie's face with their tiny fingertips. It felt like they were making patterns of little white dots there.

"Whatever do you look like?" The veins in Aunt Francesca's forehead looked fit to burst upon seeing Rosie's new look. "Wipe that off at once, child."

"I must warn you," Cecil interjected, "any such rebuke might be met with severe disdain from our esteemed hosts."

Francesca looked like she was about to protest, but was drowned out by the single, piercing blast of a horn.

The noise and excitement of the crowd subsided, and Rosie saw the chieftain and his fellow elders processing regally into the center of the group. Each villager looked upon their leader with due reverence, bowing their heads in supplication as the chieftain passed them. He looked even more splendid than before, garlanded with a rainbow of flowers and crowned with feathers that shone in the sunlight. His tribal make-up had been refreshed and was of that deeper reddish hue Rosie had seen the men in the village applying to their fellows. He held out his arms and turned on his heels. As he did so, every man, woman and child dropped to their haunches and fell silent. Then, women brought mats made from woven leaves and the chieftain sat down, cross-legged, flanked by the two men from the long house. He regarded his visitors with a noble gaze and Rosie fancied that she saw his eyes widen when he looked upon her. Then, theatrically, he held his arms aloft again and clapped, twice—the sound echoing around the silent arena.

At his cue a drumbeat began, like a steady heartbeat. The men formed groups and began to dance into and around the performance space, accompanied by shrill singing from the women and children. Rosie watched the painted bodies of the men as they wove and spun, kicking up dust all the while with their bare feet. Each dancer carried a spear and a net, which they swung and thrust with euphoric cries. Rosie thought they might be re-enacting a hunt and her instincts were proven correct when, without warning, another fellow burst from one of the huts. He was clad from head to toe in animal furs and scurried on all fours around the exuberant crowd, which clapped, cheered and goaded him as one. They laughed with delight as the "creature" ducked between one of the dancer's legs, evading capture in one net, then another.

The dancers made a great show of organizing themselves

into a circle around the skin-clad man, singing gutturally as they closed ranks around him. Cornered, the animal man made feral whinnying noises before the dancers ensnared him with their nets. Each hunter then thrust his spear at the prostrate man, feigning the act of killing him. Rosie felt her heart beat faster at the sight, which was at once uncomfortable yet compelling to her. She glanced at her aunt and uncle and saw that both of them were as transfixed as she, unable to look away from the spectacle despite their obvious discomfort. The whooping continued as the men split into two lines and danced their way toward the women carrying their still-writhing catch. An explosion of joy ensued when the men pulled their nets away so that the animal player tumbled to the ground at their feet. Laughing, the women mimed eating the flesh of their bounty.

"A primitive depiction, but a revealing one all the same." Professor Cecil spoke in a stage whisper, apparently from reverence for the tribal rites. "If the men of this culture do not succeed in the hunt, there will be no meat for the community. They share everything equally here between all the families of the tribe. Not one goes hungry while another eats. Even if only one hunter is successful in catching his prey, all benefit. It is a noble way to live, I am sure you will agree."

A communal shriek went up as the children began chasing the man in the animal skins and he made a great spectacle of almost evading them. Nobody answered the professor, save for Rosie.

"They do everything with such joy, and yet they must face such hardship sometimes. I will never complain about eating my greens again."

"Careful now. Your aunt and uncle shall no doubt quote you on that," Cecil whispered with a wink.

Rosie bit her finger in order to stifle the giggle growing within her, but it was too late. Her eyes welled up with tears of laughter. Aunt Francesca looked down her nose at Rosie, peering at her as though she were mad. Uncle Gregory harrumphed and shifted in his seat and Rosie did her best to compose herself, drying her eyes on her handkerchief. As her vision cleared, she realized how silent the village had fallen. Blinking away the last of her mirthful tears, she became aware that the chieftain was looking directly at her. His gaze was penetrating, and Rosie felt goose bumps forming as he stared, not at but *into* her face somehow. The villagers were all on their feet, even the man in the animal skins who had been frolicking with the children but moments ago. Rosie wished she could retract her head into the depths of her bonnet, like a turtle might hide in its shell, but she had no such place to conceal herself. All she could do was to squint back at the many gathered faces with the sun in her eyes. The chieftain stood up to make a proclamation and several of the women approached Rosie with their arms outstretched. Rosie looked to Cecil, who nodded at her in encouragement, and the next thing she knew she was being hoisted into the air and carried on the shoulders of the women. Cascades of brightly colored feathers and petals rained down on her like confetti as the tribeswomen carried her across the arena to the chieftain and his fellows.

The chieftain held his hands above Rosie's head, his fingers looking like the feathered tips of some monstrous bird's wingspan against the sun, and began to bellow further proclamations to his people. Rosie wished the professor was at her side to translate, however roughly he might do so, but she knew he would remain seated out of respect for the ritual. She tried to crane her head around, searching out a glimpse of his reassuring presence, but the women held her fast and she could not move. The women began to dance to the rhythm of the chieftain's voice and Rosie—still held fast—danced with them by osmosis. She was like a puppet in their hands, going through the motions of being one of the tribe as they swayed in one direction, then the other. The women began to sing, a series of orgiastic wails that made Rosie's ears ring, and they spun her between them. Like a spinning top she whirled from one woman to the next, the wailing growing louder and more oppressive in her ears until she felt like screaming and—

She came to an abrupt stop before the shaman.

Up close, Rosie realized he had colored his hair with the same red paste the men had used as make-up. The medicine man's forehead and cheeks were also slicked with the stuff, so much so that he looked like a strange re-imagining of Rosie—her features exaggerated to absurd proportions. He squawked and shrieked, his tongue oscillating in his mouth and making bizarre music of the sounds. Rosie glimpsed something thin and black between the fingertips of his right hand and then felt a sharp sting at her wrist. She cried out, but the sound was lost in the communal wailing of the women and the shaman. Looking down at her wrist, Rosie saw two red marks there. She felt panic rising in her throat like bile, believing the thin black object in the shaman's hand to be a snake. With relief, she saw it was a long, twin-pronged fork fashioned from sharpened wood. It was soot-black from having been burned in a fire and, as the shaman traced its tip through the air in front of her, Rosie caught its sharp, unpleasant odor. Her wrist had gone numb and her throat burned dry with the taste of bile.

Movement caught her eye and she saw a young boy, in his early teens at most, sidling between the press of bodies. He looked somehow different to his fellows, pale and sullen compared to the revelers all around her. He held her with his gaze and his brown eyes looked like they had seen too much for one so young. Rosie tried to speak to him, to ask him his name, but no words would come. He disappeared into the crowd, leaving a palpable atmosphere of sorrow behind him and Rosie felt a tear trickle from the corner of her eye. Her vision blurred with the tear and the women cavorted around her in a watery frenzy of color. Rosie moved with them, tumbling like a rag doll amidst their ranks. Beneath her, the ground seemed to fall away, and she had the sensation of floating. For a moment, Rosie thought the women had lifted her again, but she was mistaken. Her legs had gone as numb as her wrist, all sensation dissipating from her body below the waist. Then the numbness crept upward, making jelly of her arms and neck until she could no longer take her own weight. She folded in half like a clothes horse and tumbled to the ground, light as a feather. Fire raged in her throat together with a barbed, scraping sensation as if an entire rose garden of thorns were being dragged through her windpipe. Rosie tried to scream, but felt a queasy resignation take hold of any resolve her body had left within it. Somewhere far off, she heard the concerned cries of her aunt, but they were muted, muffled and so very far away. She was freezing cold all of a sudden, a melting glacier beneath the brim of her bonnet. She retched and vomited painfully into the dust before the blackness took her.

CHAPTER NINETEEN

Rosie opened her eyes to bright sunlight and spat dry earth from her mouth. She was lying in a fetal position on the ground where she had fallen. Expecting to see the crowd of villagers around her, Rosie was confused to find that she was lying there alone.

Rising into a seated position, she looked around to see the arena was now deserted. She listened intently for the sound of voices, but only a light breeze answered. Feeling weak and dehydrated, it took great effort to push her body up from the ground and into a standing position. The glare of the sun dizzied her as she peered into the distance looking for signs of life. She held the palm of her hand over her forehead against the sun's glare. Rosie felt sure she had been wearing her bonnet—where had it gone?

"Hello?" she said, her voice sounding oddly muffled in her ears. No one answered.

A glimmer at the outskirts of the village caught her eye, brilliant blue against the tall green grasses lining the perimeter. For a moment, Rosie thought it was a bird of paradise until its "wings" flapped in the breeze revealing it to be her bonnet, which must have become dislodged during her initiation. Rosie hurried over to reclaim it, wondering as she went if abandoning her like this was part of the rite. She scooped up the bonnet, and found that it had been festooned with colorful feathers—

a white angel who has swum the river's mysterious depths, and risen on rainbows

—Rosie put the bonnet on and tied it beneath her chin. She was about to return to the long house to see if anyone was there when she saw a familiar face peering out at her from the gloom of the forest. It was the same little boy she had glimpsed during the ritual, just seconds before she had blacked out. His eyes widened as he realized she could see him, and he turned and fled into the trees.

"Hey! Come back! I won't hurt you," Rosie said, pursuing him into the shade of the trees.

The boy was lithe, and clearly used to the terrain, unlike Rosie and she had difficulty catching up to him. Just when she thought she had him cornered, he took off again, weaving between the tree trunks as if they were reeds.

"What's your name? I'm Rosie. I'm a...friend." Then, realizing her words sounded like a plea she said, "Please stop running, I just need to talk with you."

But the boy ran on into the forest, navigating a thick copse of trees and descending into a large, natural crater carpeted with broken branches, ferns and moss. Heart beating hard, Rosie had to break into a sprint to keep the boy in her sights. She hitched up her skirts and held them tightly in her fist, holding her bonnet onto her head with her free hand. As she made her descent down the steep side of the crater, she twisted her ankle and fell. The impact knocked the wind out of her and she rolled over clutching her ankle and cursing under her breath. At the periphery of her vision she saw the child stop, no doubt hearing her anguished cry. He turned to look and even took a few steps toward her.

"Help me, please, I twisted my ankle," she said, her voice pained.

The boy considered her words and Rosie wondered if he even spoke any English. He seemed to be weighing up his next option, rocking on his feet and seemingly ready to take off again should she dare make a move. His eyes narrowed as he made his decision, and Rosie felt relief to see him walking toward her, keeping his body low and defensive.

"You have nothing to fear from me."

The boy was just inches away from her now.

"I'm Rosie." She patted her chest. "Rosie."

"Nimbo," he said, mimicking her by patting his own chest.

"That's rather a lovely name. Now, help me up," she replied, pointing upward to help him understand.

Nimbo clasped both her hands in his, revealing physical strength beyond his stature when he pulled her to her feet. Rosie dusted herself down and thanked him, then gingerly tested the condition of her ankle by putting a little pressure on it. It was sore, but she felt confident she could walk just fine. He led her to the trunk of a fallen tree where she sat, thanking him again. She watched him as he rooted around in the vegetation, searching for something.

"What are you doing?"

His reply soon came when he returned cradling a huge leaf. It was heavy with water, trapped inside like tea in a cup. He mimed drinking from the tapered end of the leaf and then held it out to Rosie. She took it carefully, finding the water to be cool and refreshing—perhaps the purest she had ever tasted. She smacked her lips in appreciation and Nimbo smiled at her, his uneven teeth making his face even more charismatic than ever. In that moment, Rosie felt a connection with the boy. Then his eyes darkened.

A shiver passed through her as she saw unfathomable despair in those eyes, which had but seconds before glimmered with the stuff of life. He was staring at something over her shoulder and her imagination conjured giant spiders, snakes, and other jungle beasts. She snapped her head around to look in the direction that he was staring. Another boy, smaller in stature than Nimbo, stood just twenty feet away from her. He was looking directly at Nimbo, his gaze unwavering.

"Pacon?"

Nimbo's voice was cracked with emotion. He glanced at Rosie and she saw utter disbelief in his expression. He took one single, tentative step toward the mysterious boy, who bolted into the trees. Nimbo broke into a sprint and Rosie called after him. She did not want to be left alone again. Testing her ankle, she started off after him at a brisk walking pace.

"Pacon! Pacon!"

Nimbo's voice urged her on and she, too, broke into a run. She careered through the labyrinth of trees, feeling damp leaves and low branches whipping at her face, but managed to increase her pace. Birds flapped skyward as she crashed through the undergrowth, and monkeys gave their warning calls from up high. Rosie gritted her teeth and pushed herself on through the vegetation until she had Nimbo in clear sight. He was slowing down now, and something about his gait suggested that he was full of dread. Rosie slowed her pace, too, and jogged over to where he now stood.

Nimbo had stopped before a great mound of moss-covered earth, topped by ancient trees. Sinewy tree roots tangled in and around the natural platform, keeping the structure tight in their grip. Rosie's gaze traced their descent across the surface of the mound, and she found the source of Nimbo's apparent dread. A dark hollow was hidden beneath an outcrop of overhanging moss held up by a natural archway of tree roots, which disappeared into the forest floor beneath the opening. Rosie and Nimbo stood side by side, staring into that dark place.

Something smelled bad inside.

"Pacon?" Rosie gestured toward the hollow.

Nimbo nodded at Rosie gravely. His lips curled a little with the fear he was trying so desperately to hide from her. She fought the urge to put her arms around him, to tell him it was all right. The stench coming from within that dark entry place was telling her an entirely different story. Nimbo gestured at her to stay put, then crept toward the opening. Rosie's heart pounded as she counted out his footfalls until he was at the threshold. He turned and glanced at her, blinking into the light.

The breath of a breeze cooled the nape of her neck. The forest had fallen eerily silent. She could not let him go in there alone, however bad it smelled. And she did not mind admitting to herself that she was motivated now by a strong desire not to stand alone at the front door of this strange place. Nimbo shook his head as she approached him, but her mind was made up.

They entered the cool, stinking dark together and found themselves in the mouth of a tunnel.

Rosie's nipples hardened at the chill inside the tunnel and every hair on her body stood to attention. Her feet slipped a little as they crept farther inside, the earth loose beneath her feet. The angle of the tunnel changed, taking them deeper into the earth. In near total darkness now, they both hesitated at a bend in the tunnel. Rosie reached out and clasped Nimbo's hand in her own. His flesh was impossibly warm. It gave her some comfort, at least.

Together they rounded the bend and Rosie discerned the faint flicker of an orange glow up ahead. Torchlight. As the tunnel straightened and stretched out before them, a shadow loomed on the tunnel wall.

The boy.

He was running away from them again. Nimbo let go of

Rosie's hand and sprinted off after him. Rosie ran, too, fighting her instinct to turn back the way they came and to run into the daylight. Torches were set into the wall at intervals in this section of tunnel. She did not wish to consider who, or what, had set them there. Struggling to keep up with Nimbo, Rosie navigated another turn.

"*Irmão!*"

Hearing Nimbo's frantic scream she skidded to a halt. And saw what he was screaming at.

It was the young boy they had been pursuing, that much was clear from his face, his now lifeless eyes. But the rest of him no longer looked human. His flesh had been peeled from his body and nailed to the curved walls of the tunnel, as taut as a drum skin. The sick exhibition of the boy's flesh formed a starfish shape that blocked their path ahead, his dangling skeleton a macabre centerpiece. Torchlight flickered from behind him, making a dark rainbow of his outstretched flesh and unraveled entrails. The soft earth beneath him was a dank soup of blood and other fluids. Rosie wanted to be sick, but a sound at her back shocked the impulse from her system. Her eyes met Nimbo's and the expression she found there made a pit of terror in her stomach.

They were not alone in the tunnel.

There, just a few feet away was the hulking figure of a man, dressed in leathery robes that had been stitched together in a crude patchwork. He peered down at her with the same black, glassy eyes she had glimpsed on the professor's film recording. He stood a good few feet higher than she, and had shoulders so broad they seemed to fill the entire width of the tunnel. His silhouette, more fearsome than any spider, shifted and moved, marching slowly toward her and Nimbo.

The boy cried out, mouthing words Rosie could not understand, and braced himself—standing firm. Rosie thought his bravery's source must have been the atrocities visited upon his fellow, whose corrupt form now blocked their escape. The huge man was upon Nimbo in seconds, his great fist closing around the boy's windpipe as he lifted him from his feet and hurled him aside. Nimbo's head hit the wall of the tunnel and he fell unconscious to the floor.

Rosie staggered back in fright. It was as though a void were closing around her—a presence so dark and ancient that her fear was matched by awe for whoever, or whatever, this man was. The obsidian pools that were his eyes loomed at her from the shadows, reflecting the hideous remnants of the ruined boy behind her. The twin images and the threat that they were telegraphing her fate turned Rosie's blood to ice.

The ground beneath her gave way and she was shocked to find her feet sinking into wet mud like quicksand. She gasped, in pain and frustration, as both her feet were sucked deeper into a hideous quagmire of blood and stench. Rosie clutched at thin air and screamed, thrashing in desperation. But all her movement achieved was to drive her deeper into the quicksand and a new panic took hold of her as she found herself up to her neck in the dark, stinking mud.

The huge man towered over her and she craned her neck back to look up at his face. His expression betrayed no emotion and she realized in that moment his eyes were covered with crude discs of obsidian glass. Perhaps designed to keep the light out—or to keep the darkness within. Rosie shuddered, wondering if his baser impulses might give him cause to extricate her from his oubliette. But he just stood there, immovable as a monolith and watched her sink into the ground. Rosie's screams became dirt in her mouth as she went under.

And fell.

CHAPTER TWENTY

The blood-drenched soil around Rosie that had, until now, been choking her solidified into a cylinder around her. She plummeted through the darkness and with her arms at her sides could do nothing to slow her descent. The sides of the tight tunnel felt granular, like sandstone, and the friction caused by her high-speed transit was burning her skin. She screamed, the sound rebounding in her ears in the confined tube of the tunnel as she continued falling. Then the space beneath her opened up and she was spat out onto a hard stone floor beneath. Her legs buckled beneath her and her hands found solid ground. Firelight flickered from somewhere above her. Spitting the foul taste of earth and ruin from her mouth, she crawled on all fours across the stone floor and took stock of where she had landed.

Rosie was in a cave, or rather a series of caves, for she could not see an end to the number of dark tunnels stemming off from the one she had fallen into. She stood and explored the chamber, which was bigger than the chapel at the mission complex. Several burning torches were mounted on the rough-hewn walls—the source of the firelight illuminating the cave. Most were too high for her to reach save one, which she managed to grasp by climbing up and balancing on one leg on an outcrop of rock beneath it. The flaming torch felt reassuring in her hand, its flame sputtering slightly as she pointed it at the nearest alcove. The torch threw shadows across the walls, revealing details unnoticed by Rosie during her initial, cursory inspection. What she had thought were the shadows of myriad irregularities in the rock face were in fact inscriptions of some kind.

She crept closer to the nearest wall to take a better look and saw a collection of symbols and images had been painted there. The ink had darkened with age to a deep brown hue and Rosie shuddered at the thought that it may have been blood red when first applied to the cave wall. She moved the torch, taking in the complexity of the cave paintings each of which had been painstakingly applied in a spidery, almost delicate hand. The cuneiform letters and symbols described a tale of some kind, she felt sure of that, but in a language perhaps more ancient than, and unfathomable as, hieroglyphics. Rosie wished Professor Cecil was at her side to help make sense of what she was seeing. Most of all, she wished not to be alone in this dark, alien place. She strafed slowly aside the wall and continued studying the cave paintings, stopping at a startling image. Rosie had within her the strongest sensation of déjà vu and, as she peered closer at the pictograph that had stopped her in her tracks, she realized why.

The image before her depicted a tall figure with dark discs for eyes. He held his arms aloft in a triumphant gesture, rather like the shaman during her initiation rite, and in each hand he held an animal skin. Rosie held the torch closer and felt her stomach churn as the intricate details of the painting revealed the skins to be of human origin. One male, one female, they dangled sickly from the hulking figure's hands above a crowd of kneeling worshippers. Something about the scene chimed with Rosie's memory and she took a step back to better see the whole picture.

Surrounding the sickening scene of flayed worship was, unmistakably, a depiction of the temple ruins Rosie and the others had explored on their arrival in the rainforest. A black sun hovered over the scene, looking as chilly as Rosie now felt. The walls seemed to be closing in, heavy with ancient secrets. The tunnel mouths that surrounded Rosie whispered to her of the atrocities depicted in the paintings. She swung her torch away from the wall and peered at each of the alcoves in turn, for now her overriding instinct was to find a way out of the cave and away from its chthonic mysteries. One of the tunnel openings seemed brighter than the others and she opted to try it.

As she entered the tunnel a waft of humid air struck her skin, a sensation that elated her by the prospect that it did, indeed, lead back outside. Her elation was short-lived when she heard a sound behind her in the cave, like a crab scuttling across rocks. She turned and the flame of her torch revealed the dark-eyed figure, watching her from the center of the cave. The way he stood there, with his shadow a mirror of the deity depicted on the wall, told Rosie she had fallen right into his domain.

His glassy black eyes reflected the flicker of her torch flame and she screamed at the sight of them. They were hard and uncaring, boring into her fragile psyche like maggots into windfall fruit. She staggered back under their harsh glare and felt the rough wall of the tunnel at her neck. The hulking man moved then, taking a step toward her. His approach turned her body to liquid adrenalin and she bolted. The torch sputtered angrily before her, the core of its flame blue as the sky she so dearly wished to see again. She rounded a corner in the tunnel, feeling its elevation and praying it went all the way up to forest level. The huge man was not far behind her and, hearing his footfalls, Rosie put on a burst of speed that caused her to rebound off the walls painfully, barely navigating them as they snaked higher. Her lungs began to burst, but on she pushed, seeing distant daylight at the top of the tunnel. Her feet slipped on the crumbling tunnel floor and she cried out, afraid she would fall beneath the feet of the black-eyed monster at her heels.

Then she was up and out, running at a sprint across the damp earth and vegetation of open rainforest. But something was wrong. She felt her feet moving beneath her as she ran, but knew that she was not actually getting anywhere. A sharp tension closed around her ankle and she toppled, seeing the man's hand clamped to her leg just above her right foot. She jabbed the still-flaming torch at his hand, but he held on fast. Panicking, she dropped the torch and set fire to his leathery robes. Still he held fast, gripping her ankle like a trap might ensnare an animal. Rosie pulled with all her might and felt a hot wave pass over her as she separated from her assailant. She ran on, powering through the trees with her hands like a sprinter and saw that they were bleeding. Slowing to a stop on impulse, she looked down at her body and saw that what she thought was blood was in fact her hidden self. She had been skinned. Turning back to look at the mouth of the cave entrance she saw the huge man towering there, holding her skin aloft in a horrific, living rendering of the painting she had witnessed back at the cave.

Rosie screamed, the rawness of her voice becoming the rage of a fire in her ears. Skinless and bleeding, she felt as though she were burning. An acrid stench filled her nostrils, the distillation of a million burning trees and her own roasting flesh. She looked about her and saw the forest had become an inferno, each tree trunk a molten pillar of flame searing into her vision. The fire spread out, engulfing everything in its wake and the trees began to topple. A domino effect of raging flames tumbled around Rosie. It was as though the rainforest were folding in on itself, and around her, a living lava flow of angry flames. Feeling the last remnants of meat cook from her bones Rosie raged inside the inferno, flesh and fire becoming one.

CHAPTER TWENTY-ONE

R osie opened her eyes.

She sat bolt upright, coughing the acrid taste of black smoke from her lungs. The stench of flame and flesh lingered, but a quick examination of her extremities confirmed that the fire had been a phantasm. She rubbed her eyes and looked at her surroundings and found them at once to be familiar in more ways than one. She was in a hammock, which hung a few feet above the floor of the long house. Nimbo sat cross-legged nearby, apparently keeping watch over her. Setting the hammock into a swinging motion as she sat up, Rosie clung to the side ropes and swung her legs over the edge. The boy, seeing she was awake, was at her side in seconds. He offered her a water canteen, fashioned from animal hide. She pulled out the wooden stopper and took a welcome drink, slaking her thirst and cleansing the last of the smoky aftertaste from her throat. A confusion of images collided in her head—Nimbo in the forest, the quagmire and those black eyes in the cavernous depths—Rosie handed the canteen back, then hugged her arms, feeling the afterglow of imagined heat pricking her skin.

"What happened?" she asked the boy.

"No English," he replied and offered her more water.

She refused and said, "Nimbo, isn't it?"

The child looked astonished at the sound of his name.

"Who is Pacon? Is he your brother?"

Without another word, the boy stoppered the canteen and ran to the doorway at the far end of the long house. Rosie heard his excited chatter outside. His rallying cry was soon taken up by other voices, some of which drew closer. Presently, Rosie heard movement at the doorway and was relieved to see Professor Cecil, his eyes brimming with excitement.

"Rosie, my dear! How was your trip?"

"My...trip?"

"The whole village is very excited, my dear. Few have walked the sacred path as you have done." The professor lowered his voice to a conspiratorial whisper. "Tell me, what did you see?"

"See?"

"While you walked in your dreams."

Rosie frowned, unsure if she wanted to speak of the frightening visions she had endured.

"You can tell me, Rosie. You can tell me anything."

After clearing her throat, Rosie said, "I followed the boy. He had lost someone—someone just like him. I saw a man, as tall as a mast and with the blackest eyes. Eyes like nightmares. I fell into the shadows and saw old cave paintings...like the carvings we found at the temple."

At this, Cecil's eyes widened. Rosie heard him utter a single word under his breath.

"*Skintaker.*" Seeing her confusion, he said, "You saw one of their rainforest deities. The Skintaker. I wonder if he also saw you."

"But he wasn't real. Was he?"

Rosie shivered. Her garlands were gone. She felt nauseous and wished she could erase the disturbing visions from her memory in the manner that she might wash her hands clean. Before she could articulate such thoughts, Rosie saw her aunt and uncle enter the long house. Both frowned with dour, concerned expressions as they approached her.

Hearing them, Cecil put on a show of joviality. "Rosie here was just telling me about her hallucinations," he quipped.

Francesca coughed in that prim way of hers. "Professor, please do not make light of the matter. Our Rosie was taken ill. Are you all right, my dear?"

"Quite all right thank you, Aunt Francesca. Apart from this dreadful taste in the back of my throat. I dreamt forest fires and I'm afraid I brought something of them back with me."

"Excellent. Quite excellent," Cecil said, handing Rosie the canteen. "You must take little sips, not gulps. The effects of the ayahuasca have been a shock to your system."

"The effects of the...what?"

"They poisoned you, the savages," Gregory rumbled.

"If we had known—if the professor had seen fit to tell us—" Francesca gave Cecil a look that could wither fresh-cut flowers.

"Let us simply give thanks that you are safe and well."

"What else did you see? You must tell me everything," the professor said, taking Rosie's free hand and clasping it between his.

"Professor. Now is not the time," Francesca said.

"It's quite all right," Rosie said. "I think I might appreciate some understanding about what just happened to me. I knew the boy's name, though he never uttered it to me."

"You see?" Cecil said to Gregory and Francesca. "How could she know the boy's name if the drug had not had some transcendental effect upon her?"

"Mumbo jumbo," Gregory said, "the boy could have spoken his name as she awoke."

"Did he?" Cecil asked.

Rosie faltered, under the disapproving looks from her guardians. "I don't know. You must understand, it was as though I was awake but dreaming at the same time."

The professor nodded. He, at least, seemed to understand.

"But perhaps there is something you can tell me," Rosie continued. "What was he chattering about with such excitement outside?"

"Why, just that very same thing," Cecil said. "The boy said you had returned to us and that you spoke his name. Word is spreading around the village that you are a spirit walker."

"Spirit walker?" Rosie rather liked that. But her uncle clearly did not.

"Enough of this heathen nonsense, Professor. May I remind you that young Rosie here was administered a powerful drug without so much as a by your leave? It could have killed her…"

"Oh, I seriously doubt that," Cecil said. "It has been known to exacerbate mental problems, but our Rosie here is as tough as a shire horse, quite, quite…"

"Don't 'quite, quite' me, Professor. Francesca, make sure Rosie is decent and bring her outside."

The professor stiffened. "I do understand your concern, however none of us could have imagined the ceremony would involve the administration of such a substance. If I have caused you any offense…"

Gregory rounded on the professor, towering over him and speaking low and clear just a breath away from his face. "You have caused every possible offense, Professor Cecil. Our association is hereby at an end. You may collect your equipment from the mission house. It will perhaps be put to better use among the savages with whom you are so enthralled."

Cecil looked crestfallen at Rosie, who felt responsible, somehow, for this falling out.

"Uncle, please, the professor wasn't to know—"

"That is my final word on the matter, Rosie. I have seen and heard enough to begin ministry in earnest on the morrow. This is a Godless place and I know now, more than ever, that my calling is a just one—to imbue every man, woman and child with His Divine Word."

The professor nodded at Rosie, a look that she took to convey his thanks for her support. He bowed his head to Francesca and Gregory in turn and walked to the doorway. Rosie watched him go, wishing she could do something to improve relations between those around her. She felt like a pawn in someone else's game, sat up in bed like a child watching the grownups, just as she had after the attack aboard the paddle steamer. She caught a look of triumph in her uncle's eyes and wondered if the grownups were behaving as anything but.

"Hellfire."

The professor had stopped in his tracks at the doorway.

"I beg your pardon?" Gregory asked.

"Hellfire. Quite literally," Cecil said as he rushed outside.

Francesca and Gregory followed him, looking as confused as Rosie now felt.

Then, hearing the frantic cries of villagers outside the long house, Rosie hurried out of bed and bolted for the door. The same acrid smell from her nightmare visions greeted her as she emerged into the daylight. She joined her guardians, the professor and row upon row of villagers, all of whom stood staring at the trees outlining the village. Above their green canopies, Rosie saw a plume of thick, dark smoke. Pushing her way forward through the press of bodies to get a better view, she then saw the source of the smoke.

A forest fire.

CHAPTER TWENTY-TWO

The entire village was in a state of flux. All around her, villagers dashed, gathering up huge armfuls of thick green leaves from the outskirts of their settlement. The professor took up the natives' rallying cry and urged Gregory to join him in helping them. Uncle Gregory instructed Rosie and Francesca to remain in the relative safety of the village, then took off with Cecil into the forest.

Out of the corner of her eye, Rosie saw Nimbo. He, too, uprooted some large leaves and ran with the adults into the smoke. She called after him not to go in, but either he did not understand her words or did not care for them. Rosie felt a hand on her shoulder. Her aunt must have known what Rosie was about to do. Before Francesca could utter a word, Rosie hitched up her skirts and ran after Nimbo.

Her aunt was shouting now, pleading with her not to follow, but her pleas only made Rosie more resolute. She could not stand idly by while others risked their lives to save the village from the threat of the fire. Breaking into a sprint, Rosie soon joined the ranks of Myahueneca and, to her delight, found that several of their numbers were female. She made eye contact with one of them, who was Amazonian in all senses of the word, a formidable, broad-shouldered and beautiful woman who looked capable of quashing the flames with her bare fists. There was a flash of recognition in the woman's eyes and a grin that made dimples form in her round cheeks as she noticed Rosie.

On they ran, following the raised voices of their fellows. The deeper they penetrated the forest, the thicker the smoke that billowed from between the tree trunks. The dense smoke made it difficult to see, but Rosie knew they had reached the extremity of the blaze because of the heat that lapped at her face and arms. The Amazonian woman put her arm out to prevent Rosie from running any closer to the fire, then called to her sisters in urgent, sing-song tones. They formed a line with such speed and ease that Rosie could only imagine they had performed the routine hundreds of times before. They each set about delving into the undergrowth and uprooting the largest ferns they could find. Rosie discovered the purpose of the plants as the women began rhythmic beating and sweeping movements in unison, each drawing closer to the flames. To Rosie's eyes, the act seemed futile at first, but she could see that the women in their numbers were having a stultifying effect on the flames. The moist leaves were choking the fire of oxygen, and the brush-like sweeping of others was kicking up enough damp earth to smother yet more of the flames. Rosie bent down and uprooted her own fern, gripping its gnarled root like one might grip the hilt of a sword. Finding her place in amongst the ranks of Myahueneca women, Rosie did her best to mimic their method, beating out flames and sweeping earth over them in order to prevent the blaze's progress.

Sweat trickled down her face, making her red patches sting a little, but Rosie did not mind. Instead of her usual glower of embarrassment, Rosie felt a glow of pride, of belonging. Back in the city, it would be absurd to see a female firefighter, let alone one of her tender age. But here, in the rainforest, the women were just as able as the men. Women and children were equals, each contributing something of value to the greater whole. As the line of beating bodies advanced, Rosie felt at one with it. She wondered if this was how her uncle had felt when he had plucked her from the fire that killed her parents, like a savior, a vessel for God's purpose.

Rosie savored the feeling for as long as her body would permit but soon enough the effects of the heat and smoke grew too much for her. Coughing, she withdrew along with several others and retreated to a clearing where she sat, drew breath and rested a while. The struggle to contain the fire went on, and Rosie watched a team of men from the village digging a trench, presumably to halt the progress of the blaze. She saw her uncle, helping the men to dig while the professor sweated and flapped about, supervising them. Gregory had been harsh back at the long house, that was undeniable, but Rosie admired him for taking his place among the Myahueneca. Rosie saw that his beliefs were backed up by his actions and, although he would no doubt castigate her for it later, she felt proud to be helping out alongside him.

A faint cry stirred her from her thoughts. She peered into the smoke from where she thought she had heard the eerie sound. It came again, muffled beneath the noise of the fire and its attendants, but unmistakably the voice of a child. She dashed to the edge of the clearing and was enveloped by thick smoke as she followed the sound of the cries. The smoke was as thick as autumn fog and she realized her mistake when, hearing the voice again, she could not retrace her footsteps. The only way was on then, to locate the child in the forest and give whatever aid she was able. It did not take long to find the child, for his cries became screams that were so loud she felt sure everyone in the forest would be able to hear them. She ran, bracken breaking beneath her feet, and almost fell into a deep pit that was partially hidden by the smoke. Teetering at the edge of the pit, she peered down and saw Nimbo. The boy must have fallen inside and become trapped. He clung desperately to exposed tree roots in the soil wall of the pit, using them to clamber up. Below him, cut tree branches and foliage littered the pit's base, indicating that the trap had been camouflaged deliberately. She called Nimbo's name and he looked up at her, his eyes filled with terror. He glanced behind him and Rosie saw the source of the boy's fear.

A dark figure, the same man from her visions, stood at the lip of the pit on the opposite side of her. He regarded her casually, his look conveying no discernable emotion. The dark man's stoicism only added to the heady atmosphere of dread that cloaked him like a shroud. Rosie's compulsion was to run from this ominous giant, but her compassion would not allow her to do so. Instead, she dropped to her knees, then lay on her stomach, reaching down to help the boy climb the final few feet to freedom. A cry of panic escaped from her throat as she saw the huge man move toward them, his steps slow and measured like those of a predatory animal. Nimbo's terror intensified as he glanced around and saw, too, that the man was approaching.

"Don't look at him, look at me!" Rosie stretched her arm until it was almost out of its socket. Nimbo's fingers found hers and when he clasped her hand, she pulled with all her might.

"Don't worry, I've done this before," she said, encouraging herself as much as the boy.

The boy was light as a feather compared to the professor, who had nearly pulled her down with him when she had saved him from the ravine. Nimbo scrambled over the side of the pit and together they backed away in fright from the towering figure bearing down upon them. Rosie screamed. Their assailant was so close she could almost feel his hot breath. She felt something whistle past her ear and saw the huge man take a spear to the shoulder. He wavered, pulling the sharp end from his flesh and throwing it to the ground in anger. More spears flew, forcing him to retreat. Rosie willed him to fall into his own pit, but he circled the edge without even looking at it. Despite his size, the huge man had a grace to him that made each movement fluid. As more spears ripped through the smoke, Rosie watched, amazed, as he dodged each and every one.

By the time the Myahueneca men had caught up to her and Nimbo, the dark man had disappeared behind the thick curtain of smoke like a specter. With them Rosie saw her uncle and the professor, who was out of breath and lagging far behind.

"Are you all right, lassie? The man who was here, did he hurt you?"

"No," Rosie said, taking some solace from the realization that the hulking figure was, in fact, just a man. Flesh and blood. Why else would he fear the villagers' spears?

Her uncle embraced her, then pushed away.

"I told you to stay put!"

It was as though he was remembering that he was supposed to be angry.

"I'm fine, Uncle. I'm sorry but I just had to help. Then I heard Nimbo's cries and had to help again."

"Nimbo? Ah, the boy."

Gregory frowned down at Nimbo, who beat a hasty retreat to rejoin the tribe.

"I'm sure he can look after himself."

"He was trapped in the pit," Rosie said.

Gregory crossed to the edge and looked inside.

"In that case, it was very Christian of you," Gregory admitted. "But do not on any account tell your aunt about this little adventure, you hear?"

"Loud and clear," Rosie said, relieved that her ticking off appeared to be at an end.

Professor Cecil caught up to them, still looking a little wary of Gregory but glad to see Rosie safe and well.

"Did you get a look at him? The man who was here but moments ago?"

"No...the smoke was too thick."

"A tribal fellow was he, like these Myahueneca chaps?"

Rosie hesitated. She couldn't be sure where the man was from. And he had disappeared so quickly she was beginning to doubt if she'd seen him at all—if it wasn't for the fact that Nimbo had been so afraid of him, and that her uncle, Cecil, and the villagers had seen him, too.

Cecil looked into the smoke.

Rosie looked, too, but there was nothing to see, save for the vague flicker of flames beyond the gray.

Cecil crossed to the edge of the pit, scanning it with his sharp eyes.

"The Myahueneca were anxious to catch him. He must be one of the blighters who set the fire. Blaze farmers they call them, arsonists by any other name. Quite. It's a travesty against nature what these madmen do, burning tracts of rainforest to the ground, farming the land dry then moving on to repeat the process elsewhere. A travesty, I tell you. They leave acres of destruction in their wake. Nothing lives; nothing grows, in the shadows of their footsteps. Ah!"

The professor was clutching the leaf of a large fern that he had plucked from the mouth of the pit. Its serrated green surface was slicked with dark blood.

"One of their spears must have wounded him. If he's bleeding then he can be tracked."

Rosie looked on as the blood trickled across the surface of the leaf, staining its green veins red. So, the man she had encountered was real, and human, after all. The thought somehow made his imposition more threatening, and Rosie suspected she might feel more at ease if he had turned out to be a figment or a phantom.

Cecil turned to one of the tribal men, who corroborated his story by displaying the bloodied end of his retrieved spear. The professor chatted with the man in excited, broken dialect before marching off into the smoke with him and his tribal contingent.

"Where are you going, Professor?" Rosie asked, concerned.

"Not to worry, my dear." Cecil paused and turned to face them, the earnestness of his expression disarming even Rosie's uncle. "You two get back to the mission house where it's safe. I'll be along later to collect my things, just as soon as we've caught this damnable fire starter."

Before Rosie could try to dissuade him, Cecil was off, accompanied by the tribal men. She hoped their spears would protect him. As she and Gregory walked away from the pit, she saw a solitary figure waiting for them. It was Nimbo, pleading with them to hurry up.

"What's got the laddie so spooked?" Gregory said.

Nimbo rushed over to Rosie's side and grabbed her by the wrist, urging her along.

"What's wrong?" Rosie asked.

The boy pointed into the smoke, where the professor had gone.

"*Skintaker,*" he said, in English.

After that, they fled the forest together in silence.

CHAPTER TWENTY-THREE

Richter crouched in the bushes, silent and still, his hand raised in signal to his fellows to remain quiet. He listened intently to the footfalls of the Myahueneca men as they stalked their way through the forest, and was surprised he could hear them at all; the professor was breathing so loudly. As the group moved down a slope to lower ground, Richter rolled over onto his back then righted himself and began to crawl to another vantage point. At his signal, his men followed. One of them snapped a twig and Richter and his men halted. Expecting to be discovered, Richter prepared to give the order to attack Cecil and his new-found allies. But the snap of the twig had gone unnoticed perhaps due to the noises from the blaze nearby.

Richter looked over his shoulder to find out who had snapped the twig; Keyser, of course. He was the only man Richter had ever seen who did not look dwarfed by the trees in the rainforest. Richter sneered as he watched Errol jab Keyser in the arm, warning him to be quiet. Returning his watchful gaze to Cecil and the natives he found that they had broken up into smaller groups, fanning out to track their prey.

But their prey was already watching them it seemed, as Richter noticed a figure so still and so solid that he had mistaken it for a high tree stump at first. Clamping his hand over his mouth to quell a gasp of surprise, Richter turned his attention to this new player in the game of cat and mouse that was unfolding before him. From the man's posture, Richter ascertained he was watching the professor, too. In fact, he looked to be following him, and when the fat man wandered off into the wisps of smoke clouding the forest, Richter was proven right. The dark figure followed after taking soft, steady strides that seemed impossible for a man of such impressive build. His interest piqued, Richter decided he had better witness how this most silent of pursuits panned out. He could not risk Keyser's clumsiness and so, with the time-honored hand gestures, instructed his men to follow the men from the village while he peeled off to observe the professor's dark pursuer.

Keeping to higher ground posed no problem at all as this part of the rainforest was formed of a ridge lined with thick tree trunks. The professor had taken a low, narrow path through the younger trees lining the forest floor below. Suspicion brewed in his gut as to why the mysterious tracker had opted to follow upon lower ground. His fears were allayed when he saw that the trees up ahead were so densely packed together that he would struggle to pass between them. He had no choice now but to shimmy down a sheer slope carpeted with leaf litter and branches and hope, or rather pray, that his descent would go unheard.

It did. Save for a slight rustle of leaves as he slowed his descent at the foot of the slope, Richter's movements would have made an assassin green with envy. He took steady, even breaths, slowing his heart rate before stealing along the faint track that his predecessors had trodden but moments ago. Up ahead, the dense fog of smoke from the forest fire had thinned out, replaced by the ever-present vapor that drifted up from wet leaves. He saw a sharp movement, and for a moment it was like a shadow had passed over his vision. Then it was gone. He slowed his progress, casting his gaze about him and looking up into the treetops for good measure. Many a hunter had fallen because he had forgotten to look up. His nerves leveled and as he picked up his pace a little, he heard a cry.

The cry was shrill, and its source could have been animal, but then it came again, and Richter could just make out the words "Jesus God." Richter broke into a run, sprinting after the sound. A garbled cry of anguish echoed around the forest. Richter's keen hearing enabled him to discern it had emanated from a break in the trees some thirty feet away. As he neared the breach in the tree cover, he slowed down again to a careful walking pace then sidled up to the thickest tree trunk he could find. Peering out from behind the tree he found he had arrived on the edge of the clearing.

"Oh Jesus!"

The voice was Professor Cecil's, loud and clear, except now his dulcet empirical tones were drowned in blood. He heard Cecil gargle and spit like a patient in the surgery room of a particularly sadistic dentist.

"Oh Jesus God!"

It seemed the man of science had turned to religion after all now that he'd met his maker—or rather, the engineer of his undoing. As Richter watched, wide-eyed, he saw the dark man towering over the pudgy frame of the professor who was pressed up against the trunk of a large tree. He had a hold of Cecil's head and appeared to be crushing the life from his skull. Richter was astonished to then see the professor's attacker lift him from the ground by his head. The strength of the man was awe-inspiring—the professor had to weigh as much as a bear. Then, without warning, the hulking figure smashed Cecil's head against the tree. The sound was sickeningly final, and an atmosphere of dread seemed to fall with the professor's body as he was dropped to the ground. The big man looked down upon his victim and Richter could see, for the first time, that he wore some kind of apparatus over his eyes. Glassy and black, they had the aspect of a raven's eyes, especially now that they were regarding the professor with their cool, unforgiving gaze.

Then the man seemed to come to his senses. He glanced around before he lifted the professor by one arm and slung his bloated corpse over his shoulders. As he watched the huge man thunder away through the forest, Richter knew he had found his prize. And thanks to the events of the day, he also knew how to obtain that prize.

Richter made sure the huge man had gone, then headed back through the forest to find his men. He had work for them to do.

Approaching them from higher ground, he heard Erroll's familiar whine before he even saw his men. His trajectory had taken him on a rough semi-circular route through dense vegetation, and then onto a mud track forged by decades of rainwater snaking down to the lower slopes. He moved off the pathway and found Erroll, Keyser, and the others beyond a thicket of gigantic ferns. Keyser stood, watchful, over a small group of native men. Each had his hands bound behind his back, and each was kneeling before Erroll.

Seamus was making himself useful by keeping watch, though not entirely effectively Richter noted—after all, he had been able to approach without detection. Erroll, meanwhile, had dropped into his natural role of inquisitor, relishing the opportunity to hand out some punishments, no doubt. Richter's lips curled into a wry smile as he watched Erroll kick one of the men in the belly. The man bent double and coughed blood onto the soil. He had already suffered quite a beating by the looks of things.

Good.

"Ask him again," Erroll said casually, his intonation so heavy and deliberate that he might have been at a board meeting.

Richter listened to his hired hands gabbling among themselves in the local lingo before one, their interpreter-elect, stepped forward and crouched next to the bleeding man. He spoke a few words and the man listened, though he looked likely to lose consciousness from the way his upper body swayed side to side. He appeared to mull over the interpreter's words for a few moments, before spitting blood into the man's face.

"Kill him," Erroll said.

Keyser reached for his gun. Richter stepped in and held up a warning hand.

"No guns," he said.

Erroll and the others looked dumbstruck. They had evidently misinterpreted his reticence for mercy.

"How would a blaze farmer do it?" Richter asked. Seeing the blank looks around him, he elaborated. "We are on a hunt, gentlemen, and our quarry is as tricksy as they come. What serves our cause better than the spark of a flame, the ignition of conflict? A jungle at war with itself enables the stealthy to carry out his mission undetected. We will become silent weapons in a quiet war amidst the white noise of conflict. If the Myahueneca here were to be murdered by the blaze farmers who also destroy their lands— well, think about it."

Realization dawned in the eyes of his men save for Keyser, who stood examining his empty hands for clues to God only knew what was going on inside that thickened skull of his.

"Divide and rule," Erroll said.

"Divide and rule," Richter echoed. "Let them tear each other apart while we, unnoticed, make a happy hunting ground of their land."

Richter pulled his tinderbox from within his breast pocket and handed it over to Erroll. Erroll's eyes burned with imagined fires, then he rushed over to their supplies and rooted around until he found what he needed to make them a reality.

The cork made a deafening sound as he twisted it from the

bottle. The kneeling men coughed and spat as Erroll sloshed raw liquor over their heads. The act looked like a profane kind of anti-baptism to Richter, who stood quietly by, enjoying it.

"A baptism of fire, then," Richter said to Erroll who set about striking the stones next to some kindling.

Chik, chik, chik.

Richter's thoughts turned to the insufferable pastor that he had dined with aboard the steamer. He had spoken of his intention to Christianize the selfsame savages that knelt before him now. Such wild things could not be tamed, Richter felt sure of that. He had seen villages burned to the ground, women raped, and children butchered while their patriarchs looked on in silent stubbornness.

Chik, chik, chik.

Sparks became flames.

Men held to what they believed, it was a truism undeniable. And the Myahueneca, when they found the torched remains of their fellows, would hold to the belief that the blaze farmers had committed the heinous act. And they would respond accordingly, helping Richter's cause. It was part of the natural order of things, part of the sacred hunt, and of the life cycle that made men like him the top of the food chain.

The screams of the men stirred him from his thoughts. He watched their faces burn, their lithe bodies writhing in agony against their bonds as their flesh began to sear. Their eyes pooled in their sockets and their scalps, until moments ago dark and lustrous, became crowns of burning flame. Some tried to run, making good sport for Keyser who uprooted them from the ground like saplings and tossed them to the forest floor where the flames took hold. The screams diminished and the air filled with the pungent aroma of burning flesh. Richter inhaled the scent as if it were a balm, then instructed his men to pack up and move out. They would travel north in the direction his tracker's instinct told him the blaze farmers had gone. Behind them, they would leave a bonfire of bodies. The Myahueneca would smell it and come seeking their fellows. It would hurt them, gouge them deep inside collectively to find so many of their kin defiled in this way. The blaze farmers would smell it, too, and know that Richter and his number were like-minded fellows—the type perhaps to do business with. And the huge killer who had slain the professor in the forest, then carried him away as if he were but a young deer, he would smell the bonfire from wherever he was hiding. And he would recognize the same primal instinct within Richter that dwelled inside of him. He would know Richter meant business, but what business—he doubted the dark hunter could ever fathom such an undertaking. At least, that was what Richter hoped.

Leaving the smoking circle of bodies behind he said a silent prayer.

Before the devil damns me all to Hell, he prayed, *let the best man win.*

Just let the best man win.

STRATUM GERMINATIVUM

The long walk carrying the body of the fat man had fatigued him. He required sustenance, but first he must attend to his workings. The body still lived, and the mind within must be tapped. He would know its thoughts, its wisdom, and all its failings.

Looking at the carcass, he saw the stark evidence of those failings. The skin was stretched to the breaking point. As he undressed it, he felt utter dismay at the damage that had been done. The stretch marks and patches of psoriasis were testament to the decadence of the West World.

Such willful waste in a land of plenty.

He felt revulsion, and not a little pity, when he sliced the stomach open to reveal thick layers of livid yellow fat. He sliced it away, barely able to control his anger, freeing the organs from their fleshy prison.

There, now it could breathe.

He slapped the face, chubby cheeks making sounds like peals of thunder in his cave.

The fat man's eyes flickered open and began to register the reality of his situation.

Now he was with him, the real work could begin.

He took the longest of his probes, so sharp and so precise, and located the entry point into the man's skull. He paused for a moment before sliding it in. Here he stood at the threshold to conscious thought, about to open the gateway to the stuff of dreams and hopes.

And nightmares.

CHAPTER TWENTY-FOUR

It took three days for the fire to die out. The glow and the smoke not only provided a constant reminder of her adventures in the forest, both real and visionary, but of the professor's absence. Since her uncle's disagreement with him, Cecil had not returned to collect his belongings. Her aunt instructed her not to worry about the professor, reminding Rosie how impulsive he was, and positing the theory that he had gone native. She went to some lengths to reiterate her disgust at his behavior at the Myahueneca village. Her nose wrinkled as she outlined the casual way in which he had put Rosie in such danger—by subjecting her to what Francesca described as "potions of witchcraft most foul."

Rosie protested, insisting that Cecil would never knowingly do her harm. She knew that he was a scientific man to his core and, as such, would never leave his precious equipment behind for too long. Her attempts to convince Francesca to allow her to visit the Myahueneca again fell at the first hurdle. She pleaded with her aunt but she was resolute on the matter and so Rosie had no choice but to worry about the professor on her own.

Rosie had watched the eerie orange glow from the mission house balcony before bedtime each night, wondering where the professor had gone to and now, finally, it was gone. The blackness of night had finality to it, and Rosie's heart wrenched with the knowledge that something bad might have happened to the professor. She tried to cheer herself with flights of fancy that he may have gone on a vision quest of his own. Perhaps he was, even now, lying in one of the tribe's comfy hammocks surrounded by his new friends and the watchful spirits of their forebears. But then her thoughts wandered to a memory of those gleaming, obsidian eyes—their omniscient gaze sweeping the forest like a dark thunderstorm.

Next morning, Rosie roused herself from the chill that had washed over her and decided to rise early and walk the grounds of the mission house in an attempt to coax some warmth into her bones.

Trotting downstairs, she found the house staff in a state of industry. They were each carrying huge bundles of cut flowers outside. She tried to ask them what they were doing but they hurried on with their tasks so single-mindedly that she could only imagine her uncle to be the cause. Taking a bouquet of flowers from the many that were stacked up in the foyer, Rosie could not help but notice that the last of the professor's luggage and equipment had been removed. Had he returned to claim them after all? If that was the case, Rosie already felt dismayed and more than a little annoyed that he had not thought to say goodbye to her. The last time she had seen him, in the forest amidst the chaos of the fire, had been far from closure for the kinship that had been cut short too soon.

Carrying the bouquet outside, Rosie followed the staff to the chapel door and heard her uncle's booming voice echoing within. She found the chapel to be transformed when she stepped inside. The musty smell had gone, replaced by the succulent sweetness of the cut flowers, which stood in vases and large earthenware pots. A rapture of color and scent had been created either side of the aisle, and Rosie felt lifted as she moved between the bouquets. She found Uncle Gregory next to the altar, instructing Pedro on the placing of the flowers. Pedro teetered atop a chair that looked too old and infirm for such a task, filling hanging baskets with fistfuls of blooms—the beginnings of an impressive altarpiece.

"Ah, Rosie," Gregory said. "You are most welcome here. I need a woman's eye on all this. How does our décor strike you?"

"It is very pleasing to the eye," Rosie said, "like all the color of the rainforest has assembled here in praise of nature."

Her uncle smiled. "In praise of the Lord most high, as we welcome our first congregation."

"So, the villagers are coming?"

"On the morrow. Pedro tells me a considerable number of the villagers are interested in learning the Word of God."

Rosie figured they might be more interested in learning English, but she let the thought pass. "Well, they will certainly feel at home here. The blooms are as vivid as their dress and make-up."

"That is the intention, of course," her uncle replied. "I am heartened that you think it so beautiful. I had hoped to glean your aunt's opinion on it, hers being of the botanical bent..."

"Where is Aunt Francesca? I did not see her on my way down."

"Alas, you would not have done, child. Your aunt has complained of a sore throat since we visited the tribal village. She took to her bed this morning."

"Strange, she did not tell me she was feeling ill."

"You know how your aunt is. Perhaps you might look in on her? She must take a luncheon of hot broth. Cook is preparing some, it really is the only thing. Make sure she does so, yes?"

Rosie nodded. Her uncle returned to his instruction, but turned back to her when he realized she had not yet moved from the spot.

"What is it, Rosie?"

"Did you hear from the professor? His equipment was gone from the hallway when I..."

"Ah, I had the staff move Professor Cecil's things. They were rather cluttering up the place. Everything is safely stowed away in the stores."

"But it has been three days since we heard anything."

"Your aunt told me of your concern. Don't fret, child, the professor is safe in the eyes of the Lord—even when he goes out of his way to denounce Him."

"But—"

"The professor is a grown man, Rosie. Big enough to look after himself. Now, you can see that I'm busy so I'll say no more on the matter."

Rosie backed away. She wondered if even the eyes of the Lord could penetrate the depths of the rainforest but did not have the courage to voice her concerns any further. And what point would there be in doing so anyway? Her worries would fall on deaf ears.

"Don't forget your aunt," Gregory called after her.

"Hot broth, I know," Rosie sighed.

"The only way," he said.

His way was the only way, and how Rosie knew this. But as much as she loved the man, she could not escape the confine of the flower-filled chapel a moment too soon; its scent, so soothing just moments before, was now clogging her throat.

CHAPTER TWENTY-FIVE

The fires were nothing but smoke by the time Richter and his men caught up to their creators. Tracking the blaze farmers had not been hard—they made little effort to conceal themselves so far from the Myahueneca's village—but they moved fast. Twice Richter had come upon the remnants of their camp, the ashes of their campfire still warm, their leavings still fragrant, and twice he had missed them. This time, he was lucky. The blaze farmers had gone fishing.

A tributary of the main river snaked its way through the forest here at the northern reaches of Myahueneca territory. Chopped tree trunks gave evidence of boat building activities on its shores, which lapped against the tall grasses on the forest's edge. Sunlight gleamed on the water, making silhouettes of the men who stood in its flow, spears held at the ready to catch any passing fish. Victorious cries rang out as one of the blaze farmers speared his prey, holding it aloft. The sunlight twinkled on its scales, which glimmered in bright rainbow colors.

They did not see Richter's men coming.

He had them surrounded before they could react. Seeing the hunters' guns, they lowered their spears, knowing in an instant that they were no match. Richter nodded to them to drop their weapons. The spears floated away like driftwood atop the fast-flowing river.

"What's the word for parlay in your twisted tongue?" Richter asked.

His interpreter shouted at the blaze farmers and their leader stepped forward. He was the eldest and looked to be in his fifties, though Richter could not be certain—the natives of these parts kept themselves tight well into their old age. One thing he did know was that this guy was also the shortest of the group, a real

Napoleon Bonaparte. Now he knew exactly how to work with him. They parlayed.

The equation was simple, or at least as simple as Richter made it out to be. The blaze farmers were nomadic, snatching land here and there wherever they could along with the spoils—the occasional rape of a rival tribe's womenfolk, the abduction of their strongest children who would work like oxen in their newly-razed fields. What they wanted were the riches of those that had settled here. The Myahueneca were the greedy landlords, and the blaze farmers the revolutionaries poised to take what was, perhaps not so rightfully, theirs. But theirs all the same. What they lacked was a strategy. Their methods were opportunistic and entirely reactionary. Richter and his men could give shape and purpose to the chaos of their fires. If they worked together, they could overthrow the Myahueneca and enslave their land, their women, and their children. Richter would help them achieve this because he was on the side of the underdog. All he wanted in return was a little help with his hunt. A hunt for big game. The blaze farmers' skills would come in handy. And with allies such as them in control of the region, Richter's paymasters might establish a strong foothold there. Trade routes would open, and they could plunder the other rich resources the Amazon basin had to offer. The blaze farmers were forward-thinkers, businessmen like Richter and those whom employed him. Not like the Myahueneca. They were blinkered, backward—archaic traditionalists.

Richter and the blaze farmers parlayed some more. Then they cooked and shared the fish that had been plundered from the river. They handed around hipflasks of the white men's *fire water* and laughed as they drank toasts to one another in the shade of the ancient trees. Trees they would gladly hack and burn in the name of progress. In pursuit of the riches. By the time their meal was over, they had reached an agreement.

Together, the men gathered up their things and began the steady march south. Thanks to Erroll's interrogation of the Myahueneca men they had slaughtered, Richter knew exactly where and when to find a congregation of the villagers. They would be away from their village's defenses and he would have the element of surprise.

If he kept the pace up, they would reach the mission house in time.

CHAPTER TWENTY-SIX

The housemaid was adamant that Francesca was not to be disturbed, and Rosie's attempts to the contrary were exacerbated by the language barrier between them. After several minutes of attempting to make herself understood, Rosie shrugged and feigned compliance then marched off to the kitchen.

She found the cook mixing a large pot of warming broth in the hearth. It smelled delicious, and Rosie's stomach did cartwheels as the cook filled a bowl for her and another for her aunt, which she set aside to cool a little. Rosie sipped the broth from a wooden spoon and let its warmth fill her extremities with renewed vigor. The cook slid some freshly baked flatbread from an alcove above the fire and placed it before Rosie. It, too, was delicious, and Rosie savored each strip as she tore it off, using the last piece to mop up the broth from her bowl. The cook cut some more bread with her knife and placed it beside the bowl of broth on a silver tray. Full, Rosie stood up and was about to pick up the tray when the cook stepped in, protesting and shaking her head.

The woman uttered Jorge's name and Rosie understood her outrage to be borne of the fact that the work was beneath her. "It's quite all right," Rosie said, "I must visit my aunt to make sure she is well, my uncle expects it of me. Please, you understand, Father Gregory insists."

At mention of Gregory's title, something seemed to register in the cook's eyes and she let go of the tray. Rosie took a napkin from the basket by the fire and quickly folded it into a shape befitting of her fussy aunt, then set about her ascent of the stairwell. The climb was slow and deliberate as necessitated by the broth, which kept threatening to spill over the sides of the bowl. A couple of steps from the summit, and Rosie almost lost her footing. She was so intent on not spilling any of her aunt's lunch that she had misjudged her step. Propping herself up against the wooden banister, she just managed to right herself without spilling the broth. Rosie hoped Francesca was awake and hungry after all the trouble she had gone to in order to deliver room service. When she neared her aunt's room, she heard coughing.

Rosie felt impolite even thinking such a thing, but her aunt looked dreadful. The moment Rosie entered carrying the tray, Francesca sat bolt upright in bed, struggling to compose herself. But the act was far from convincing; her eyes were ringed by dark circles and her hair, which was normally a testament to precision grooming, had come undone and spilled over her shoulders. Francesca's breathing was labored, and she pulled her bed sheet close to her like a shawl, which only added to her frail appearance. Rosie could not recall a time when she had seen her aunt in a state such as this. The woman always prided herself on her iron constitution, and Rosie had often heard her making disparaging comments about the sick, preferring to support the belief that common ailments were "all in the mind." Seeing her aunt now, it appeared she was having great difficulty maintaining an attitude of mind over matter.

Francesca was about to speak, but before she could utter a coherent word she had a coughing fit. The dry rattle coming from her throat made Rosie concerned for her aunt and she set the tray down on the nightstand before helping Francesca to sit up straight. She plumped a pillow and set it higher behind her aunt's shoulder blades so she might better draw breath. The maneuver worked, and Rosie waited patiently while the coughing subsided and her aunt got her breath back.

"Your uncle put you up to this, did he?"

"He was quite clear on the matter, Aunt Francesca. He said you were to take a lunch of warming broth. Cook gave me some flatbread, too, though it might catch in your throat. It is delicious, though, I tried some."

"Room service and chief taster, I feel like I'm in the Savoy," Francesca said. Her quip fell flat through the strain of her raspy, constricted chest.

"I'm sorry, Aunt," Rosie said.

"No need to be sorry, dear, can't be helped, it's this damnable climate."

"I mean to say, well, I'm sorry I didn't notice you were taken ill.

I've been so worried about the professor and that was all I could focus on. You must think me very selfish in the light of things."

Francesca propped herself up on one elbow, perusing the contents of the tray. "Nonsense, child. Firstly, I have not 'taken ill.' I merely have a head cold brought on by the process of relocation to a part of the world that evidences new and unparalleled quantities of damp. A head cold that will pass in a day or two, I hasten to add. Secondly, you are a dear sweet girl but you do worry too much. An over-emotional trait inherited from your late mother, God rest her soul."

Rosie was quite taken aback. She had not heard her aunt make mention of her sister in such a long time that she thought she may have misheard.

"Don't look at me like that, child," Francesca continued. "Like a startled rabbit. You are becoming a woman, are you not?"

Rosie nodded, feeling her skin burn.

"Then we must have womanly conversations from now on. Pass me the soup, my dear, I will partake of some sustenance, it may indeed help to rid me of this inconvenient malaise."

After passing the soup to her aunt, Rosie then unfolded a cloth napkin and placed it over her aunt's lap. She watched as Francesca lifted the spoon to her lips and tasted the broth.

"It's rather bitter from the greens, which I am not convinced are entirely edible." She grimaced. "If this is the quality of the hospital food then I will be motivated to feel as right as rain in no time."

"Uncle Gregory will be pleased to hear that."

"You will tell him nothing of the sort," Francesca said through another mouthful of soup.

"But if you're feeling better…"

"You misunderstand me, Rosie. If I were to be feeling restored, then I might be looking at another few years in this hellish place. Living in the woods, surrounded by savages, is that any way for a lady to pass the years when she is in her prime? Well, is it?"

Rosie remained silent.

"You might enjoy going native with our friend the professor, scrambling around in the dirt making those infernal film recordings, but I—I am simply not designed for this way of life, my dear. It is beyond me why anybody, even those in the service of the Lord such as we, would ever wish to establish roots in a cesspit such as this."

She watched as her aunt slowly, and deliberately, placed the spoon back inside the bowl of broth and left it there.

"Tell your uncle I was too weak to take much of the broth when you came to me. Tell him this interminable climate is the root cause of my ailment. Remind him my health would be much renewed by my—by our—swift return to the temperance of the city."

She fixed Rosie with those sharp little eyes of hers. It was as though their gaze could cut through stone, such was the power of her aunt's single-mindedness.

"I will try."

"Take the tray with you, there's a dear." Francesca handed the bowl back to her then lay down again in bed, gathering her bedding around her. She looked to Rosie like a spider in its web, waiting.

"Close the door behind you, child. I am not to be disturbed."

Rosie did as her aunt requested, balancing the tray on one hand, while pulling at the handle with the other to make sure her aunt was properly contained.

CHAPTER TWENTY-SEVEN

Avoiding Uncle Gregory was not difficult due to him being so busy with preparations at the chapel, and for that Rosie was thankful. She knew he would be disappointed to learn that Francesca might be too "ill" to attend the inaugural service and so decided to avoid him for as long as she could. That way she could delay having to impart her aunt's words to him, a prospect that filled her with dread.

Rosie retreated to the dining room and watched the comings and goings around the mission house complex. Unseen on the balcony, she peered down at the staff who were busy putting the finishing touches to the chapel. Jorge teetered atop Pedro's shoulders, removing dead leaves and detritus from beneath the chapel eaves. The scene was pastoral to Rosie, and she found that if she narrowed her eyes a little she could almost be watching small-towners back home getting ready for Easter Parade. But Francesca's voice was still ringing in her ears, with all her remonstrations about jungle life hanging heavy in her thoughts.

Opening her eyes wide, she reminded herself that the balcony on which she stood was attached to a house on stilts, built that way because its foundations were mud and leaf litter. The roof above her head was all that separated her from the awesome, fickle elements of nature. And all around her she could still hear the distant cries of birds and other forest creatures, celebrating their dominion. To Rosie, this was still a magical place, a place in which to lose herself for a while. And perhaps it could be a place in which to discover something new about herself, too. She had certainly discovered a hitherto unknown passion for the botanical and anthropological sciences. If only the professor was still around to tutor her further in these disciplines, but alas he was not. Spying her uncle as he emerged from the chapel, Rosie ducked out of view and decided to retire to her room.

Rosie wished her room held more distractions. Her mind was alive with questions following her stressful encounter with her aunt. At least her complexion seemed to have calmed down, despite the stress. She risked exploring the surface of the skin on her cheeks and forehead, finding that it felt softer and smoother than it had in a long time. Perhaps there was something of medicinal value in the white paste the Myahueneca children had applied to her face on the day of her initiation. Again, she wished she could speak with the professor about it. He was, after all, the man who had finally given her a name for her condition—something tangible, along with the hope that it might get better with greater understanding and advancements in medicine.

In lieu of the professor himself, perhaps a peek at his library of textbooks might quiet her restless mind. She was in the kind of dither that could only be assuaged with a good book. Rosie fancied she might steal downstairs and take a look through his remaining luggage in the stores. But only if she was certain her uncle was not abroad to catch her and ask her about her aunt's well-being. The prospect put paid to her flights of fancy. Instead, she picked up Francesca's book of Psalms in desperation but only managed a few lines before her mind began to race again. Leaving the book on her nightstand, she took to pacing the room instead. After a few minutes, she realized there was only one thing that could calm her. She crossed to her bed and knelt down beside it to retrieve her little suitcase.

The newspaper clipping was where she always kept it and she extracted it gently so as not to damage it. The gossamer texture of the paper felt soft as skin beneath her fingertips, and as she stroked its creases and folds, she became calmer already. Unfolding the paper, she read the headline again as she had done a thousand times before. The typeface was so familiar to her she felt certain that if she blinked she could read its afterimage. She knew every word of the reporter's commentary, of course, she could recite it in her sleep, but she read it through again in one sitting, each word resonating within her like a heartbeat. She tried to give form to the ghosts of her mother and father, to somehow make them real inside her head. Their story began to come to life behind her closed eyes. It was given a soundtrack by her memories of how the fire had crackled and roared in the rainforest just days ago. The smell of smoke flooded her senses, dry and dark, and she could not tell if the sensation had stirred from the reality of firefighting alongside the villagers or from the *danse macabre* of her hallucinations. Either way, she felt as though she were losing air, and toppling. The ghosts of her mother and father had eluded her; it was all so long ago.

Rosie felt the familiar sting of tears streaking her face and toppled onto her bed, clutching the paper in her trembling hand. She closed her eyes again and let the tears come. She had learned long ago how to weep quietly, so as not to bother anybody.

Dreaming of fire, and timbers falling all around her, Rosie became aware of urgent hands on her. She felt lifted, just as she had been as a child when Gregory had claimed her from the burning house. But as she came to, Rosie realized the hands belonged to a woman, and they were shaking her awake, not lifting her at all. She opened her eyes and saw the maid, wide-eyed with panic.

"*Signora. Signora,*" she said.

"My aunt?"

"Yes. Come," was all the woman could say before crossing again to the door, which was wide open. From the scant light in the hallway beyond, Rosie guessed she had slept through until early evening. Pulling a shawl around her as she climbed up from her bed, Rosie rubbed the sleep from her eyes and followed the maid out of her room.

The sight of her aunt shocked Rosie to her core. The defiant woman she had left in bed just a few hours earlier looked as pale as a ghost now, her tangled hair and pallid skin slicked with perspiration. Her lips appeared yellow and were flecked with the vomit that stained the uppermost corner of her bed sheets. Pedro and the cook were trying their best to clear up the mess that had also spattered onto the floorboards, but Aunt Francesca was making the task nigh on impossible for them to perform. She flailed and writhed beneath her sweat-sodden bedding, scratching the cook's face so severely that she drew blood, and a scream of pain, from the poor woman. Taking the woman's place at Francesca's side, Rosie spoke in a calming voice and asked her aunt to relax. The sound of her voice seemed to chime with her aunt, who stopped thrashing and peered up at Rosie. Her eyes were red, her pupils impossibly large and her breath came in erratic rasps.

Rosie heard footsteps and Jorge appeared at the doorway with Uncle Gregory. Both looked horrified at the sight of Francesca in the throes of fever. Gregory joined Rosie at her aunt's bedside. He placed the palm of his hand on Francesca's brow. Rosie knew from his expression that her aunt was burning up—and she knew he could see the concern in Rosie's eyes, too. He sighed, deep in thought for a few moments, and then appeared to reach a decision. He went back to the boy and, speaking slow and clear, instructed him to travel to the Myahueneca village. Once there, he said, Jorge was to ask the tribe to bring Professor Cecil when they came for the service, along with any medical supplies he carried with him. The boy nodded and ran away down the hallway, his footfalls echoing the pounding that Rosie could feel in her chest.

She told her uncle that she would keep a close eye on her aunt until morning. Gregory placed a hand on Rosie's shoulder and told her that she was a caring soul, that there were places reserved in Heaven for those who exhibited such kindness. He insisted that he would take the first vigil, watching over Francesca in the hope that her fever might break.

CHAPTER TWENTY-EIGHT

Unable to sleep for the commotion coming from her aunt's room, Rosie got out of bed, dressed, and went to do whatever she could to help.

Aunt Francesca's condition had worsened as the night wore on, and she was in turmoil when Rosie arrived. Poor Francesca's face was slicked with sweat and her dry lips spouted fevered gibberish. Gregory did his best to placate her, holding her down with his gloved hands while she writhed, spat, and attempted to tear the garments from her burning body. He remained resolute throughout his wife's unseemly remonstrations, speaking to her softly until finally she lay back and drifted off into an exhausted sleep. He withdrew, looking tired, and the maids stepped in to make Francesca more comfortable. Seeing the fatigue written in Gregory's knotted brow, Rosie insisted he retire to one of the guest rooms to get some rest. He protested, and Rosie admired his dedication to his wife for he clearly did not wish to leave her side. But Rosie reminded him that the service was but a few hours away, and that he needed to take some rest for the sake of his ministry. Reluctantly, he withdrew, thanking Rosie again for her kindness. As he sloped out of the room, she sensed some relief in him. The night had been an ordeal for them all thus far. Now that her aunt was sleeping, Rosie dismissed the house staff, and told them she would watch over Francesca for the remainder of the night. By her reckoning, they each needed some sleep, in order to better help her uncle with his first congregation. The maids closed Aunt Francesca's mosquito net around her and left the room.

Alone in the room with her aunt, Rosie began to feel drowsy. The air in the chamber was hot and still, and Rosie wished she could open one of the shuttered windows. Listening to Francesca's rasping breaths, she wondered if some fresh air might not be so bad after all. But she dared not disturb her aunt for fear she might awaken and be given to the same convulsions that her condition had visited upon Uncle Gregory earlier. Rosie closed one of the shutters over the single lamp that lit the room, subduing its light but not extinguishing it. This way she could keep an eye on her aunt and watch for the coming dawn through the slatted window shutter.

For how long she had dozed off she did not know. When Rosie awoke with a start, she found a long shadow had fallen over her. Aunt Francesca towered over her like a statuesque apparition. A sheet of the mosquito net had traveled with her as she had left her bed and it was draped over her head and left shoulder like a macabre shroud. Francesca's eyes were ablaze with a manic gaze that seemed to pierce the fabric of the net. Her aunt's left hand twitched and tugged at her nightgown beneath the net veil as she stared at Rosie. Her expression made a pit of Rosie's stomach, churning in sudden discomfort—and fear—yet Rosie could not avert her eyes from that terrible gaze. Aunt Francesca's eyes burned with portent and, just as Rosie was about to ask her what was wrong, Francesca began to scream. The sound came as a whining rattle, the sound a coffee pot might make if left on the stove to boil dry, then exploded into a shrill series of anguished shrieks. Rosie flinched, unable to hide her fear of the now unrecognizable woman who now stood before her wearing her aunt's clothes and howling like a banshee. Attempting to flee, Rosie lurched from her chair but that twitching, tugging hand came down on her shoulder forcing her to sit once more. Rosie gasped as her aunt picked up then thrust the lamp into her face. Recoiling from its heat, her hands leapt to her face instinctively and she cried out as the lamp brushed her fingers, burning them.

"That burns! Please!" Rosie said, trying once again to get up out of her seat.

But her aunt was still looming over her like a shadow.

"How are you here? Speak, phantom, speak!"

"I am no such thing, I am your niece, your Rosie."

"Impossible. You burned. Why are you here to torment me so?"

"You are ill, you must take to your bed, I'll get Uncle..."

"Foul spirit. Trickster. You burned," Francesca said, "like your bitch mother and that fool she married."

"What did you say?" All the fight had gone from Rosie. She

just sat there, numb in her chair.

Her aunt looked disoriented for a moment, like she had awoken in a strange room. She looked at her hands, at the lamp.

"Rosie? You're alive?"

"Of course, I am, Aunt Francesca. You're just ill, that's all, a fever..."

Francesca peered into the lamp, entranced by the flickering flame. Then her eyes sharpened and showed her teeth once again.

"You should have died in the fire like them. My life was to change for the better, not for the worse, you hear? You hear me, you selfish, useless girl?"

Rosie screamed as her aunt lunged at her and tore a clump of hair from her head. Pushing Francesca away, Rosie got to her feet and backed away. The door was on the other side of the room, with her aunt standing in the way.

"I set that fire to kill all of you," Francesca muttered, as if recalling a dream. "*All*. Of you. You're a specter, come to torment me. Well it won't work, you hear? It won't wor—"

Rosie's mind reeled. She gripped the arm of the chair, riding a wave of nausea as it passed over her. Then, she saw Francesca urinate on the hardwood floor before collapsing into the fetid pool of her own leavings. Her aunt had fainted and dropped the lamp beside her. Its flame flickered and died.

CHAPTER TWENTY-NINE

Her aunt's fevered ramblings echoed in Rosie's ears as she ran from the room to rouse her uncle. He was not in the guest room and his bed was still made. Calling for aid as she raced downstairs, Rosie found the ground floor deserted of staff. In desperation, she pulled her nightclothes tight around her and headed outside.

The sky above the rainforest wore the faintest glimmer of purple and gold, heralding the impending sunrise. Beneath it, Rosie could see the sharp silhouette of the chapel, and her heart leapt to see lights burning within. She ran across the clearing and up the steps, bursting through the doors. The maids were busy making final preparations for the service, moving to the booming rhythm of Gregory's recitations. Her uncle was in the pulpit, his Bible on the lectern before him, in mid-rehearsal for that morning's sermon. He looked down at Rosie as she skidded to a halt in the aisle.

"Aunt Francesca." Rosie tried to get the words out whilst drawing breath. "Uncle, you must come, she's much, much worse…"

Gregory closed the book with a thud that echoed off the walls of the chapel. Descending the wooden steps of the chapel he almost lost his footing and had to steady himself on the banister before picking up his pace once more and bolting for the door. He was past Rosie before she could say another word, and so she took another breath and dashed out after him.

"She was here but moments ago," Rosie said.

Her uncle glanced at the part of the floorboards that was shiny and wet.

"What happened here?"

"I'm afraid Aunt Francesca had an accident."

Her words sank in and Gregory blanched. "Dear Lord above,"

he muttered. "Well, she can't have gotten far, not in the state you described anyway."

"You'll help me look for her?" Rosie had an encroaching feeling of guilt, though she was uncertain why she felt that way.

"No," her uncle replied. "We'll have the staff search the house and grounds until they find her, safe and well."

"But what if she has taken a fall? Anything might have happened to her."

"Fretting will not help your aunt, she's made of sterner stuff as well you know. My dear Rosie, the congregation will be here soon and we must be ready for them. I must ask for your help with this."

Rosie fell silent, a silence her uncle took to be compliance to his wishes. He nodded and strode toward the door—and almost walked straight into Jorge. The boy was sweating and spoke urgently, his native language lost on Rosie and her uncle.

"He must have brought the professor," Gregory said, "in the hour of our greatest need. Come, Rosie."

Gregory and the boy were gone before she could reply. Rosie attempted to gather her thoughts. The way her aunt had looked upon her—like a ghost—was embedded in her consciousness. The things Francesca had said, such hurtful things as to be unbelievable. And yet something about her disturbing encounter with the woman she had called "Aunt" for all these years had left her feeling cold; perhaps because beneath it all, if she was honest, she had grown to think of her aunt as a surrogate mother. It was time to help Francesca, as she herself had been helped since her salvation as a child. Rosie just had to find her first. The professor would help and, elated by the prospect of a reunion with her mentor and friend, Rosie rushed out of the room.

The sight that greeted Rosie was a strange one indeed. A large contingent of Myahueneca, dressed in their finery of feathers and body paint, had formed a semicircle outside the chapel, standing two or three bodies deep. The chapel loomed behind them, and seemed to Rosie like a reminder of the change Pastor Gregory was so intent on invoking within them. Beneath their bright colors the villagers seemed subdued and on edge. Rosie searched the rows of glum faces, looking for Cecil, but she could not make him out. Then she spotted her uncle, speaking with the Myahueneca chieftain through Pedro, who interpreted at his side. Rosie sidled over to

Jorge, who also stood near to her uncle and asked about Professor Cecil, repeating his name so that the boy would understand. But Jorge just shrugged and turned his attention to Pedro, who said a few words before the boy ran off inside the chapel.

Rosie edged her way closer to her uncle and in the end had to push her way through the ranks of locals crowding the space around him.

"Ah, Rosie," Gregory said, "quite the turnout, isn't it? No sign of the professor, though."

"Any word on his well-being?" Rosie asked, concerned.

"From what I can glean, he went hunting with a group of men from the village."

"But it has been days—"

Just then, a shock of make-up and feathers caught her attention—it was the shaman, pushing his way through the crowd toward his chief. They spoke animatedly, and Rosie watched the chief's expression darken yet further. The Myahueneca chattered quietly to each other—the subdued atmosphere becoming a crashing wave of remorse. Several of the women began to wail and at their cue, children began to cry.

Uncle Gregory looked lost, apparently not even hearing the babbling voice of the shaman as he shouted at him. The clanging of the mission bell started up, adding to the noise of the throng. It promised no comfort to Rosie.

"What is going on?" she asked.

"I instructed the boy to ring the bell in welcome to our congregation," Gregory said, floundering.

"Why are the villagers so upset?"

Her uncle's lip moved, but he did not have the words. Rosie turned instead to Pedro, who spoke in dialect with the shaman. The shaman's voice filled with bile and he spat his words into Pedro's ear above the racket. Pedro's face fell, and Rosie knew it was not good news.

"Myahueneca found men, few men, burned in the forest," Pedro said.

The shaman railed on again and with such force that Pedro had to cover his ear with the flat of his hand.

"He says this happened now you are here. He says a curse follows the white men of the West. He says your God makes their gods angry…"

The villagers began chanting along with the shaman's rallying cry. Rosie saw tears of disbelief in her uncle's eyes. He had clearly been expecting a new congregation, not an angry mob. And then she heard screams. The sound was coming from inside the chapel. The doors burst open and a blazing figure tumbled down the steps before them. The stench of burning flesh tainted the air, evoking a thousand of Rosie's nightmares. Jorge thrashed at the foot of the chapel steps, his clothing and hair on fire. His cries were awful, like those of a pig facing slaughter. Rosie's hands flew to her ears in an instinctive attempt to negate the dreadful sound.

Pedro screamed the boy's name and rushed over to him, trying desperately to douse the flames with handfuls of dry earth. Frantic, he rolled the boy on the ground and put out the flames. But the child was badly burned, the skin on his face and hands blistered and blackened beyond recognition. As Pedro knelt helpless before the burned boy, a series of distraught cries ripped through the gathering.

CHAPTER THIRTY

The chapel tower was now aflame, smoke billowing from the window frames.

Rosie saw her uncle standing agape at the sight. A new chant started up among the crowd, and Rosie could feel its meaning in the pit of her stomach as she pushed through to her uncle's side.

"Good God. They think this is our doing, Rosie."

Gregory's words echoed her suspicions. She wanted to tell him that it would be all right, that they would just go back to the house, pack their things, and begin the search for Aunt Francesca so they could return home.

But now the chapel doors were open, Rosie saw that her aunt had already found them. And at the sight of her, Rosie began to wonder if this was indeed their own doing, if they had brought some madness, some curse with them to the rainforest.

Francesca stood raving before the pulpit, which was now a wall of flame. Her nightclothes were stained with mud and the Lord only knew what else, and her hair in such disarray as to make her look like a wild woman. For that was what she had become—gesticulating before the tumult of flames like an insane preacher. The fever had made red pockets of her eyes, which saw through and beyond Rosie, as though Francesca bore witness to an entire congregation of phantoms.

Francesca swooned and collapsed to the floor.

Gregory shouted her name and was bolting up the steps, taking them two at a time, before Rosie could say a word. She flinched as the growing fire brought supporting beams down from the ceiling. Gregory managed to dodge the first flaming beam, but the next struck him on his left shoulder and knocked him down as it fell.

Rosie, too, started up the steps then but was forced to stop when the pews nearest to her went up in flames. The heat and smoke stung her eyes as she searched out her uncle. He lay morbidly still just a few feet from where her aunt had fallen, at the foot of the altar. Rosie bit her lip, fearing the worst—and then her uncle moved.

The agony of those movements was evident in his gait but move he did—first getting himself up and onto his knees and then, with sheer determination of will, he stood and staggered toward Francesca.

She was on fire.

Rosie found her voice and called out above the din of the fire. Gregory's frantic cries joined his wife's own exclamations of terrified, mad distress. Rosie bit down on her knuckles, watching as Gregory tore his morning jacket off and used it to beat his way through the flames. Reaching Francesca, he smothered her with the garment and lifted her to her feet. There they stood in the aisle of the burning church, a strange parody of a couple on their wedding day. As her vision blurred with tears, Rosie saw Gregory and Francesca take a step toward salvation. His arm was clamped tight around Francesca, who clutched on to his morning jacket like a bridal shawl, and together they staggered to the chapel door. Rosie saw them, stark and still as shadow puppets against the billowing amber of flames. She reached out her hands across the conflagration.

Just a few more steps.

Her uncle and aunt staggered through the last of the flames, their clothes smoldering. Rosie helped her uncle support Francesca and together they tumbled down the steps. As they fell into the dust the chapel roof collapsed with a deafening crash of burning timbers.

Coughing from the smoke and the dust, Rosie helped Gregory move Francesca away from the ransacked chapel. It was only when they set her aunt down that Rosie was able to see the full extent of her injuries. Francesca's face was a corrupt mask of blistered flesh, the remnants of her hair blackened to a crisp from root to tip. Her eyes were molten pools, a feverish fire burning in her pupils. The rest of her body was raw from the burning and she twitched uncontrollably from shock. Gregory sobbed at the sight of her, rocking her in his arms as though she were a frightened child. Rosie had no words. The sight of her aunt in the throes of her fever had been shocking enough, but this was beyond that. She was watching her aunt die.

"I'm sorry, child, sorry for everything."

Francesca reached for Rosie with blackened fingers and gripped her dress tightly. Gregory shushed her, urged her not to speak. But the words tumbled from Francesca's mouth, in a race against her body, which was shutting down.

"I set the fire," Francesca said.

For a moment, Rosie thought she meant the chapel, but then she caught something in Gregory's expression. Something dark and until now, hidden.

"I despised my sister for what she had, so I took it from her. And for that I am eternally sorry. I hated my life, the pious, piteous life of a pastor's wife. Your parents, living out of wedlock, went against everything we had been raised to believe in. Free spirits, they called themselves. They were an affront and I...I killed them."

Rosie looked from Francesca to Gregory in shock and disbelief.

"You knew about this?"

She could see as much in her uncle's eyes, and she knew that what she had always mistaken for piety was in fact a lifetime of guilt, there to see for anyone who was looking hard enough.

Rosie looked hard enough now and her uncle averted his gaze.

"Why?"

Francesca coughed.

"Money. I wanted to *live*, Rosie. To travel. Away from small towns, and small minds. We sold the farm, and travel we did. You know this, Rosie, and I think you enjoyed growing up on the road."

Rosie said nothing.

"But what you didn't know was that your poor, dear uncle was so racked with guilt, our new life together became a damned pilgrimage. Instead of a pleasure trip."

Francesca laughed. It was a hideous, liquid sound. One that spoke of her body's unmaking.

"Damn you, Gregory. I don't want to die here."

The tears came then, in torrents. Rosie blinked through them at the blistered death mask that was her aunt's face. She wished she could snuff that selfish face from memory, but feared it would haunt her from that moment on.

"How could you..."

"Oh, don't blame your uncle, Rosie. He saved you, loved you as his own daughter." Francesca looked at Gregory, wearily. "I hated you for that, too, you know."

"I know," he said.

"Is there really a Hell? I don't want to go to Hell," Francesca said, her voice no more than a cracked whisper. "Bless me, Gregory. Please. Give forgiveness for my sins…"

Gregory clamped his lips shut against his grief. He held the words in, his agony making tortured sounds of them, until Francesca breathed her last. Then he let her gently down onto the earth and closed her eyes. His own were filled with tears. He reached out a gloved hand to Rosie and she recoiled.

"Don't touch me."

"Please…"

"Don't."

What Rosie had thought were her aunt's fevered ramblings had become a deathbed confessional. Every fiber of her being was cold with anger. She felt sick to her core.

"Every day, Rosie," her uncle said, "every single day I had to bear the weight of what your aunt conspired to do that night. I have tried to make amends, Lord help me, I have. Raised you as my own, gifted you the divine teachings of our Lord God…"

Tears tumbled from his eyes as he peeled off his gloves and looked down at the gnarled skin of his hands.

"Rescued you from hellfire and damnation…"

Rosie looked at his hands, too, wishing he had never used them to pluck her from the fire.

"You did not rescue me from anything, Uncle. You took me from those I loved, and who loved me. And why? To assuage your own crippling guilt. To try and make good with God for what *she* did to me, to my family. If only you had let me burn. Better to die once in ignorance than over and over in this…betrayal."

She saw true despair in him now, and the same look of regret she had caught in his eyes many times. Rosie knew the source of that regret now and wondered if she could ever forgive him— could ever forgive *them*—for what they had done.

"Save yourself," she said.

Ignoring his pleas, Rosie walked away. Around her, chaos reigned supreme, as scores of Myahueneca shrieked and ran, scooping up their terrified children in their arms as they beat their retreat from the fire. Rosie glanced back at the smoldering chapel and the liar cowering in its shadow.

She knew, for once and for all, that her uncle's God had no place in the forest.

The umbilical cord cut for the third time in her life, Rosie floundered, lost in a fog of smoke. She stumbled and turned, then ran to join the Myahueneca—for she did not know where else to go.

CHAPTER THIRTY-ONE

Rosie ran, urged on by frantic voices ahead of her.

She caught up to them and heard Pedro's raw, yet familiar tones. He stood at the edge of the mission house clearing, cradling Jorge in his arms. The boy's left arm dangled lifeless, the flesh there puckered and blackened from the fire in the chapel. Rosie's eyes filled with fresh tears as she realized Pedro was speaking to the boy in anguished whispers, his fractured ministrations making a lullaby for the dead. She spoke his name, placed her hand on his arm, perhaps hoping to quell her own torment by consoling him for his. But Pedro was in a state of shock, gazing down at the boy, his posture bent in anguish. Another childhood stolen by her aunt.

She walked on, across the clearing toward the mission house and automatically began climbing the steps. She was halfway to the door when she understood why she was going there—to retrieve the only truth in her life, the precious scrap of paper that confirmed her parents' passing. Pausing at the threshold, Rosie looked down on Pedro, still clutching the dead boy to his breast. She wondered if this might have been how her parents had last seen her, from above, being stolen from the fire as they ascended to the heavens. Her mind swam, a turbulent sea of contorted emotions, as she stumbled inside the mission house in search of her precious paper.

Rosie already had a feeling of liberation from the deeper truth that lurked between the lines of text on the newspaper cutting. All her pain, her confused gratitude for having been saved now had new focus, a new channel in which to define itself. She crushed the soft scrap of paper in her hand and held it close to her furious, beating heart. After all these years Rosie felt on the cusp of something greater than herself, something deeper than her everyday existence under the guardianship of her aunt and uncle. Now they had gone it felt as though a veil had lifted and she was passing through the membranes of guilt, confusion and loss—and navigating toward womanhood. Despair at her childhood loss had eroded her spirit all these years. But now she was unpacking all of her hatred and anger, she felt these powerful new emotions were rebuilding her, shaping her anew.

She picked up the hand mirror from her nightstand and glared into it. The fire in her cheeks and forehead no longer offended her. Crimson was the color she felt burning inside her most of all. For once, she was proud to give it shape and form through the corruption of her skin. The face that glared back at her from behind the looking glass was her true face, her markings no less proud, flamboyant, nor powerful than the body paint worn by the Myahueneca tribe.

Rosie heard their panicked voices before she realized the mission house was on fire. She pocketed the paper and rushed from her room, careless of her other belongings for she had no need of them now. She hurried down the stairs and was about to descend farther when an appalling sight stopped her in her tracks. Men, some of them familiar to her from the paddle steamer, had rounded up the house staff. Each servant was on their knees, their hands held, trembling behind their heads. The men reached down and, for a moment, Rosie thought they were throttling their captives. She realized her error when the men withdrew their hands and she saw each was brandishing a machete. The necks of the kneeling servants opened up, giving vent to cascades of arterial blood that pumped across their clothing and into their laps. The bodies fell, tumbling like skittles to the wooden floor. Each body spilled its life's blood in dark pools on the floor. The cook was screaming at the sight of so much blood. Her protestations were soon silenced.

Rosie's hand flew to her mouth, in part an attempt not to cry out in anguish, in another to stop herself from vomiting. But the men had seen her on the stairs, their faces flushed with the heat of murder and other feral desires that she had no wish to witness. She backed up the stairs, for to continue her descent would mean certain capture. The first of the men began to climb after her. Despite his injuries, she recognized him as the deckhand who had entered her room aboard the paddle steamer. And she knew from the look in his eyes that he meant to visit his most bestial of instincts upon her. His lust had been denied on board the vessel, but here she was alone and more vulnerable than ever.

Rosie counted her options and concluded she had only one. She would have to jump from the banister at the top of the stairs and hope to Heaven that the fall would snap her neck. Retreating to her chambers and barricading herself in would only keep her safe for so long—these half a dozen men would make light work of breaking down her door. Rosie was almost at the top of the stairs now. She took a furtive glance at the landing to her left, the banister looming like a shadow. Her frantic mind conspired to quash her will and she felt her legs weaken. But she could not falter. Collapsing like a frightened girl would make the men's victory all the easier. If she were to accomplish anything in her final moments, then it would be to deny them the pleasure.

Rosie had a hold of the banister and was just about to clamber up onto it when the first shot rang out. The sound was deafening as cannon fire, echoing around the confines of the foyer and stairwell. Her pursuers stopped, two of them, on the stairs and peered down to locate the source of the sound. Smoke billowed from below, not from the fire but rather from the firearm that a lone figure was, even now, reloading before aiming it at the men on the stairwell. The man nearest Rosie gasped as the shot blasted his jawbone into pieces. Blood and bone spattered on the wall, and he fell to his knees before tumbling down the steps. His descent knocked his fellow from his feet with such force that the man seemed to levitate for a moment, a full three feet above the stairs. He plummeted, his face cracking open on the sharp edge of the wooden stair beneath it. His cheek gushed blood and several of his teeth spilled from his mouth as he spluttered in shock and pain. Rosie, still clutching the banister, peered over the edge hoping to identify her savior. As the smoke cleared, she saw his face.

Pedro.

Rosie had never felt so relieved to see someone in her life. He was frantically reloading his weapon, an archaic hunting rifle. As the remaining men closed in around Pedro, her relief turned to new panic. He managed to fight the first one off, using the butt of the rifle as a cudgel to disintegrate the man's nose. The second went down from Pedro's well-aimed blow to the side of the head, but the third man ducked and weaved, stabbing Pedro in his exposed midriff with the blade of his knife.

Pedro's defiant look fell from his face. His mouth dropped open and blood trickled out. Through the shocked silence, Rosie heard him utter a single word.

"Go."

CHAPTER THIRTY-TWO

R osie was at the foot of the stairs before the remaining men could react, the door just a few tantalizing feet away. She could see smoke and flames beyond, could hear the screams of women and children, but any danger outside would be preferable to death at the hands of the savages who had murdered Pedro and the others. One of the men, the wiry fellow from the paddle steamer, shouted at his larger friend not to let her go—to grab her and bring her to him. His words put fresh fear into her heart and she propelled herself toward the door. She was almost within reach when she slipped on something wet and crashed onto the wooden floorboards.

Winded from her fall she saw that she had slipped in the slick of blood created by the mass murder of the house staff. Their bodies lay around her, lifeless eyes glistening with their last tears. Rosie gasped in horror at the carnage all around her. She scrambled backward, trying to get to her feet so that she might reach the door before her pursuer. He thundered toward her, looking like a bull in a fight with his head lowered and his teeth bared. A cry of fear escaped from Rosie's throat and she heard the wiry fellow laugh at her. His cruel cackling made her stomach churn, for one so lacking in empathy could only mean to destroy her in pain and humiliation. She threw her arm over her face and braced herself for her attacker's assault.

It did not come.

In its place, she heard a gunshot.

Blinking, she moved her arm away and looked up at the colossal man. He had stopped running toward her and stood stock-still with a dumbfounded expression on his idiot face. His right hand reached up and patted his chest. He looked at the blood on his fingers as though he had never before seen its color. The bullet had gone right through him, punching a hole where his heart used to beat. It was as though someone had popped the cork from a barrel of claret. Red torrents pumped through his shirt, driven by his dying organ.

Uncle Gregory stood clutching Pedro's rifle. He looked at Rosie, his face pale with relief and fear. He looked as shocked as she was that he had managed to take down the huge hunter. Her uncle had saved her again, and this time she felt grateful.

The hunters appeared to forget about Rosie for a moment and turned their murderous attentions to Gregory. He pulled the trigger, but the rifle was spent. The first of the hunters to reach Gregory thrust a machete so deep into his abdomen that Rosie saw the tip of the blade appear through his back. Gregory gasped, then tried to speak through the thick globs of blood spilling down his chin. He was denied his final words. They cut his throat first, and then removed his withered hands at the wrists. Rosie tried not to scream as Gregory was hacked to bits where he stood.

Nimbo stepped in through the doorway and helped Rosie to her feet. He dragged her out through the doorway, away from the angry cries of the hunters. She heard a sickening thud as her uncle fell, dead, to the floor. Rosie resisted the urge to look back as she and Nimbo kept running, away from the burning mission house and the murderous men who had defiled it.

They ran into a living nightmare. Frightened Myahueneca dashed in all directions around them. The source of their fear—new fires that had taken hold of the tree line surrounding the mission house compound. Rosie looked back at the house and saw the rear of the building was now ablaze. The intruders meant to raze the compound to the ground.

She saw them exit the building, the weasel-faced man barking instructions to his fellows. He peered out across the chaotic crowd, searching her and Nimbo out. She pulled Nimbo close and led him into a crowd of villagers who were making for a break in the trees that was, as yet, untouched by the forest fire. They scrambled together, close knit and moving as one.

Rosie saw the smoldering remains of the chapel as they passed it by and felt a chill on her skin. She thought of the graves behind the chapel, a long lineage of missionaries lost forever in a foreign land. Francesca and Gregory had joined their ranks, a thought that did little to calm Rosie's troubled mind. But the simple matter of survival yanked her out of her morose thoughts. She and Nimbo, along with the locals, had been spotted by the men outside the mission house. Gunshots rang out, and a couple of the group fell away from Rosie's side. Others farther ahead started yelling as figures sprang out of the undergrowth in the clearing before them. Rosie's eyes widened in terror as she saw they were tribesmen, but not Myahueneca. The men wore black body paint on their arms and faces, giving them the frightening aspect of living skeletons. Two of the men put blowpipes to their lips and, after drawing air into their cheeks, launched a volley of tiny darts into the crowd of would-be escapees. Several tribespeople fell, and Rosie knew that the tiny darts protruding from the flesh of their necks and faces must be carrying a deadly poison. This new danger sent the Myahueneca into a frenzy of fear and, to the apparent delight of their attackers, the group broke ranks and peeled off in separate directions in a desperate attempt to evade the deadly darts. Nimbo ducked, dodging one of the blowpipe darts, then dived onto his stomach as he and Rosie reached the tall grass at the perimeter of the forest. Rosie followed suit and together they began to crawl toward the trees. The frenzied Myahueneca around them were the perfect cover. As the rival tribesmen focused their efforts on picking off the disoriented adults, Rosie and Nimbo were able to crawl to safety.

Once inside the cover of the trees, Rosie and Nimbo helped each other to their feet and ran on, keeping low so as not to be detected. They realized their mistake when they ran into a thick blanket of smoke—the fire was on both sides, closing in. Rosie coughed, her lungs filling with acrid smoke. Nimbo looked around, the whites of his eyes brilliant in the fog-like gloom. They both saw the shadows of more tribal men. They were setting fires all around them with flaming torches. Rosie figured they must be the same blaze farmers who had burned the forest near to the Myahueneca's village. They had somehow forged an unholy alliance with the men from the paddle steamer and their aim was clear—to wipe the Myahueneca from the face of the earth and take their lands. Rosie's eyes filled with tears at the betrayal of those who had treated her with kindness in the short time that she had known them. Her indignation bolstered her resolve, however, and she vowed to do everything in her power to help Nimbo survive the catastrophe that had befallen his people.

The smoke was overpowering, the heat intense, and Rosie had no choice but to urge Nimbo farther on into the forest. Behind them, the shrieks and cries of the villagers continued on, punctuated by the rhythmic hissing of the blowpipes as the blaze farmers continued their genocide. The horrific sounds propelled Rosie and Nimbo on, but they soon hit a wall of flame so high that they could not see over the top of it. The heat shimmer was so strong that it created the illusion of the forest melting all around Rosie and her ally. She held on to his hand and looked into his eyes. He looked younger than his years, and his clear attempt to cover up his dread made him all the more noble and innocent to Rosie's eyes. She remembered her vision quest, recalling the tunnel where she had stood with the dream version of Nimbo and how she sank into the ground powerless to help him.

Not powerless this time. Rosie knew what they had to do. She peered up through the smoke and the shimmer and looked for the tallest tree she could find. Pointing at it, she shouted to Nimbo to climb, to climb as high as he could because it was the only way he could survive the blaze. He shook his head, but then seemed to realize she was right—this was his only way out. She urged him on, marveling at the nimble way he began his ascent up the tree trunk. Rosie tried to follow, but her dexterity was no match for Nimbo's astonishing, innate ability to climb. He peered down at her as she slid from the tree trunk and back to the ground.

"Keep climbing!"

But he did not listen, opting instead to shimmy back down the tree trunk almost as quickly as he'd climbed up.

"What are you doing? Get back up there!"

He held his hand out to Rosie and his intentions became clear to her. Nimbo was offering to help Rosie up into the lower branches with him. Once there, she might be able to climb the rest of the way herself, albeit at a slower pace than the boy. She stood on the tips of her toes and strained to reach him. Her fingers outstretched, she felt his fleeting touch then lost it again. She prepared to jump up and make another go of grabbing on to his hand.

A sharp, stinging sensation took hold at the nape of her neck. Nimbo cried out and she whirled around to see the dark shape of a blaze farmer through the smoke and the tall silhouettes of the trees. His blowpipe was as plain to see as the look of triumph in his eyes. Rosie's fingers found the dart at the center of the stinging feeling, which was now spreading through her body like a warm wave of nausea. She mouthed Nimbo's name but could not tell if she was yelling or whispering it. The hot sickness was taking her down and, just as in her vision, she felt sure she would sink into the earth beneath her feet.

As she fell to her knees the sky went out. A black shadow had fallen upon her, negating her line of sight. She heard the sharp snap of breaking bones and was vaguely aware of someone falling in the forest before her. Her head tilted back, and she caught a whiff of something that smelled like the old tanning barn at her parents' farm. Her vision snapped back into focus, and she saw the monolithic beast-man standing just a few feet away from her. He was holding the broken body of the blaze farmer in his hands. She screamed and heard the sound this time, her own fear a clarion call to get up and flee. Staggering to her feet, Rosie bolted into the forest. Nimbo was crying out somewhere above and behind her, but she could not understand his words, much less heed them. Mortal terror took hold, and she used the last of her diminishing energy to sprint through the trees, away from the black-eyed monster.

Smoke filled her mouth and lungs, causing her to gag and to almost stop breathing before she was forced to slow her pace. Flames danced all around her as the forest fire raged on. She heard the splintering, aching roar of a giant tree trunk and it fell just feet away from her, causing an explosion of flame as it crashed to the ground. The aftershock of the blast knocked her off balance and she fell into the fire, the skin of her hands blistering as she tried to break her fall. Her skirts went up in flame and she could smell the hair burning from her scalp as she tried, desperate, to right herself. Screaming in silence, she felt the flames rise up and over her torso as the rest of her clothing caught fire. She fell backward and rolled over, now completely enveloped in burning flames. The trees were bent over her like funereal mourners, their leaves weeping fire.

Rosie reached into her clothing and felt the burn of smoldering flesh against flesh. She opened her hand and realized she was clutching the little scrap of newspaper she had rescued from her bedchamber at the mission house. Her tears evaporated on her blistering cheeks as she watched the scrap of paper blacken to ashes in the palm of her hand. The ashes rose on the heat shimmer like tiny, black question marks.

The world around her seemed to vibrate in brilliant hues of gold and sunset yellow as she blackened and burned, too. For a moment, she was transported back to the fire at the farm and felt that same stomach-churning feeling of despair as she realized she was about to die.

Then, just as she had as a child, she felt powerful hands searching her out in the blaze.

I must be dreaming, she thought, *dead but dreaming,* as the powerful hands lifted her from the flames.

She looked up, expecting to see the phantasm of her uncle's face peering down at her. She struggled against his grasp, reluctant to allow him to carry her down into Hell with him—and with her murderous aunt. But as she peered through the unbearable heat that made her eyes feel ready to burst, it was not her uncle's face that greeted her.

The last thing she saw before she lost consciousness was her screaming reflection—in the black eye coverings of the monster that had haunted her in visions and had now, in death, come to claim her.

CHAPTER THIRTY-THREE

Rounding up the remaining Myahueneca was not an easy task, given the rapid spread of smoke and flames, but one that provided much sport for Richter's men and the blaze farmers. As Richter made his way up the slope to the patch of higher ground where they had made their base camp, he savored the feeling that only satisfaction in a job well done could provide. He scanned the area through his binoculars, humming along to the soundtrack of screams and dying cries. A shame they had lost the girl from the paddle steamer, though. She would have been quite the prize for his men after their arduous day of arson and slaughter. Richter knew that Erroll, in particular, would be eager to punish her for Keyser's untimely demise. The big man's death had come as a shock to Richter initially, but then he'd reminded himself how astounding it was that someone so dumb could have lived for so long in the first place. The burning mission house had become a funeral pyre for Keyser's sizeable corpse, along with so many other casualties of the day's activities.

Richter heard more of them dying, even now. He closed his eyes in order to increase his focus and was rewarded with a rich soundscape of rape and murder. His acute hearing had picked out the unmistakable screams of Myahueneca women, imploring their gods to end their lives and put an end to their ordeal. Good. So, his men, and the blaze farmers, were partaking of their spoils after all. Richter opened his eyes and let the light in. He rarely felt the post-violence sexual urges that he had witnessed in so many men during his hunting years, but he respected such things for what they were: ritual. In his travels, he had met the descendants of countless conquered territories, their blood still burning with the infiltration of the usurper. To Richter, rape and pillage expressed the same innate drive to replicate oneself—to continue one's creed and bloodline—that any mating creature exhibited in the wild. Wherever there was wilderness, along came the urge to command and conquer. It was the natural way of things, and who was he to stand in the way of nature? The smart money had always been on using such instincts to his advantage. The current situation provided a stark case study through which to defend his thesis. Here he stood, in Planet Earth's most impenetrable wilderness, penetrating it all the same.

Erroll's scratchy voice roused him from his victorious thoughts, something about prisoners, and another about the fair-skinned girl who had escaped. He turned to face Erroll and snickered at the man's appearance. He looked like a firefighter who had gone the extra mile to save someone from the flames. They both knew different of course—the scratches on Erroll's rodent face were testament to his true activities. Tears streamed down the man's cheeks. Richter assumed they were the product of acrid smoke rather than remorse at his crimes.

"I said someone..." Erroll hesitated, drawing breath, "... something took hold of her. Killed three of the blaze farmers and left them broken in his wake. Snapped they were, like twigs..."

"Heading?"

"East, toward the ruins, far as we can tell. It's difficult with all this God's damned fire. My eyes are still stinging, boss."

"And your dick, too, no doubt. Move everyone out, we're heading east."

Richter caught a flash of something in Erroll's wet eyes. It looked like genuine fear. When he blinked he looked weak, like a child. Richter deconstructed the man who stood limp before him. A loathsome creature born to follow orders and inflict his misery on those further down the food chain than him.

"What a piece of work is a man, hey, Erroll?"

"Boss?"

"It's just, I'm sure I'm mistaken, but for a moment there it looked like you were crapping your pants at the prospect of the hunt."

Erroll flushed, on the tipping point between anger and despair. Life was a mere cycle of abuses for men like him—a cycle perpetuated by the ever-darkening requirements of his masters. Now was the time to take care of such requirements.

"Get to it then."

Richter watched Erroll scurry away like the rat he was. As he watched him slither down the slope, Richter saw a shape, high in the tualang trees. It was a boy, one of the Myahueneca tribe from his attire, making his way down a tree trunk through the drifting clouds of smoke. Richter hissed at Erroll to halt then drew his attention to the child in the tree. They both watched as the boy dropped to the forest floor, agile as a monkey, and searched around. The boy crouched low, studying something in the dirt. Then he set off, keeping his eyes trained on the ground. Richter caught up to Erroll and gestured for him to follow. Without even speaking, Richter felt sure that his intent must be clear. They had a guide now—one who was following the tracks of the man, or rather the thing, that had carried the fair-skinned girl away.

They followed the boy until they reached the extremities of the blaze. Richter instructed Erroll to go round up the rest of their little hunting party while he continued on after the boy. A bottom feeder like Erroll would find it easy to follow Richter's tracks—he'd make sure of that. Erroll snuck off in the direction of the mission house complex, or rather, where it had once stood. Keeping a safe distance from the boy, so as not to spook him and thus ruin his delicious game of cat-follows-mouse-follows-cat, Richter found the tracks taking him deeper into the forest, then out again and onto higher ground. The remnants of the blaze looked a million miles away from this vantage point and could be mistaken for an everyday mist to the untrained eye. Richter's eyes were sharp, however, and he knew for sure that the Myahueneca were finished. A grim smile twisted his lips as he contemplated how easy it had been for one culture to usurp another.

The blaze farmers would make a clean sweep of the Myahueneca's village and take what they wanted, or simply install themselves as the new inhabitants. The remaining women would be taken in hand to rear children for their new masters. The combined bloodlines would beget strong children and ensure the blaze farmers' superiority in the region. Their openness to collaboration, demonstrated by the way they had worked alongside Richter and his men, suggested trade would be possible with the new landlords. And where trade was possible, actual trade routes opened up, too. Within five years, Richter's employers would be mining for gold, oil, and anything else precious they could get their grabbing hands on. And to whom would they owe their gratitude for deliverance of such riches? *Lord Richter* had always had a ring to it, he had to admit. He would retire somewhere warm, but not quite as humid as the rainforest, and enjoy his autumn years in a state of luxurious retreat—with the occasional hunt to keep him sharp, of course.

He was almost at the ridge now, the tangle of roots gathering at his feet signaling the elevation. Stooping low, before he reached the top where the trees grew steeper and thinner, Richter readied his sidearm. He heard the boy before he saw him, circling the shadow of the ruined temple. Dozy kid must have stepped on a fallen branch. The cracking sound that followed was loud enough to wake the dead. Upon hearing the sound, a flock of bright birds took to the wing directly above him. Richter pressed himself to the ground so as to remain undetected. He waited a few moments, listening to the dull rhythmic thud of his heart as he counted down the seconds. When thirty had passed, he risked a peek over the ridge and into the shadows.

The boy was no longer there. It was as though the ruined temple had swallowed him whole.

CHAPTER THIRTY-FOUR

R osie dreamed.
A fathomless death-dream, one from which she felt she might never escape. She had faint awareness of thinking that its edges were too fuzzy. Too hot to go near somehow, blood and fire just inches from the extremities of her inward vision. Dark space folded around her like a sentient shroud. She could sense its molecules trying to keep her cool. Each particle was like a cold hand, ferrying her down into blackness and void. Her awareness spiked with the recognition of having endured this sensation before, but where? Of course, during her vision whilst under the effects of the Myahueneca shaman's potion. Only then the cool brushing all around her body had felt like the soil into which she had descended. This time the hands crossed over each other, lowering her like they had purpose. A prickle of panic started to form in the small of her back as she felt the heat of that purpose there. Rosie wondered if this was to be her descent into Hell. She had died in the burning forest and was now to be punished for eternity in recompense for her mortal sin—to have lived and flourished in the house of murderers while her parents had died. The heat at her back grew in intensity, and if she had a voice, she felt sure she would be screaming. Soon, the cool hands would give way and lower her, or let her drop, into a lake of fire.

She fell, instead, to earth with the gentlest of bumps. The heat at her back felt warming now and no longer threatening—a cradle of earth that was soft and granular, yet held her firm. Void gave way to light, and she tried to focus as countless dust motes swam before her eyes, like sand in an hourglass. Squinting in a vain attempt to peer through them, Rosie instead found that they were solidifying, joining together to create form and function. Structures of atoms danced, sprouting from their endless pools and swirls, building upon one another. Recognizable shapes began to make themselves known to her—the foundations of a building, the roots of massive trees, the halo of the sun beaming down on them. Rosie sat up, for she, too, was taking on more defined form. The kaleidoscope of her mind's eye had been shaken, and the pieces were coming together. With each glance at her new surroundings, they sharpened into focus, and she knew she was in the rainforest once more. But it looked different, *wilder* somehow, if such a thing was even possible.

Rising to her feet, Rosie saw she was atop a plateau, high above the rainforest. The ground beneath her feet had hardened to stone, and she realized she was standing on a man-made structure. Giant trees that grew all around cast strips of dark shadow across the stones, dividing them up into jagged sections of light and dark. A light breeze picked up, and Rosie smelled the combined flora and fauna of the Amazon, scents so pure and so beautiful that they were dizzying. She drifted across the structure, passing between the shadows and the sunlight, enjoying the transition from cool to warm and back again. She blinked with eyes anew and felt purified, perhaps even sanctified.

This was not Hell. It was paradise.

Hearing a multitude of voices, Rosie crossed to the nearest edge of the stone platform. Peering over the edge, which gave way to a sudden drop of some fifty feet or more, she saw a crowd of tribal people gathered in an enclave of statue, stone, and dust. There the stone had been worked and hewn into designs she recalled from the ruined temple near the mission house. But these looked as though they had been sculpted yesterday, the fine details of the animal iconography standing out in the blazing sunlight. The crowd sang out in exaltation, a discordant choir of shrill tenors and guttural baritones, their voices swelling and shrinking on the breeze. Each was dressed in tribal finery, and Rosie caught flashes of paradise bird feathers as they glinted like mother-of-pearl in the sun. At the head of the crowd stood a wild, dancing man. He tumbled and whirled before the crowd, his chirruping voice urging them on into a frenzy of celebration. The mood of the people seemed to drift upward to her, weaving a spell around her. She felt lightened by the voices and the colorful movement, intoxicated by the crowd's evocations. As they lifted their voices to a crescendo, Rosie yearned to be among them.

Descending the rocks, Rosie thought how strange it was that she seemed to know the intricacies of their layout. It was as though she had climbed over them dozens of times, even their texture was familiar to the skin of her hands as she clambered down the largest of the tiered drops before reaching the bottom. She dusted off her hands and stood erect in the enclave, watching the dancers and their shaman. The warmth coming off their bodies was like a sirocco, penetrating her flesh and igniting something there—a glow of understanding, perhaps, and of belonging. She ran, then, to join with them and they parted ranks to let her in. The press of bodies all around her was life affirming—sweat and flesh combining to remind her of the stuff of life, of brotherhood and sisterhood, and of passion and ritual. She reveled in the closeness and joined in the dance and the song. Like the shapes of the stones during her descent, Rosie seemed to know the ritual movements and more surprisingly the words of the song, despite them being in dialect. She knew their meaning, too, and felt the surge of adoration within her breast as she sang them. Each word was a totem, a metaphysical form made real by the simple act of intoning it, and each was meant as an offering for their god—for her god—the Skintaker.

Her colorful kaleidoscope world tilted, and she felt light as a feather, then realized the crowd had gathered together to lift her up high into the sunlight like a gleaming jewel. She looked down and saw their hands all around her, felt the warmth of their blood pumping, unlike the cold digits that had ferried her down through the void to this wondrous place. Only then did Rosie notice the difference of her own form. She blinked in disbelief at her body, her arms and hands, as she saw not the body of a nineteen-year-old girl but that of a young tribal boy. The shock of her new form rocked her, but the hands all around her held her upright. She felt some of them close around her limbs, gripping her arms and legs too tight. Something was wrong. The hands felt hard all of a sudden, like leather. Rosie imagined each one had become gnarled, disfigured, and clad in Gregory's sable gloves, their vise-like grip ready to drag her down into the hellfire that had misshapen them.

She cried out—her voice not her own but that of a young boy's. The crowd paid no heed to her discomfort. She blinked in the harsh sunlight as they carried her toward the opening in the temple. Struggling as they paused at the entrance, Rosie implored them to let her go. The shaman, standing high on his podium, bowed over and smiled at her with all the warmth of a proud uncle. The sound of the crowd fell away and all that Rosie could hear was the whisper of the breeze. She felt her clothes being torn away and the cool kiss of oil on her skin as the shaman anointed her body. The fluid dripped into her eyes and nostrils, mingling with the snot and tears that welled there. It smelled of deep earth, an ancient, hidden scent that she had only before experienced at her parents' graveside on the day they were buried. She remembered the sound a crow that had been digging for worms had made with its beak. She also recalled the sound that the shovels had made as the gravediggers tossed the earth in over the coffins. Bodies went in and worms came out, the cycle of life in a synergy of sound. Rosie had fainted soon after to be carried away, once again, by her uncle—the false hero.

Rosie wished she could faint now, but she did not know if it was possible to do so in a dream, or in purgatory—or wherever the hell her burned brain had taken her. She began to laugh, a sound that frightened her, but which appeared to move the shaman to paroxysms of joy.

She's ready, his eyes said, *ready for the rite. Ready for him.*

Throwing back his head he bellowed that one must die so that one might live. Again, Rosie understood the words.

The crowd beneath and all around her joined the shaman's frenzied call, and she felt them moving her again. As they carried her across the threshold, Rosie saw the carvings beneath the arch of the temple entrance above her. There, hewn into the sharp texture of the keystone, was a face she recognized from her darkest nightmares, its disc-shaped eyes like those of a watchful insect, glaring down at her from above. She felt sure it would reveal itself as real any moment, sliding its body from the cracks and crawling down from its hiding place, a ravenous thing come to feast upon her bones. Then it was gone. She had passed through and into darkness.

CHAPTER THIRTY-FIVE

Torches were lit. Rosie heard their crackle and felt their heat about her. The tunnel interior was astonishing. Carved out of the rock, it must have taken decades of patient chiseling by countless hands to create such a space. And it seemed to go on forever, twisting and sloping with the demands of the strata through which it had been forged. The crowd chanted on, their voices sounding ever more unified in the tunnel's tight space, reaching a frenzy as they processed through the last leg of the tunnel and into a chamber.

Setting their torches into alcoves in the wall, the tribe lowered Rosie onto a stone altar at the center of the chamber. As the flames flickered and her eyes adjusted, she saw yet more carvings in the walls of the chamber. They were exactly the same as the ones she had seen in her vision quest, as familiar to her as the words to the hymns she had learned off by heart for evensong in her uncle's ministry—

He descended unto Hell.

On the third day he rose again.

The resurrection of the body.

And life everlasting.

—her memories echoed in the silence of the chamber. The throng had ceased their chanting. Rosie tried to move, but their hands held her firm on the dais. The stone beneath her curved into her back, as though it had been worn into shape by countless bodies before hers, a thought which made her feel sick. Strange that this body was not hers, but she could still feel sensations within it. That thought, too, filled her with dread and the oil-drenched sweat turned cold on her skin. A gasp went up among the crowd and Rosie sensed movement at the head of the altar.

Craning her neck back as far as it would go, she saw the shaman standing behind her. He was upside down to her, an inversion of all things that were holy. The warm, paternal look had gone from his eyes, banished by something dark and primal. His pupils had widened in the torchlight, making his eyes look black, their gloss surface evoking the obsidian orbs of his god. Worshippers at his side removed his tribal dress and as he stood, naked, Rosie saw the glint of a knife blade in his hands. He raised the weapon high above his head and Rosie felt her mouth go dry as she anticipated the cut of the blade as he brought it down.

But it was his own flesh he pierced. Rosie watched in abject horror as he cut into his own throat and down through his sternum, all the way into his belly. The tribal men and women at his sides reached into his abdomen and grabbed at the spools of his innards, releasing them for all to see. Hot blood splashed onto Rosie's face and chest, and she gagged at the unwelcome salt-metal taste invading her mouth. An orgiastic cry rippled through the crowd as they tore into one another, mimicking the self-immolation of their shaman—but with their bare hands. Fingernails ripped skin from flesh and teeth gnawed flesh from bone. The very air in the chamber turned red with arterial blood as it gushed from so many writhing bodies.

No longer held by hands, Rosie was instead held by fear. She looked down at her borrowed body, still that of a tribal boy, and tried to will it to move so that she might flee this new horror and live again. But paralysis had taken hold and she watched as the tribe skinned one another, their cries at an orgasmic pitch somewhere between death and ecstasy. The warm glow of belonging that she had experienced outside had become a hot frenzy of wounding. The tribe painted the walls and floor of the chamber with so much blood that it began to froth with the violent churning of their bodies. Rosie felt her body heave and she vomited stomach bile onto her clammy skin. She sat up then and turned to see the shaman, his entrails pulled to the breaking point as the revelers danced with them, ducking and weaving in and around them. It was as though his intestines had become lurid ribbons, strung from the maypole of his dying body.

All around her, flayed bodies fell, splashing into pools of blood and excrement. The wailing subsided as the life started to leave the bodies, and in the hush, Rosie knew something else was now among them. The presence was dark and heavy, and before she saw him, she knew he was the Skintaker. His glassy eyes reflected the scarlet madness of the scene before him, but his face betrayed no emotion other than the faintest hint of approval. This was his domain, his ritual—it was meant to be.

His shadow fell across Rosie's naked form, a spike of intense darkness cutting through the tumult of flame and blood. Her throat tightened as he stepped closer, the draft from his robes of flesh enveloping her in its pervasive, almost surgical scent. He sighed then, this behemoth of a man, his head lowered ever so slightly, and Rosie detected melancholia somewhere behind those black eyes of his. He lifted his hands up and considered them, and Rosie knew from his movements that he was weary. Perhaps she had mistaken sadness for exhaustion—at what she could only guess. Perhaps this life he lived, as a god to so many frenzied faces, or maybe he was exhausted at so much death. Whatever the root cause, he ambled closer still and held Rosie flat against the stone with one massive hand. She almost welcomed its weight on her, if only because through its pressure she could feel the ferocity of her heart beating. For that moment she was alive in this borrowed body, more alive than she had been in her own. The blood that coursed through young veins was driven by the engine of a heart so much younger, and more innocent than hers.

He felt it, too, this man who smelled of flesh and ruin, she knew that now. He revered it for a moment, holding still as the pulse in his hand dropped into sync with that in her chest. They were connected, as one, and a stark thought entered Rosie's mind. The beast before her had been a boy once, wearing the same skin that she wore now.

The thought was still with her as the Skintaker plucked the boy's eyes from their sockets and tore into his flesh, opening him up as though he was in search of Rosie, hiding inside him. At his touch, she knew that he had found her. And she knew that she would never be able to hide again.

CHAPTER THIRTY-SIX

Nimbo crawled farther into the tunnel. It was narrow, even for him, so much so that he had almost missed spotting the entrance when he was topside. The smell had alerted him to its presence, that sickly sweet stench like over-ripened fruit. It was the smell that reminded him of Pacon, of his little brother. It reminded him of the day they had gone out hunting and he had returned to the village alone. And it instilled him with renewed anger and indignance at the beating he had suffered at the hands of his father for daring to speak the name of his brother's murderer in the presence of the tribe.

"Skintaker."

He whispered the name now, sucking in his fear and spitting it back out. The name was a totem, a dying word to be uttered in one's last moments. And so perhaps it could be a killing word, too, to be exclaimed into the face of such awesome death. He uttered it again, and sucked it back in. Something scuttled across his back in the tarantula dark, and he flinched momentarily before pressing on down the tunnel. Soil caked his fingers as he crawled ever on. He could feel the skin on his knees breaking against sharp stones. But he did not slow his pace. The murderous man-thing had brought the pale girl down here. She was trapped, just like his brother had been. He could not save his brother, nothing could change that. But perhaps he could save her. She had shown him kindness and they had shared visions from the animal spirit guides. He did not know what part he had to play in her story here in the rainforest, but he knew he had to try to do something. As far as he knew, he was the last of his tribe. That made him chief now, so no one could tell him not to do a thing. No one could beat him for making the wrong decision. His path was his and his alone. He just wished it wasn't paved with quite so many creepy crawlies.

Pulling a centipede out of his ear and tossing it aside, Nimbo glimpsed light coming from the end of the tunnel. Not much farther now, and the crumbling earth walls began to widen and solidify around him. Within minutes he was able to walk on at a low stoop, and then a little farther along he could stand fully. Such a place was anathema to Nimbo. Only nocturnal creatures burrowed this deep. He whispered the name of his nemesis again and swallowed it whole, an act more bitter even than the vilest of his medicine man's concoctions. No use wishing the shaman could be at his side now to share his wisdom and bring light to this shadow place. His spirit was on the long walk with that of Nimbo's father, up high among the trees. Not down here in a spider hole with the corrupt dead.

He was nearing the source of the light now. It lay just beyond a turn in the tunnel. Gods above but the air smelled ripe down here, and worse the closer he got to the light. Every fiber of his being screamed at him to turn tail and run, to crawl back up into the light and take his place as chieftain in whatever was left of his burned-out home. But Nimbo knew that was weakness calling him, his own lack of confidence in his ability to do the right thing even if it meant facing his destruction. Better to end his waking life with his head held high rather than descend into a dream death on his knees, staring into the maggot earth. He balled his hands into fists and turned the corner.

She was lying atop an altar of rough stone, and for a moment, Nimbo thought she was deep in the throes of death-dreaming. But then he saw her chest rise and fall and he knew that she lived, though how she could live like that, his poor traumatized mind could not fathom. The fire had inverted her coloring so that the parts of her body that had once been bone white were now stark red. And those patches of red that she had worn so defiantly as a tribe-sister to Nimbo and his brethren were now a sickly yellow-white. His eyes mistook the horrors visited upon her earth-body as the work of the Skintaker. But as Nimbo took a step closer he saw that her body had instead been ravaged by the fire.

He cast his mind back to the moment when he had been forced to abandon her to her fate, and to climb the tree. By the time he had ascended to the high branches and looked down upon her, she had gone. Judging by the way her flesh had blackened and bubbled, Nimbo now knew the flames must have claimed her before the

Skintaker did. He crossed to the altar and reached out, staying his hand before he touched her for fear that he might add to her pain. Her breath came in agonized gasps, the sound of which moved Nimbo to tears. Here, lying before him was all of the pain that had been unleashed upon his people, and hers, encapsulated in a single, frail body. That she still lived humbled Nimbo beyond words and he bowed his head in reverence, then dropped to his knees. He pleaded with the Great Spirits to release her from the earthly plane, to take her to higher places where she might be wrapped in clouds and the fire of her flesh doused forever.

The silent prayer was still on his lips when he heard a footfall behind him. Nimbo did not move, but rather listened. The crunch of another footstep told him who had entered the chamber. That and the leathery smell. He gazed up at the wall beyond Rosie's body and watched as flickering torchlight made the frescoes carve their dance before his eyes. The carvings told a living narrative of sacrifice, torture, and death. And of resurrection. As the great hands of the man at his heels closed tight around his throat, Nimbo held an image from the wall carvings in his mind's eye. A boy, not that much younger than him, was being put to death on an altar like this one. But his death was not in vain. That revelation gave Nimbo cause to laugh, even as he was being strangled.

So, his last expression was to be one of joy. As the breath left him, Nimbo finally knew what the spirits required of him. He felt proud, and not a little afraid, as he slipped out of earthbound consciousness and into his death-dream. Nimbo welcomed its dark embrace. With Rosie laid out as a goddess of death and resurrection before him, he welcomed it. Nimbo prepared to join with his little brother and lead him out of the darkness. Together they would climb the highest tree, up into the rainbows.

He swallowed his fear and spat it out again and died.

CHAPTER THIRTY-SEVEN

Rosie awoke in flames.

She gagged at the pain, a raw exclamation forming in the depths of her throat. Every inch of her body was burning, and she patted at her flesh to quash the fire. The touch of her hands sent her flesh into shocked shudders of renewed agony. She had to peel her palms away from her torso before she realized the burning was coming from her ruined flesh, and not the flames of a forest fire. Looking down at her body, she imagined she was experiencing another nightmare vision. Just as in her dreams, where it had been so alien to see the dark boy's body instead of her own, here she was faced by a cooked cadaver in place of her own pale body. The clothes had been burned from her skin. A few tatters remained here and there but they were barely discernable from the blackened hair and skin they clung to like weeds. Between the black, her flesh had blistered and opened up in livid displays of corruption. The more she looked, the more she could feel, her sense of sight informing the pain centers in her fevered mind. She held up her right hand and opened it, a dark mark in her palm all that was left of the scrap of paper she had been holding on to when she died.

Died?

If she was dead, then how could she be feeling such excruciating pain? Her hands dropped to the stone surface either side of her. She was on a raised structure of some kind. Rosie peered over both sides and found it was like an altar. Her blood had pooled into the little indentations and cracks, making a horrific rock pool of the stone surface.

A voice, deep and low as a cat's purr, startled Rosie, and alerted her to the fact that she was not alone. She looked about, searching the shadows for its source. All at once she remembered the black glossy eyes, the strong arms that had lifted her from the pyre, and this chamber. She knew this place, knew its smell, its acoustics, and its dreadful purpose. As her eyes adjusted, she found the imprints of the carvings in the wall, recalling their depictions of sacrifice and adulation from her visions. And standing among them she could now make out a deeper shadow, one that was now moving toward her.

The huge man was carrying a limp form in his arms, and Rosie knew it was Nimbo before he even got near to her. The shock of dark hair and the tribal bands around his powerful little arms told her it was Nimbo without a doubt. Hot tears filled Rosie's eyes at the sight of him. His arms, once strong enough to help climb the tallest of trees, now dangled lifeless from their sockets. How anyone could destroy such a vital thing as Nimbo, Rosie did not know. But even as she wept for him, her pain-addled mind was making connections between the boy she had seen in her visions and the dead friend hanging from the clutches of his huge killer. She blinked the tears from her eyes and watched them splash blood red onto her fingers. Panicking, she wiped her eyes with her fingertips and her entire field of vision turned the color of stigmata. A wash of images bled into her eyes, the orgy of flesh from the ritual she had witnessed in her dream state becoming one with the tableaux on the walls all around her.

The huge man stepped closer, giving a centerpiece to the confusion of images that were bombarding her. He held the boy aloft and Rosie heard a sickly, wet sound as he lowered Nimbo's neck onto a hook that hung from a chain set into the chiseled rock ceiling. She heard the voice again, chanting in that strange feline growl, and looked up to see the man with his arms outstretched in a gesture of exultation. Her eyes found the pictogram on the wall behind him and she saw the similarity immediately—a priest and his offering, a man and his boy. The intensity of his chanting built into an engine-like hum as the huge man invoked the names of his gods. Names so alien to her she would scarce be able to repeat them even if she wished to—which she did not, given their currency.

The chanting ceased and was answered by a whisper—or rather several gossamer thin voices that lilted through the cavern and turned her innards to ice. The whispering became a maelstrom howl of utterances so hideous that they gave cause for Rosie to clamp her damaged hands over her ears. But she could not shut out their concert and it burrowed deep into her ears, piercing her brain with thoughts and feelings so dark, and so ancient somehow, that they turned her very being into a well of unfathomable despair. Darkness gripped her, filling her veins with ice and her bones with the corrupt movement of dead, scurrying things. She fought back now, writhing at the hallucinatory invasion of these terrifying invocations. She focused on their vanguard—the huge man standing before her in his patchwork robes of skin—and clenched her teeth so tight that she could feel them move in her gums. Opening her mouth, Rosie tried to scream, but the black whispers had her tongue. Then she tried to move, but the arcane utterances that gripped her agonized body held her rooted to the spot atop the altar.

She watched the man pluck out the boy's eyes. He carried them over to a stone bowl a few feet away from the altar. Or rather, he cradled them with a delicacy of touch that belied the size of his hands. Rosie watched, transfixed in horror and awe as he washed them and whispered dark blessings over them. Leaving the orbs in the bowl, he returned to the altar and untethered something from deep within the folds of his robes. Turning his attention to Rosie, she realized he had not until now looked directly at her. Under the blank, impenetrable gaze of those glassy eyes, Rosie wished he would look anywhere but at her. Cold terror provoked her body into action, freeing her from the mental shackles that the death-whispers had conjured around her. She scrambled back across the hard stone surface of the altar, removing yet more of her burned skin in the process. Crying out in pain, she rolled to one side and pitched her body off the altar, landing in a crouched position on the cave floor. Her reddened vision made it difficult to navigate the floor beneath her feet, and she lurched clumsily toward the nearest opening in the cave wall.

But he was on her in seconds.

She felt his massive fist close around the back of her neck and was still running when he lifted her from her feet—her legs making mad, flailing motions in mid-air as he swung her back and onto the altar. Knocking the breath from her as he slammed her down, Rosie kicked and lashed out at him in fury and pain. Her fist brushed against something hard and cool and she looked up to see the obsidian discs dangling from his face. They were indeed crudely fashioned eye coverings of some kind, and she had managed to knock them loose in her struggle. Rosie gasped at the sight of the eyes behind the glass. They were the bright, young eyes of a child and they glimmered at her in the cave—dark as diamonds. But they were set into the puckered frames of ruined, red-raw flesh. Eye sockets so damaged, so old, that they must have played host to hundreds of pairs of such young, stolen eyes.

Their eyes met, hers bleeding, and his borrowed. He let her look, let her *see*, but for a breath before he pulled his eye coverings back into position over his bright eyes. Now she could see her own again, reflected in the cool indifference of the glass. Black became red as her tear ducts pumped a film of blood across her vision. Her sight swam as the huge man pinioned her body with one hand and lowered the object—that he had taken from within his robes—to her face with the other. It looked like a sculptor's trowel, curved handle cradling a diamond-shaped head that was delicately sharpened to a tip. The device was the last thing Rosie saw before the man used it to scoop out her left eye from its socket. She heard the wet twist of her optic nerve, spaghetti around the fork that was his tool, followed by a sharp snapping sound as he first tugged, then severed it. Rosie sobbed, a cracked, dying sound. She felt fluid streaming from her eyehole, felt the man move his hand to cradle her head almost tenderly before his soft, dry lips kissed away the fluid from her face.

When he made a start on her other eye, Rosie went under.

CHAPTER THIRTY-EIGHT

Rosie came to and a smell like overripe fruit invaded her senses, making her gag. She opened her eyes and squealed in agony, clamping them tightly shut again. Her vision swam red, a hot lava flow behind her lids. The pain in her eyes was excruciating, dwarfing even that of her burned flesh. She felt something cool and wet splash onto her eyelids and within seconds the white-hot pinpricks of pain behind them numbed to a dull throb.

She opened her eyes afresh.

The huge man stood at the foot of the altar, attending to Nimbo's corpse, which still dangled from its hook and chain. He had removed his robes and Rosie tried not to look at his impressive physique, a landscape of muscles tethered by his flawless skin. She could not put the two together—this man and his pale, hairless body—because the latter made him look gentle somehow. He had the alabaster sheen of an angel, or what Rosie had imagined angels to look like when she was a young girl, listening to her uncle's sermons about their kind. He turned to look at her now, perhaps sensing that she had regained consciousness, and then returned to his work. And what dark work indeed. An angel would not be covered in blood so, she reminded herself, and he would certainly not be wrist-deep in the viscera of a poor, dead boy. She heard the dull clanking of a metal tool from deep within Nimbo's ribcage as it scraped against bone. Swallowing down hard to stop the bile from rising to her throat, Rosie tried to look away, but she could not. And for a moment, she was looking out from Nimbo's body, past the naked monster of a man and at her own face as if with Nimbo's eyes. She saw her face streaked red, like she had cried out torrents of blood. Perhaps she had. She blinked and snapped back into her own head, her own field of vision again.

As if with Nimbo's eyes.

She knew then what her insane captor had done, though she could scarce believe it. The eyes in her sockets were not her own but the boy's—Nimbo's. The dark knowledge to achieve such a transplant was beyond her, but she knew it to be true. She was watching Nimbo's evisceration through his own eyes. She could not stop the bile this time and leaned over the side of the altar to vomit on the earthen floor. Wiping her mouth on the back of her hand, she heard the huge man exhale a single peal of dry laughter. He paused for a moment, then proceeded with his task.

Rosie watched as he opened the boy up—gasped as she saw his mysteries unfurled. Through her new eyes his body seemed to glimmer like sunlight through cut crystal. Every organ, vein and dermal layer glistened in the torchlight—each aspect of the boy's viscera an individual color of his rainbow. Rosie wept tears of bloody anguish for the bright boy who had been opened up like this before her. She was powerless, unable to repair him, to help put him back together.

There-there, dear.

But her new eyes seemed also to enhance her tears, to distil them, adding a swell of joy and of pride to her anguish for his physical death. For she now knew he was not merely a sacrificial victim but also a celebrant of life, and of the flesh that gave it form. Nimbo's body had become venerated by his murderer's dark workings. Rosie blinked, her new eyes washing clearer.

She felt a powerful hand entwining with hers. The man stood before her, naked and unashamed, his dark eyes piercing her heart with a wicked truth. She understood how legions had come to worship such a man and become his acolytes. What he offered was the very stuff of life. He cradled it in his hands and transmuted it into the cool surfaces of his surgical tools. He had given her the gift of true sight and Rosie felt a part of his alchemy, immutable. Her fingers slotted into his—so warm and slick from the boy's blood—and she took her first unfaltering step toward the open cadaver, and salvation. He was like a magician, pulling back the curtain of Nimbo's flesh and inviting her into the inner sanctum to reveal his secrets. She willingly followed. Entwined in the wonder of life after death they made love and Rosie's body became his body. Joined by the conduit of the bright boy's viscera, Rosie could feel everything her lover felt, could sense his every thought. And memory.

She was atop the temple again, the one from her nightmare vision after the forest fire.

Voices were chanting, people screaming, the wanton tearing of flesh.

Heat at her groin, a spike of fire in her belly, cool waves washing over her torso and back, rushing down her legs like waves receding into a freezing ocean.

Back in the dark boy's body, acid taste of copper in the back of her—of his—mouth.

Huge man towering over her.

Skintaker. He is the Skintaker.

Huge hands on her body, pushing her down, crushing the very breath from her. But soft so as not to bruise. Don't damage the skin, he needs it, he wants it.

Blood everywhere, an orgiastic torrent anointing the dark boy's body. The huge man scooping the eyes from their sockets and planting them like seeds in his own sockets. A transplant. Opening the boy up now, little red corridor beyond, a conduit into his next life.

He is the Skintaker.

The dark boy.

He is the Skintaker.

His old form nearly worn out, new flesh needed to continue his work. New eyes for seeing, new skin to wear for the hunt. He had been a boy once, this monstrous man. The dark boy carried by the throng into the temple. An offering of flesh and youth and longevity, now playing host to the Skintaker. A vessel for his power, renewed.

In the dark, she saw the cave carvings. One by one they sprang to life before her, etchings on the surface of distant memory. She knew now that the pictograms did not simply depict child sacrifice, but rather that *he* was the child, becoming the new Skintaker. His story grew in her mind's eye and she traced it back as far as it would go, down dark decades into a time long before white men had ventured to these shores.

The time of a king.

The carvings wrote the tale in stone. She saw King Venturia—a vain and beautiful man, perhaps the vainest that had ever lived. He was ruler of the unbroken lands that stretched from the volcano at their center and as far as the sea. Rosie saw their map unfurl through stone and time, vast and awe-inspiring. But she knew how he wanted more. He wanted life eternal so that he may be worshipped forever, here in this garden of earthly delights. His demigod walked the forests, a being with the power to extend life, to repair and renew the ravages that time visited upon all flesh. They called him Skintaker and heeded his totems in the lands above the river, which he made his hunting grounds. Venturia poured offerings, some as young as babes, into the Skintaker's territories. He erected a vast temple in his name and that of his god Poré, and his goddess Perimbo, who were creators of all things and masters of worlds.

The Skintaker accepted Venturia's offerings and restored his fleshly form in return for his sacrifices. The barter continued, a ritualistic exchange that balanced ruler and deity to their mutual benefit.

But Rosie saw another figure take her place among the etchings in the cave story.

Marena was a beautiful woman who had traveled across the ocean to give worship to Venturia and his dark demigod. Within days, the king made her his queen. At the wedding, which lasted seven days, men and women wept to see such a beauty as their rulers' and put out their own eyes in frenzied rituals for fear they would never see its like again. All rejoiced.

Marena gave birth to a daughter, Moxica, and promised her to the Skintaker when she had come of age. The king and queen noticed how the Skintaker watched over their daughter, his black eyes betraying his lust. So, the demigod had urges that placed him closer to humankind after all. The king and queen became greedy and wanted his secrets for their own. They ensnared him using his obsession with Moxica. No sooner had she revealed she was bearing the Skintaker's child, they imprisoned him. Subjecting him to a campaign of tortures both physical and mental, they thought they could extract his dark methods. He watched, unblinking, as they eviscerated Moxica, their own flesh and blood, before his eyes. The atrocities they visited upon his infant son would surely break him, they thought. But the Skintaker remained faithful to his gods and the art they had bestowed upon him. King Venturia made a banquet of the Skintaker's son's flesh. Driven mad with the desire to ascend to godhood, Venturia conspired to kill his demigod and offer him to Poré and Perimbo in return for their dark knowledge that would forge him into a new Skintaker.

But the true Skintaker lived yet.

With the help of his most loyal of disciples, he broke free. His retribution was absolute. He slaughtered King Venturia and Queen Marena, undoing years of reparation gifted to them by the same hands that now undid them. Then he laid waste to their entire kingdom, skinning countless numbers of the king's subjects alive. He stretched out and displayed their skins like a feudal emperor marking his boundaries with banners. Those who did not die by his hands put out their eyes, driven mad by the sight of such atrocities. All despaired. Hundreds took their own lives in fear of the Skintaker's wrath. And, finally, he stood alone atop an empire of death.

Abandoned to exile by Poré and Perimbo, the Skintaker roamed the rainforest for dark decades. He was no longer a demigod to be revered, but a demon to be feared. He had to take a new body to continue his life cycles—each one becoming shorter than the last. The skins he wore grew paler with each ritual. They were both a blessing of eternal life, and a curse of the wretched alchemy he was doomed to continue...

Rosie wept for him then, drowning in an age of death and resurrection—the slow sand in the hourglass of his time on this earth. Her salt tears mingled with the blood that was pumping between them, a shared life force. She felt him join with her, sheathed in the new skin that was becoming a part of both of them, and gasped. She felt the cool, delicious envelope of flesh close tight around her, quenching the fire of her burns. He was inside of her and surrounding her all at once, his dark workings healing her from within and without. She felt his rush of seed inside her, warmth coating her inner thighs. The two sensations fused together within her, ice and fire, and she swooned. Together they fell as if through all the layers of one another's skin, through their cells, and to the very heart of their histories. And Rosie went deeper still. No longer caring how she might be changed when she emerged—or if she were to emerge at all—she cleaved to him in the dark.

CHAPTER THIRTY-NINE

"There. Tell them to set the fire there. We'll smoke him out." Richter waited as Erroll sloped away through the trees to issue his instructions to the blaze farmers. Two of them were more than enough to warm things up the way he wanted. It seemed those guys could make a forest fire by clicking their fingers, a skill that had proven invaluable to Richter—and was about to once again.

Turning his attention to Seamus, Richter found the freckle-faced lad warming up with stretches by one of the larger trees that overshadowed the temple building.

"You ready, kid?"

The lad nodded to Richter.

"Don't get too close. He's big, really fucking big, this guy. I saw him lift the fat guy without even breaking a sweat. You get close enough to pop him, then we do the rest, understood?"

Seamus nodded again, breathed out hard.

Yeah, he'll do. He'll have to, thought Richter.

He reached into his waistcoat, pulled out the pistol and handed it to the kid.

"It's already loaded. Shoot low, kneecap the fucker and take him down. This is big game—you do this right and you'll be on the beach before Christmas with all the local pussy you can worry. Good to go?"

"Yes, sir."

Richter watched the kid tuck the pistol into his pants and led him away from the trees. He took his field binoculars from their case and focused on the men working at the temple entrance. The flames had already taken hold of their tinder and smoke began to billow into the opening.

"It's time, kid, circle round in back and keep your eyes peeled. If he sees you first, you won't even know about it, I can guarantee you that."

Richter saw a lump appear in Seamus's throat, his first real hint of fear. Good, it might keep him on his toes.

"Don't worry, we won't be far away," Richter said, "it'll be just like the wild boar, pincer movement, remember?"

"Sure I do, sir," Seamus replied. "I come up behind and, pop."

"Attaboy. Now skedaddle."

Seamus shook out his arms and legs, and then sprinted around the perimeter of the temple building, disappearing behind a nearby thicket of trees. Richter watched him go, through the twin viewfinders of his binoculars. Now all he had to do was track and wait.

STRATUM SPINOSUM

The stench of men roused him from his slumber. He could smell their sweat and their desperation at his door, polluting his cocoon of sacred coupling and conduit.

The sacred rite had depleted his life force and he ached for sustenance. His body tingled, a sensation he had not experienced for lifetimes. He rose and pulled on his robes, then gazed down at the smooth form of the girl upon his altar.

No longer a girl, a woman now.

He brushed the hair from her face, approving of the new skin she wore. And she wore it well. The childish blemishes were gone, superseded by the purity of rebirth. He inhaled that purity, willing it to expel the rank intrusion of the men outside his chambers. But a new smell was carried in on the air. The acrid smell of smoke.

He tucked his killing blade inside the folds of his robes and left the woman to dream while he went outside.

To hunt.

CHAPTER FORTY

Rosie started at the smell of smoke, half-expecting to find herself in the midst of the forest fire once again.

Instead, she felt the cold, hard surface of the altar beneath her.

At first, she thought she was still dreaming, her visions brimming over into the real world, expecting the raw pain of her burns to return to her with a vengeance. But even before she opened her eyes, she could feel it, soft and supple beneath her now undamaged fingertips. She sat up and surveyed herself, taking in every pore, every crease in the landscape of skin covering her body. She was naked and yet felt fully clothed, clad as she was in new skin. Holding her trembling hands up, she marveled at the soft translucence of her palms and fingers. Moving them closer to her eyes, she gasped as she saw that her fingertips were devoid of the usual whorls and lines. They were completely smooth and if she had dipped them into ink and pressed them onto paper, she would leave no fingerprints. She liked that, the feeling of having been reborn, anonymous now, and not as the wretched young girl who had been plucked from her parents' funeral pyre.

Rosie slid off the side of the altar and stood fully erect. The skin that covered her was as soothing as a soft blanket. She ran her fingers through her hair, which felt lustrous and new, enjoying the tickling sensation against her hands. Elsewhere, her body was completely hairless, as smooth as a newborn babe's. Rosie wondered if it would remain like that forever. She hoped so.

Her chuckles rebounded off the walls of the cave and echoed around her—a proud proclamation of joy where there should perhaps be shame. Shame because of what still dangled from the hook and chain nearby, the flayed corpse of the young boy she had once called a friend. His life had been utterly drained from him and put into her so that she might live again, young and beautiful. Strange, if that was the source of so much shame, such extreme guilt, then why did she feel neither? Perhaps she had lived a young lifetime of those tortured emotions and now the time had come to cast off such youthful things. Rosie stood proud against the backdrop of alchemical carnage created by her savior, the Skintaker. And only then did she wonder where he was.

She held the faintest trace of a memory of his departure, from her dream or from almost waking she could not tell. He had risen, naked like she was, before climbing into his robes and leaving the chamber.

Where are you going? her mind asked in silence.

I need sustenance, her memory of him replied.

Must be an after-effect of the rite, she thought. *I'm still connected to him somehow.*

She felt warmth at her groin, where he had been—her former nightmare—now her lover and pastor. Rosie wished for the sensation never to stop. She sniffed the air, searching him out on the cool breeze that moved through the cave from tunnel mouth to tunnel mouth. There was the smell of smoke again—so she had not dreamed it after all. She could see it hanging above the cave floor like a sea mist, its source one of the tunnel openings. Rosie moved away from the smoke and toward another tunnel opening.

That way.

A hint of cured leather scent marked his route. It was a smell that would have scared her witless and given her cause to flee had she smelled it just hours ago, but now it was a balm and she followed it. She passed a low table, formed of a throw slung over two makeshift wooden boxes. Wooden bowls, like the ones at the mission house but dulled with age and the stains of unspeakable fluids, sat atop the table alongside votive candles. Rosie's eyes widened at the sight of the bowls' contents. A collection of human teeth—small enough to be those from a child, or rather several—were stacked inside one of the bowls like candy corn on All Hallows. Another contained dried tongues, each coiled in an approximation of the agonies that had silenced them. Most surprising of all was the human brain that sat in another bowl, stark gray in the subdued light of the cavern and swimming in a soup of neural juices. Rosie moved the bowls aside carefully, finding the one containing the brain to be heaviest of all, and lifted up the tablecloth. Its colors had faded but the Myahueneca, or perhaps their ancestors, had clearly woven it. Maybe once it had been an offering to their demigod, their beloved demon. How fitting that it should become a gown for his newborn. Rosie shook the dust from it and wrapped it around her body, fastening it into a makeshift toga. She followed the path into one of the tunnels that, somehow, she knew he had taken.

CHAPTER FORTY-ONE

As she rounded a corner, she looked at the flickering shadows on the walls, seeing within them the dancing shapes of the worshippers she had seen in her visions. With so many bodies and so many skins there must also have been so much blood. She felt damp earth beneath her feet, wondering if these very tunnels had run red with the blood of the Skintaker's offerings—back when he had been worshipped as a demigod, not exiled underground to live off scraps. Rosie had begun to feel the weight of all his years on her shoulders, their connection helping her to understand the stark nobility beneath the man's fearsome, bestial frame. He was, she thought, a noble beast—no different to any of the rainforest's denizens she had met on her brief travels. He was agile like the howler monkeys that used the treetops as their paths through the forest. He was as defensive as the Myahueneca, keeping close watch over his subterranean abode, just as fiercely as they had protected their culture. And he was as brilliant as the paradise birds, his flawless, alchemical skin a match for their rainbow-colored feathers. She smoothed her hands over her new skin—that which he had gifted to her—and felt grateful. A shiver passed through her, new nerve endings forming and fusing within her, consolidating the difference she felt in herself. Her parents were in Heaven, her aunt and uncle were in Hell, and here she walked—in limbo between her old life and something entirely new.

Twilight glistened at the mouth of the tunnel, a golden beacon that beckoned for her to walk, renewed in green and pleasant lands. Rosie was about to answer its call when she heard a sound, so slight at first as to be missed. She stopped walking and listened intently and, hearing it again, realized she had heard a low whisper coming from farther along the tunnel. She followed the sound and discovered a low doorway cut into the tunnel wall. Beyond it, she saw the flicker of torchlight and heard the voice become clearer. It was a man's voice, soft but strained, and whispering rhythmically. As she entered the chamber Rosie could pick out a few words here and there in the whispered stream of consciousness spilling from his lips. He spoke of equations and the mating patterns of migrating birds, of the distance traveled by some species on their seasonal flight south of the equator. He spoke of blood and fire, and of hot, white terror at the aspect of the thing that had dragged him down here into the cloying dark.

Rosie knew his voice. She knew he was the professor.

Or what used to be him.

He hung, suspended in a wooden frame that had been lashed together with what looked like reeds. As her eyes adjusted to the firelight, Rosie saw that the reeds were in fact lengths of viscera from the professor's own body. His flesh had been carved and unfolded, forming a pink, red, and purple mosaic around him. His skin was stretched taut, holding him tethered within the confines of the frame. If he had been able to struggle free, it would be fatal to do so, as his arteries and vital organs, too, formed an intricate part of the insane diorama of flesh. Even his face had been opened up into a rich, red flower, making a stamen of his skull and spine. And at the heart of it, his eyes were gone. Rosie gasped to see his eyeless face, smiling at her.

"Rosie."

His mouth spilled blood as he whispered her name.

"Rosie Shields. You're quite shiny and new."

"How can you…"

"Curious, is it not? I can smell you. Can smell him on you, his magic touch. I can smell everything since he…" He cleared his throat, and a glob of discharge sputtered from his lips. "He fixed you, didn't he?"

Rosie nodded and her new eyes filled with tears to see Cecil like this, as her old heart remembered his friendship. He leaned forward from his cage of skin and Rosie saw the contents of his open belly shift and shudder as he did so. Her hand flew to her mouth, anticipating the wet unspooling of his innards should he venture any farther. His panicked eyeless expression revealed that he was aware of the danger, too, and he leaned back again amidst a quiver of slopping organs. The smell of him was atrocious, an overpowering cocktail of ripe, excremental decay. She gagged and swallowed, thankful there was nothing in her stomach to regurgitate. She focused on his face, on the twin pits where his now-absent eyes had once twinkled. His eyes had seen so much in his fifty-plus years. Rosie knew, even before he spoke again, that the last thing he had seen was the same obsidian eyes she had seen before the fire and smoke had taken her.

"He claimed me, in the forest. I felt certain—to kill me. But here I am, somewhere between life and death. Malformed. He took my mind from me. Every memory, every scrap of knowledge. I can't get them back. They're slipping away from me. It *hurts*, Rosie."

Cecil's words were contorted and pained. How he could even speak, let alone still breathe, was beyond Rosie's understanding. But even in the face of such terrible mutilations, Cecil forced a smile again and a crimson tear formed at the corner of his mouth.

"Did you see his mysteries, when he remade you?"

Rosie felt herself blush, pulling the woven cloth tighter around her. She disliked succumbing to the old prudish ways ingrained in her by her aunt, but perhaps some things went deeper than flesh.

"I saw glimpses, my dear child, glimpses of a forgotten time. How he walked with kings and queens on temples constructed beneath his feet. Oh, what I wouldn't give to see more, but he has me at a disadvantage, see?"

Foul yellow bile dripped from the professor's empty eye sockets.

"It hurts, Rosie. You have to help me."

"But I don't know how to...or even if I can..."

"Hush, child. Brave child. You saved me once before, and you can do it again."

His voice became as stretched as his skin and he coughed, sending his flayed frame into spasms. Parts of him fell at their feet, steaming in pools of their own juices. Rosie shrieked in horror and recoiled. The professor moaned in agony. He sounded like a dog, chained to its kennel.

Rosie steeled herself and prepared to speak the truth to her old friend.

"I don't think I can do this, Professor, don't think I can undo this torment. Its intricacies are beyond me, I'm sorry."

"Worry not, child," Cecil said, his voice paper thin now.

"I'm so sorry."

"Do not feel sorrow for a silly old man. I've seen things I would not have dreamed possible. I shall take them with me, when I go. And go I must."

His eyelids closed over their ruined sockets. For a moment, Rosie saw the man intact, as he had been on their field trip in the forest, a dreamer and a scientist reveling in new worlds.

"Reach through, Rosie, and pull. You can do it."

His whispered words echoed in her ears.

"You alone can save me, dear girl. Just reach through and pull."

It took a few seconds for the dread meaning of his words to become clear. Then Rosie stepped forward until the professor was within reach. She closed her eyes, clamped her teeth together in a grimace of determination and reached deep inside of him.

Her hands found something wet and beating.

Sobbing, she pulled with all her might.

CHAPTER FORTY-TWO

Richter pressed his back to the crumbling temple wall and took a breath. He had to admit that he felt nervous. All his travels, all his hunts, had brought him here to this place and this time. His lifetime retirement plan depended on the next few minutes. He cast his gaze at the treetops and saw the last golden streaks of the setting sun there. Time now to act.

He signaled to Erroll and the remainder of his men and they followed him, crouching low, through and beyond the smoke that still billowed from the mouth of the cave. If his tactics had paid off, and they usually did, his quarry would have left its nest by now and would surely be moving in Seamus's direction. He hoped the boy was as light-footed as he bragged. Richter tried not to succumb to self-doubt about his choice. The kid had shown skill during the boar hunt and there was no reason to believe any different now, especially with the promise of so much to gain.

Ten feet.

The corner of the temple was looming large.

Five feet.

Richter signaled again and his men dropped into position, one covering him and another two ready to launch themselves into the fray.

Base.

Richter sucked in breath and pushed his back against the stone structure. He counted down, exhaling slowly, then pushed himself away. His momentum exposed him, and he crouched quickly, dropping out of sight behind the tall ferns that formed dense scrub at the base of the temple. He glanced at Erroll and the others. They were well camouflaged and held their positions, awaiting his signal. Richter peered over the top of the foliage, searching out the slightest indication of movement in the forest beyond. For a few moments, he could only hear his heartbeat. The long grasses and taller ferns encircling the forest swayed in a sudden breeze, and then stood still again, a breath before the fray.

In one split second it came, the shock and the noise. A shape so large and dark that Richter mistook it, at first, for a gorilla. Seamus crashed through the trees after it, his weapon trained on it as he ran. Richter remained in a crouching position and watched as the lumbering shape drew near. It was but feet away—its sharp, black eyes and leathery robes making it look alien, even amidst the awesome science fiction of the rainforest. Seamus cackled and took aim, low at the legs. This was his shot.

"I got him, Richter! You can come out now, I got the bastard bang to r— "

The mirth fell from his lips at the hollow click of an empty chamber. The huge man turned to face him, and Seamus fell into his shadow, a crushing darkness creeping across his face. He fired again and, hearing another empty click, he actually whimpered.

Richter watched intently as the kid snapped open the pistol.

Here it comes, thought Richter, *the dawning realization.*

"Never meant for me to shoot him at all. Bastards set me up."

Seamus's shocked expression upon seeing the unloaded gun was an absolute picture. He looked like a stick man with a bubble for his head, his mouth forming an idiotic O. The kid had fulfilled his promise just as Richter had hoped. Not as the hunter he'd vainly imagined himself to be, but as the bait in Richter's trap.

"Bloody bastards set me up. Where are you?"

His eyes searched, frantic, but he saw nothing. Nothing except the dark man, closing in.

"Where are you? Help me!"

Richter heard the kid's pathetic shriek as his former prey approached him. The giant figure stood a full two feet above Seamus. Richter watched in grim fascination as one of those huge hands came down and swatted the kid to the ground like a fly. The other hand went to work on the kid's jaw, crushing it in one snapping movement. Seamus's mouth was no longer an O but a horribly distended red oval. Teeth tumbled from the dark orifice like hailstones as the huge man shoved his other hand inside. Seamus made sounds that Richter had never heard from a human being before as his attacker rooted around in the back of his throat. The guttural gags and ear-shattering shrieks gave way to wet sobs, and then silence, as the huge man pulled hard.

Richter winced as he watched him pull the tongue out of the boy's destroyed mouth. A shower of blood arced through the air and spattered the foliage just inches from where Richter crouched. Seamus's body dangled, broken, as the huge man lifted him up. He wrenched the kid's upper and lower jaw apart with such force that his dead face folded back on itself. Richter tilted his head, following the body's trajectory as it was tossed to the ground. Seamus looked like a book that had had its spine bent back until it broke. At the center of the mess one of his eyes glistened, accusing, at Richter.

"Now," Richter said, and an instant later the lithe forms of his men sprang into action.

They had the net over the huge man in a second. Richter heard him inhale, preparing to fight them off. Then, just as they had rehearsed, each of Richter's men sprinted around their quarry, ducking and weaving in a precise maypole dance until he was completely entangled in their web. The men then dropped to the ground in a wrestling dive, upending their captive who fell to his side with the breath knocked out of him.

Richter fancied he saw rage behind his captive's impenetrable black eyes and then realized he was seeing the fire of sunset reflected there. The image made him smile. A wild, ferocious thing, trapped in his net. Richter's masters would pin a medal on him for this one, he was sure of that.

He lowered his rifle, pointing it at the man in the net.

"This one is loaded," he said.

Then he heard a girl, screaming.

CHAPTER FORTY-THREE

Rosie emerged from the cave draped in her new colors, and her new skin. Professor Cecil's blood dripped from between her fingers, still warm from his last moments. She hoped she had set his spirit free, to walk with those he had striven to understand all his academic life. From the mouth of the temple entrance, Rosie saw night's glorious fanfare in full sway over the rainforest. The sun was going down behind the trees, snaking through their branches and leaves in bright, golden fronds. The moisture in the air had conjured a mist that hung low over the vegetation, cloaking it as though in preparation for the coming night. And the sky was the color of amethyst, the first pinpricks of bright starlight emerging from its canopy.

A shout echoed out from the trees nearby, and Rosie felt her skin turn to ice. She heard a roar and for a moment could not tell if it had come from the same direction as the shouting, or from inside her head.

Both, she decided. *We are still joined, he and I, and some trouble befalls him.*

She ran, careless of the loose stones and dirt leading down the rough track into the trees. Her heart beat faster in her chest as she ran, the roaring and screaming growing in her ears, propelling her onward into the trees.

Rosie was running so fast that she was almost upon them before she could stop. She screamed and skidded to a halt on higher ground, just above a grim circle of men. There before her were the arsonists who had attacked the mission house. Among their number was the same troupe that had made niceties over dinner aboard the steamer—minus the giant whom Gregory had toppled with the shotgun, she noted.

But Rosie looked beyond the men now, intent on seeking out the Skintaker, for his plight had taken root like a cancer in her head. Her psyche was spiked with pain and blackness and she felt a clinging, tugging sensation all around her. She was vaguely aware of the men falling to the ground, and for the briefest moment she thought their quarry had defeated them. With dawning dread, she realized they had pulled the huge man down with them, and that he was ensnared in a trap of their making.

Of *his* making.

She acknowledged their ringleader then. The overdressed, snake-like man who had kissed her hand and made such a show of rescuing her from the amorous deckhand. A shock of ginger hair alerted Rosie to the ravaged corpse of the deckhand himself, who lay dead just a few feet away. At least her savior had removed one equation from the world before they took him down.

"Well, well. The one who got away, hey boys? Looking prettier than ever, if you don't mind me saying so, miss."

The lankiest of the group chuckled at this, his eyes narrowing as he looked at Rosie. She knew she was just a piece of meat to him, as he was to her. She wished her lover could open him up and gut him. She could taste the metallic tang of blood on her tongue, the dying tears of an unrepentant man. She could feel how hollow his heart would feel if she crushed it.

Her heartbeat pounded in her ears and pulsed at her wrists. Her vision turned black and she could see the men looming over her in a dark circle. She knew she was seeing through his eyes, so cold and clear. But when she blinked the connection was severed.

The ringleader had a rifle trained on the Skintaker, freeing one hand for a moment to tip his hat to her in a gesture of pure arrogance. She saw his eyes drink her in, lingering over the new skin she had been gifted in the rite. He seemed particularly interested in her neck. She pulled the woven blanket tighter around her throat but knew that the ancestors' garb would not be enough to protect her from the likes of him.

"Leave him be."

Her words stirred something within her. The connection fused again, stronger than before. Feeling another, altogether more powerful heartbeat in her chest she blinked again and saw the men in a wheel through black glass. Each was a point on the Skintaker's compass. To him, and to Rosie through him, the men were machines of flesh and blood powered by the most vulnerable of engines. Unblinking now, she saw the access point in each man's body that would stop his heart and put him to the ground for good. She saw sinew, veins, and nerves untangle, signposting death. And before she blinked again, she heard his answer. His voice so deep and beautiful inside of her.

Run, he said, and live. If you can.

She blinked and took a faltering step back.

Black vision turned red. The men screamed. Their horrible sounds cut off by the surgery of his fingertips. One by one they fell as he sliced his way through the net. Jugulars snapped like guitar strings. Arteries opened, spilling blood in torrents as they were torn apart. The men had no time to react. Such was the speed and the fury of his retribution upon them.

A single gunshot rang out.

The Skintaker stood, monolithic in the sunset. For a moment he seemed to tower over even the oldest trees. He was a symbol, a shadow of something that had always been part of the forest, a primal force of nature. Then he toppled, a flash of color at his throat. Rosie saw the bright plumage of a tranquilizer dart, embedded in his neck.

The hunter spun, reloading his rifle.

She ran.

CHAPTER FORTY-FOUR

Rosie scrambled up the steep bank that led to the temple. She had no idea how to fend off the hunter at her heels, no instinct but to flee. The Skintaker's last words to her echoed in her brain, a mantra that pushed her on, willing her to live.

If she could.

Her feet skidded over wet pebbles and roots as she climbed, frantic, to the top of the incline. She could see the dark hollow of the temple entrance, but it was still something of a sprint away. Looking about her, she saw a fallen branch and on instinct, stooped to pick it up. It was sturdy as a baseball bat in her hands, and reassuringly heavy. Clinging to the branch, she pushed on toward the temple entrance. Flashes of memory each time she blinked perspiration from her eyes. Something important, some detail lodged in her mind somewhere between her visions and her waking terror. She imagined the congregation, carrying the dark boy over the threshold, heard their rallying cries, the baying of blood sacrifice.

"Where you running to, little lady?"

The hunter's voice paralyzed her with fear. Rosie lost her footing and stumbled. She crawled as fast as she could, feeling the skin, the precious skin, of her knees tearing open as she went. The sharp crack of a rifle being cocked rang out, echoing off the stones of the temple. This place had witnessed so much blood, so many sacrifices. Hers would just be one more in a long line.

"Don't run, there's really no need. My employers will find uses for you, I'm sure. And I'll enjoy the reward for bringing them such a bonus. Think I'm gonna build me a big house."

Rosie rolled over onto her back and scrambled backward, still clutching the branch. If only she could deflect the shot with it, stop him from shooting her. She guessed the ammunition in the rifle must be another tranquilizer dart, but Rosie wished it was a bullet. She had seen far darker prospects in the hunter's eyes than she ever had in the Skintaker's. Rosie threw her head back in dismay, and saw his unmistakable eyes looking down at her.

Impossible.

Then, the illusion became clear. She had seen this before, in her visions of the sacrificial rite. The boy had been carried beneath this very threshold and the face that looked down upon him had been a carved keystone. It had been fashioned into the visage of their demigod—the Skintaker.

"Don't fret, little girl. When you wake up, some folks are going to have a few questions for you is all. About your new look."

The hunter took aim. She saw his arm flex as he prepared to pull the trigger.

A loose stone jutted out from the array that supported the keystone high above. It was but a few inches away from her, but she did not know if she had the time to act. It was her only option. With all her remaining strength, Rosie pushed her body up and across the tunnel, lunging with the branch as though it were a lance. The tip of the branch connected with the gap between the loose stone and the wall. There was a sharp cracking sound as the branch snapped, and then another as the stone fell from its socket.

She heard Richter fire his rifle. Closing her eyes, she awaited the dull pain of impact. But it never came. The removal of the loose stone had started a chain reaction of falling brickwork. She leapt back, into the shadows of the tunnel.

The keystone fell, crowning her achievement. Rosie glimpsed the hunter's face for a moment before he was obscured by falling rocks. He had looked at her with something like admiration. As more masonry tumbled, blocking the mouth of the tunnel in a flurry of dust, Rosie turned and made her descent into darkness.

She was not afraid.

STRATUM BASALE

*H*e regained consciousness in darkness. He knew only darkness. Buried in the gloom, he felt the deep thrum of some infernal machine, some dark heart-engine. He heard water, and a paddle churning through it. He was afloat and abroad at the behest of his captor.

He performed his checks. His eye coverings were still there, all his extremities intact. The foreign object at his neck troubled him though. He gripped it and tore it from his neck like a gardener might remove a weed. A dart of some sort, machine-made, not a thing of elegance like those fashioned for the tribal blowpipes of his homeland. He crushed it in his fist, heard the dull clank of it as it hit the floor. Lowering himself flat against the floor, he pressed his ear to the cold, wet surface and listened. Cogs turned, gears grinded, man's cacophony gone mad beneath his cell.

He stood and looked aloft, keen eyes searching the darkness. Above him was a thin square of light, growing brighter. He imagined it would grow brighter still as his floating prison moved beneath alien skies. He knew it was a hatch of sorts, and hatches were designed to open.

Above him, men talked. They spoke of a paradise called Meditrine Island, a place where their dreams would come true. Men always grafted their dreams onto such places. But he knew that every paradise had a rot at its core. Dreams could so easily become nightmares.

He sat and waited. For soon they would come. Come to try and glean his secrets, his methods, as others had before them. He sighed, dust of eons spilling from his mouth in a single breath. Let them come. He gathered his fleshly robes around him. The scent of the fabric comforted him and reminded him of who he was, the many lives he had *endured, and the many skins he had worn.*

He had always been, and ever would be, the Skintaker.

"Welcome home," *they said when they finally came for him.*

They took him above decks, chained and bound. He did not struggle, did not fight. The time for that would come later. He breathed in the salt air of a new land and saw a white tower on a plateau of rock. Strange huts, made of metal ore and glass, were being constructed in the hills above. He had glimpsed their like in the dying mind of the fat man. A tribe of bright faces awaited him in their shadows. They were so pale—white angels in the sunlight—men and women of science becoming his congregation.

They baptized him with a new name in the fierce glow of their egos.

"Here he is, our very own Skin Mechanic."

A new name for a new age. An age of greed. And they cheered. Some wept, their gleaming eyes exulting him like a god.

"Bless us with your alchemy," *those eyes seemed to say,* "keep us young forever, and in return we will betray you."

As they led him from the ship and onto the island, he vowed to pluck each and every one of those eyes from their sockets before he was done.

EPILOGUE

Rosie walked the deep dark until the torchlight revealed itself at a turn in the tunnel. She sloped back to the innermost chamber where the altar stood, now empty. Nimbo's carcass hung like a painting from its hook. The bones of worshippers lined the walls, pining for their master. The smell of death and sex and resurrection overwhelmed and exhilarated her.

After lighting one of the votive candles, Rosie walked over to the place where the wall carvings began. The flickering candle flame brought them to life, and she probed their grooves with her soft fingertips. She knew the hand that had made them, could still feel its touch remaking her in his image. Rosie read the inscriptions with her new eyes, seeing new detail in them each time she looked. They had started out as cave paintings and were now etched in stone. Her silent pledge was one of scholarship—she would not leave this place until she had committed the Skintaker's story to memory. She had everything she needed here in the temple, and in the rainforest beyond, enough to sustain and nurture her for the rest of the bright days, and the darkest of nights. Enough to write the next chapters in her own memoir.

A smile curled her lips at the first pictogram of that brave, luminescent boy. One of the tribe, chosen above all others to ascend to adoration. What a legend he had become, what a legacy he had left behind. Rosie closed her eyes, reaching for him in the darkness, but she saw only a rainbow of light as vivid as paradise birds' feathers.

She smoothed a hand over her belly and gasped at the warm spark of life she felt there.

New flesh from the Skintaker.

ABOUT THE AUTHOR

Frazer Lee's first novel, *The Lamplighters*, was a Bram Stoker Award® Finalist for "superior achievement in a first novel".

Frazer's other published works include the novels *The Jack in the Green* and *Hearthstone Cottage* and the *Daniel Gates Adventures* series of novellas.

Also a screenwriter and filmmaker, Frazer's movie credits include the award-winning short horror films *On Edge*, *Red Lines*, *Simone*, *The Stay*, and the critically acclaimed horror/thriller feature (and movie novelization) *Panic Button*.

Frazer is Head of Creative Writing at Brunel University London and resides with his family in leafy Buckinghamshire, England, just across the cemetery from the real-life *Hammer House of Horror*.

Official website: www.frazerlee.com
Facebook: www.facebook.com/AuthorFrazerLee
Twitter: www.twitter.com/frazer_lee

Curious about other Crossroad Press books?
Stop by our site:
www.crossroadpress.com
We offer quality writing
in digital, audio, and print formats.